# The Shadows of Absence

## A Pride & Prejudice variation

## Elin Eriksen

# Contents

# Introduction

**After a couple of lofty swings, they threw Mr Darcy into the cold, murky water...**

Darcy is loath to leave Hertfordshire three days after the bewitching Miss Elizabeth Bennet accepts his second proposal. Yet he must return to Pemberley as the executor of his neighbour's will. To avoid spending their engagement period apart, he invites the entire Bennet family, and Mr Bingley, to Derbyshire.

Elizabeth admires Mr Darcy's compassion for the bereaved widow, but the execution of the will proves challenging, as he spends most of his days trying to determine the baronet's successor. In the shadows of his absence, she is left much to her own thoughts and the influence of others. And after Mr Darcy's involuntary dip in the lake, his mortification renders him even more taciturn and unsociable.

The widow was Mr Darcy's first love, who spurned him for wealth and consequence. Lady Baslow's rejection turned Mr Darcy into a reserved and cautious man who guarded his emotions from public display. It is up to Elizabeth to determine whether he is cold and aloof or if passion burns brightly beneath his austere mien.

The Shadows of Absence is a Regency era Pride and Prejudice novel of approximately 74,000 words. This emotional story ends in a happily ever after for our dear couple and focuses on

Darcy and Elizabeth. It would be an advantage to be familiar with Jane Austen's Pride and Prejudice to fully enjoy the story, because it follows canon up to the second proposal.

This work of fiction is created entirely from the author's imagination. At no point in this body of work has Artificial Intelligence (AI) been employed to write it.

# Chapter 1 Sad Tidings

**Thursday 8<sup>th</sup> October 1812**

Elizabeth waited eagerly for Mr Darcy to arrive. Jane had already paraded Mr Bingley around the neighbourhood, as their engagement was of a longer standing, but it was Mr Darcy and Elizabeth's first appearance as a betrothed couple. It was only a small dinner party with the Lucases, but still…

Elizabeth found herself in the unusual position of Mrs Bennet's favourite daughter. Her mother was fussing over her appearance and pinched her cheeks just as Elizabeth stole another glance out of the window. Mr Darcy had promised he would arrive early, and she would not mind a private moment to speak to her betrothed. Just the thought sent a shiver through her body. Fortunately, her mother had turned her attention to Jane. She did not notice her quiver, or she would have surely deemed her ill and marched her off to bed.

Elizabeth stood by the window and stared longingly into the wilting garden. Her vigilance was rewarded by the sight of the Darcy carriage rolling ever so slowly towards the entrance. Elizabeth tried to hide her anticipation behind a nonchalant mask, but her perceptive father was not fooled and had the audacity to wink at her.

"Oh heavens! The gentlemen are already here. Girls, make haste! You should greet your gentlemen out of doors, not dawdle inside like indifferent, overbearing princesses!" Mrs Bennet scolded and pushed her two eldest daughters towards the entrance.

To avoid making a scene, the sisters complied and hastened out of the door.

Mr Bingley alighted first and only had eyes for Jane. He whisked past with her sister on his arm, when Mr Darcy's long legs appeared at the carriage door. He looked contrite, which was not the expression she preferred upon her betrothed's handsome face. Approaching her with his familiar long strides, he painted the very picture of health and manly prowess.

"I am so sorry, Elizabeth—"

Which were not the words she had wanted to hear, and she dreaded what would come next. *Surely, he cannot have changed his mind?*

"A circumstance beyond my control has arisen at home. Unfortunately, I must return forthwith. Please believe me, I would not leave you if it were not strictly necessary..."

"Pray, is something the matter with Pemberley or, God forbid, Miss Darcy?" Elizabeth fidgeted with her skirt and hid her hands behind her back.

"No, fortunately not, but my neighbour has died, and I am the executor of his will."

"I am so sorry for your loss. Were you close?"

Mr Darcy did not reply immediately but turned his head to gaze across the withering garden. Perhaps the neighbour had been such a dear friend that it was difficult to talk about him, and she had pried where she had no business. Elizabeth clutched her hands together and prayed she had not brought him pain, because once said, words could not be unsaid. She would be more circumspect in the future and wait for him to elaborate rather than speak out of turn.

At last, he spoke. "He was a close friend of my father's. I inherited the role in his will when my father died. I hope that

I shall not be gone for too long, but Sir Lawrence left no direct heir. I pray the successor to the baronetcy will be easily found and allow me to return swiftly to your delightful presence."

Elizabeth could not bring herself to look him in the eyes when he expressed his tender regard for her. It was too soon after fully recognising the feelings in her heart, but a smile erupted whether she wanted it to or not. It was disconcerting to be so little in control of her expressions and emotions. She should reciprocate the gesture, but not a word of affection sprung to mind. His sweet endearments rolled so naturally off his tongue, but then he had had longer to adjust to being in love than she. Elizabeth would strive to do better and return his sentiments —once her embarrassment had abated. It was perturbing how easily her cheeks warmed and her heart raced in these days that had passed since she had accepted him. He was solicitous and so heart-warmingly dear that she had to touch him. She boldly grabbed his hand and dared to raise her eyes to meet his.

"Then I shall wish you Godspeed and pray your business ends swiftly with a satisfying conclusion and returns you to me very soon."

Mr Darcy smiled briefly and tucked her hand around his arm. Thus linked together, they entered Longbourn's parlour. The other guests had yet to arrive, and her mother ushered the couple to a sofa seating only two. It was exhilarating and unnerving to be so close to the man you loved. Especially when your time with him would be short and the date of his return unknown.

"Pray, when are you leaving?"

"Who is leaving?"

Elizabeth had spoken too loudly, and her mother's extraordinary hearing had caught the essentials.

"I regret to announce that news from home demands my immediate return, but it is my intention to make my absence of as short duration as possible."

"I hope your family is well, Mr Darcy."

"Yes, they are, Mrs Bennet. My neighbour, the baronet Sir Lawrence Baslow, has died, and I am the executor of his will."

"I hope you will return soon, Mr Darcy."

"Yes, so do I…"

"Are you expecting someone to contest the last wishes of the baronet?" Mr Bennet enquired.

"No, not per se. I have concerns about finding and even determining who is the successor to the baronetcy. Sir Lawrence died childless and has no living brothers or nephews. His heir presumptive is an officer. He is deployed and might prove difficult to find."

Mr Darcy did not mention the obvious; that in times of war, not all men returned.

Mrs Bennet clutched her hands to her chest and swayed on her feet. Elizabeth closed her eyes, praying that her mother would not swoon.

"Then we should all join you, Mr Darcy!" Mrs Bennet cried. "What a merry party we would make, and Lizzy may familiarise herself with the house she is soon to keep."

Elizabeth studied the floor, utterly embarrassed that her mother had invited herself and her family to Pemberley. Mrs Bennet's manners were ill-adapted to do credit to her sense.

"What an excellent idea, Mrs Bennet. If it would not be too much of an inconvenience to travel, I should like to invite you all to Pemberley, including Bingley."

Mr Darcy had not mentioned Miss Bingley and the Hursts in his invitation because Mr Bingley had come alone to Netherfield. His pernicious sisters had chosen not to join him, which was not so strange when considering their treatment of Jane.

"You would travel as far as Derbyshire in the cold, my dear?" Mr Bennet interrupted and poured icy water on Elizabeth's pleasant musings about Pemberley's park.

"'Tis only October, and it is neither too cold nor too dark to travel. It is not the dead of winter, and what is a hundred and fifty miles in a well-sprung carriage? I declare it is nothing at all!"

"You have no fear of autumn storms and heavy deluges, then?"

"None at all, Mr Bennet. I dare say we can take shelter at an inn if the weather turns foul. I am certain Mr Darcy knows all the best hostelries."

"Yes, I have several that I recommend. It would also be convenient to draw up the marriage settlement at Pemberley," Mr Darcy mused.

Mr Bennet looked at Elizabeth, clearly hoping for support against the scheme from his favourite daughter, but she had none to offer.

"Pemberley's library is one of the finest in the country," Elizabeth teased her father. "It is the work of many generations and reaches the ceiling—of two storeys..."

Mr Bennet shrugged but nodded at his wife, whose effusions were as violent as could be expected from a woman who had travelled but little. Her effervescence by no means abated when the Lucases arrived, and the anticipated journey was the sole topic of conversation around the dinner table.

Mr Darcy sat beside Elizabeth and smiled tentatively.

"I hope you do not mind this turn of events?" he whispered in her ear. His breath wafted down her neck.

"On the contrary, Mr Darcy, I am relieved we need not separate for an unknown duration so soon after reaching an understanding."

Elizabeth immediately worried she had said too much and had

spoken too candidly about her wish to remain in his company. But the smile he bestowed upon her removed all doubts, and she returned the gesture until her cheeks begged for rest.

# Chapter 2 A Bygone Love Lost

Elizabeth did not know what she had expected, but she had not anticipated seeing so little of Mr Darcy once they reached Pemberley. She had hardly had an opportunity to speak to him, as he left for Edensor House after breakfast and did not return before supper. She counted every hour and thought them far longer than sixty minutes.

Mrs Reynolds and Georgiana were her solace in the absence of her affianced. Both had welcomed her with open arms, and her second day was spent touring the house with the ladies. The extensive building took all day to explore, and she postponed the garden to the following day. She had hoped that Mr Darcy would be at home to escort her because there was a maze not too far from the house. One could easily become lost between the tall hedges and steal a kiss... At twenty, she was more than ready to experience her first kiss, and the mere thought made goose-flesh erupt on her skin.

With Mr Darcy busy at Edensor, she had to settle for the company of his trusted greyhounds, who usually followed their master around the house. When their owner was away, they adopted Elizabeth as the leader of the pack and ambled with wagging tails in her wake.

To while away the hours of her fourth day at Pemberley, a trip to Lambton was decided upon. It suited Elizabeth particularly well because she had a letter to send. Her grandmother lived in Ireland, and circumstances forbade her from revealing that fact to all and sundry. Though she must inform Mr Darcy of the particulars before their wedding—a feat that had proved much more difficult than she would have surmised. She could no longer deny, at least not to herself, that she had hoped for more of Mr Darcy's time. It need not be much more than a minute or two, preferably alone…

Under Mrs Annesley's gentle chaperonage, Georgiana introduced Elizabeth to the denizens of Lambton as the future mistress of Pemberley. It was a pleasant excursion, and she met several local ladies who had the potential of becoming friends. She even caught a glimpse of Mr Darcy, talking to the blacksmith. He raised his hat but did not approach them, and Elizabeth would not disturb him while he conducted his business.

The vicarage was also due a visit on her fourth day. The current holder of the living was a young man whose wife had recently delivered a healthy boy he proudly presented to a symphony of adoring cries from the ladies.

In the evening, it did not escape her that Mr Darcy looked tired when he returned soaked from a downpour. His complexion was pale and his features drawn when he joined the party in the dining room. She yearned to enquire how close he was to completing Sir Lawrence's affairs but would not stoop to prying. What she *could* do was try to ease his mind when he was at home by curbing her mother's foolish chatter. The matron venerated the grandness of the estate to exhaustion. Mrs Bennet need not repeat every new discovery to the man who had lived there all his life. Manoeuvring placed her mother at the opposite end of the table at supper. Elizabeth prayed that Miss Darcy would forgive her. The young lady was gentle and unassuming, with sense and good humour to boot, so she was not too concerned. She smiled at Miss Darcy, who frowned whilst studying her brother. This would not do…

"Mr Darcy, I enjoy your company, but I would not be cross if you spent the night at Edensor when the weather is as inclement as it is tonight." She nodded at the windows where the rain was pelting against the panes. "I shall not have you compromising your health for my sake, and we shall spend plenty of time in each other's company once your business is concluded. When it is, I am of a mind to monopolise you entirely for one afternoon. I have spotted your hunting tower upon the hill and would like a tour when a convenient opportunity presents itself."

Mr Darcy looked at her with such warmth that her cheeks bloomed with excessive heat.

"An opportunity may present itself much sooner than you imagine. I have no obligations at Edensor on the morrow. We are waiting for news from town, and the execution of the will is at a standstill until I receive answers to my letters of enquiry."

Elizabeth was pleased. To have a moment of Mr Darcy's time, all to herself, was everything she could have hoped for.

"We shall have an additional guest for supper tomorrow. I hope you do not mind that I have invited Sir Lawrence's widow, Lady Baslow, to join our family meal. Her relations have yet to arrive. They are travelling all the way from Falmouth, and she is lonely in that big house. I believe I mentioned before that Sir Lawrence died childless?"

He had mentioned that the baronet had no offspring but not that there was a Lady Baslow equally denied. Elizabeth imagined the old lady must be in despair, losing her husband after decades of felicity with no close kin to comfort her.

"Certainly not. If you can bring her any relief, it should be done without delay. I can only imagine how she must be suffering..."

"Thank you. My acquaintance with Lady Baslow is of long standing. I shall tell you more about it on our excursion. Let us hope the weather improves."

"I shall pray for sunshine," Elizabeth quipped.

#

**The next morning.**

Elizabeth's prayer proved efficient. There was hardly a cloud in the sky when the betrothed couple set out for the tower. They walked in comfortable silence, breathing the fresh air and enjoying the soft rustle of the autumn leaves.

"I need to inform you about Lady Baslow before she arrives for supper."

Elizabeth halted abruptly and faced her betrothed.

"Oh no, Mr Darcy. I mean no disrespect to the grieving widow, but I am a selfish being. Our jaunt is for pleasure only. We shall forget all sadness and sorrow for an hour or so. You may tell me anything you like about Lady Baslow when we return," Elizabeth replied impishly. Mr Darcy had been much too serious during the week they had been at Pemberley, and she had every intention of providing him with a reprieve, ladled with an ample amount of teasing. He regarded her doubtfully but exhaled and appeared more at ease than she had seen him in recent days. Elizabeth judged it as proof she had been correct in denying him the chance to think any more about the Edensor estate and its future.

She was a little unsettled. She had, presumptuously, ordered a picnic set up at the tower. It was simple fare—wine and fruit—and although it was not yet her place to direct the servants, she hoped he would be pleased. In the event that the ground was too wet, she had requested a table and chairs to be delivered, but to her relief, the tower was bathed in sunlight. The floor beneath an old oak was completely dry, and she chose that spot to spread the blanket.

"It may not be the comfort you are accustomed to, but please, take a seat. You may rest your back against the trunk."

Elizabeth was smoothing out the blanket when she noticed Mr Darcy's crestfallen expression.

"I am sorry, Miss Elizabeth. I should have thought of something special for our expedition."

"Nonsense! You have too many weighty matters on your shoulders to arrange silly little gestures. You must remember, in the future, that I enjoy creating these small kinds of pleasures for those I love."

Elizabeth busied herself pouring wine, with her back turned, until her bashfulness dissolved. She had just admitted that she loved Mr Darcy, and she would not have him believe he must return the sentiment. The affectionate words had crossed his lips but once, though he had stated, less than a fortnight ago, that his feelings had not changed...

Mr Darcy sat leaning against the trunk of the oak with his legs stretched out and crossed at the ankles, his eyes closed, and his head tilted upwards to the sun. She put down the bowl of fruit, fetched the drinks, and sat at his knees. He opened his eyes, and she handed him his glass.

Elizabeth squirmed under the weight of his discerning gaze. What topic of conversation should she broach? And what layers were there yet to peel back before she truly understood him?

She had been granted the duration of her life to learn, and the thought made her smile. He returned the gesture and lifted his hand to caress her face. His thumb outlined her cheekbone, and a sigh of contentment escaped his lips. No words were needed; just sitting together felt intimate and comfortable, once she let her guard down. Elizabeth closed her eyes and leant into the soft touch until he took hold of her hands. Then he tugged her forwards and kissed her. The first kiss she had ever experienced. It was over so quickly that she barely managed to savour the exquisite tingle.

"Pray, excuse my forwardness," he whispered in a voice like the bourdon of a distant organ.

Elizabeth's heart soared in delight at her first kiss, and she comforted him with assurances that there was nothing to forgive. She shifted her weight from one arm to the other, and in doing so she inadvertently grabbed Mr Darcy's knee. He jolted at her touch and shifted away. Elizabeth was absolutely mortified at the liberty she had, by accident, taken upon his person.

\#

The dinner gong reverberated through the house. The two Bennet sisters attended to each other in the hour before dinner; Mrs Reynolds had appointed a maid for their use until Elizabeth had selected a proper lady's maid, but the sisters chose to do it themselves this evening, to be able to speak in confidence. Jane was dressing Elizabeth's hair, and Elizabeth would return the service once her sister had finished.

"Lady Baslow will join us for supper today," Elizabeth said whilst trying to keep still.

"How lovely. I shall enjoy making her acquaintance," Jane replied. "There, you are done."

"Thank you, dear Jane. I believe I have never looked better."

Elizabeth admired her reflection. The auburn ringlets Jane had arranged over her shoulder looked particularly attractive, and she anticipated watching Mr Darcy's response. He had been so solicitous on their picnic; he had even kissed her and admitted that he longed to be wed. His expression of such sentiments warmed her heart and eased her mind, even though her dress was not of the latest fashion and bore the tell-tale signs of frequent use. But dark blue was her favourite colour...

It was Jane's turn, and they swapped seats. They complemented each other, although their appearances could hardly be more different. Elizabeth was short, dark, and shapely, whilst Jane was tall, fair, and willowy. She was wearing her pale blue dress and looked like an angel after Elizabeth had removed the curling papers from her hair.

"Let us leave these ringlets unbound to frame your face." Elizabeth showed Jane what she meant, and her sister acquiesced to her suggestion.

"There, now we are both finished, and what a lovely pair we make." Elizabeth smiled at their reflection and hugged Jane.

"Careful, or you will undo all your effort. Let us make for the parlour whilst we are still presentable."

Elizabeth acquiesced and, arm in arm, the sisters joined their family. Mr Darcy met her halfway and complimented her appearance, which pleased Elizabeth very much. Especially when he gently touched one of her curls in an absentminded manner, as though it was not a conscious act but an urge.

"Lady Baslow, sir," the butler announced, and her betrothed looked away. Mr Darcy's Adam's apple bounced as he swallowed hard, and his restless eyes settled on the door. How deeply bereft the widow must be to affect him so. Elizabeth turned to greet the grieving old lady, but to her astonishment, the newly arrived guest was neither old nor particularly downcast. On the contrary, she was an alluring young woman whose beauty rivalled Jane's. Miss Bingley's description of an accomplished woman sprung to mind. There was something in her air and the manner of her walking. With ethereal poise, she glided across the room, tall and elegant, with captivating pale-blue eyes and shiny golden hair. She was beyond beautiful in her fine black crepe frock over a black sarsnet slip and a tastefully ornamented body with deep vandykes of velvet. The lady wore no mourning cap—as was also the custom in Meryton, but mourning traditions varied between town and country, and even from village to village. She gravitated towards Mr Darcy, the only person present who was familiar to her.

"Lady Baslow, may I introduce my betrothed?" Mr Darcy enquired.

"Yes, please do. I am grateful to her for allowing me to occupy so much of your time." Lady Baslow smiled tentatively and offered her hand to Mr Darcy, who bowed low over it.

Mr Darcy performed the introduction. Elizabeth dipped into a curtsey, and the celestial being nodded in return.

"Miss Elizabeth. I must thank you for your patience. I have stolen away your betrothed, who has been indispensable since my dear husband died."

"I am so sorry for your loss," Elizabeth offered. "If I can be of service to you, please do not hesitate to ask."

"Sir Lawrence is gone, and yet I am still here... How happy I once was when I was young and thought that nothing would ever change. Do you remember, Darcy? How very foolish I was. I did not even know my own mind."

Mr Darcy cleared his throat and seemed unable to respond. Elizabeth suspected that Lady Baslow was no simpleton, but it was cruel to force a gentleman to choose between agreeing she was foolish or to call her a liar. She decided to rescue him from the conundrum.

"I did not know you were acquainted from childhood." Since the lady appeared not so very much older than herself—perhaps a similar age to Mr Darcy—she assumed she was speaking of her youth. "I was under the impression that your family came from Falmouth."

"Oh no, the Conksburys' estate, Haddon Grove, is in Bakewell. My parents were dear friends of the late Lady Anne and Mr Darcy. My father was Lady Anne's cousin, and we spent much of our youth visiting each other's estates. But I understand your confusion. I have a married sister who lives in Falmouth. My parents and brother were visiting her when my poor Lawrence drew his last breath. I am anxiously awaiting their return. Ladies need someone to speak for them in matters of business. I pray my family will arrive very soon. Dear Lawrence's body is decaying, and the smell can no longer be concealed, even by the most aromatic flowers."

With the heavy rains they had endured lately, Elizabeth was

not surprised the Conksburys were delayed. The rutted roads must be nearly impassable, and Falmouth was so far away.

Mr Darcy offered to introduce Lady Baslow to the rest of their party, and they moved away. Elizabeth did not follow but studied the widow's walk with the intention of emulating it in front of the mirror later in the privacy of her chamber. A refinement of her bearing would not go amiss...

Supper proceeded with the usual fare and conversation. Georgiana entertained on the pianoforte afterwards, and when her concerto ended, Lady Baslow called for her horse and bade them good night.

"You cannot ride home alone in the dark! Why did you not bring the carriage?" Mr Darcy enquired, clearly aghast.

"I enjoy riding," Lady Baslow replied, as if it was the most natural thing in the world for a gently bred lady to brave a darkened path alone at night.

"I shall escort you. There have been reports about poachers of late. It is not safe."

"If you insist." The lady had the audacity to appear miffed. "Miss Elizabeth, would you care to join us?"

Elizabeth tried to remember whether she had ever had occasion to inform Mr Darcy of her barely passable horsemanship, but he did not meet her eyes.

"I have not brought my riding habit," she finally remembered.

"You can borrow one of mine," the ever-obliging Georgiana offered.

"If you do not mind the wait, Lady Baslow?" Elizabeth enquired.

"It is of no consequence. I must change myself."

Elizabeth hastened to Miss Darcy's dressing-room and donned a lush green habit that would have looked lovely on someone with a taller and slighter frame. Fortunately, the cloak would cover the most glaring deficiencies. If only her bonnet matched in colour; but alas it could not be helped that the ribbon was brown.

"Please excuse my lack of mourning attire," Lady Baslow said when Elizabeth arrived back downstairs. "The seamstress has not yet completed everything."

Her excuse was unnecessary. Lady Baslow's exquisite purple habit, adorned with a dainty hat, suited her golden tresses and pale complexion. Elizabeth tugged her cloak tighter and hid her trepidation as best she could.

Three saddled horses were waiting for them by the entrance. There was no mounting block, so Mr Darcy lifted Lady Baslow into the saddle, then approached Elizabeth.

"Would you allow me to lift you into the saddle, Miss Elizabeth?"

She nodded, and Mr Darcy's large hands enveloped her waist, raised her effortlessly onto the horse, and left a warm imprint upon removal. It was quite thrilling, and a look passed between them that made her heart flutter in delight.

"Thank you, Mr Darcy," she whispered.

The darkness would not allow for galloping nor cantering, and for that, Elizabeth was grateful. The moon was almost full, and the path was wide. Lady Baslow took the lead and trotted lightly over the grass. Mr Darcy gestured for Elizabeth to follow, but she shook her head. She preferred to bring up the rear because, that way, no one could observe her deficiencies.

They rode through the heathland with a few scattered trees here and there. Within minutes, Edensor House rose before them, and the torch-lit garden allowed Lady Baslow and Mr Darcy to race the last hundred yards. Elizabeth, for obvious reasons, chose to follow at a sedate pace.

"Ha, you still cannot catch me!" Lady Baslow laughed.

"I was not trying to," Mr Darcy defended himself.

"If that was true, you would have stayed at your betrothed's side."

"I beg your pardon, Miss Elizabeth. I forgot myself. It was our habit, when we were young, to use any excuse to race," Mr Darcy excused himself, looking rather contrite.

Elizabeth rather believed it was she that he had forgotten and not himself.

Mr Darcy's steed stomped the ground, and he had to walk him in a wide circle around the ladies. It would appear that the stallion resented admitting defeat as much as his owner.

A stable boy took the reins of Lady Baslow's horse. She dismounted elegantly without aid, and the servant called for someone to take Mr Darcy's horse.

"That will not be necessary. I shall return to Pemberley," he said.

They bade Lady Baslow good night and turned their mounts towards home. Upon arrival, Elizabeth waited until Mr Darcy was ready to lift her to the ground and thoroughly enjoyed the experience. She was walking off when the horse grabbed her skirt with its teeth, tugged her backwards, and licked her face. Elizabeth gasped, swallowed a shriek, and chuckled at her fright. The fabric on her too-tight riding habit had ripped, and she pulled her cloak closer.

"Blaze likes you." Mr Darcy smiled at her.

"I thought he was trying to eat me," she admitted with a laugh.

"He might have been. Your habit is a particularly lush green."

"Then I should hasten to my chamber and change before another animal decides to have a taste," she quipped and ran up the steps, remembering belatedly that ladies do not run and glancing at Mr Darcy. He was, unfortunately, following her with his eyes.

She hastened inside and leant against the door until she had calmed her racing heart. Then she enquired after the whereabouts of Miss Darcy. She found her at the top of the stairs.

"I am so sorry, but I have ripped the seam on the body of your dress. I promise I shall mend it first thing in the morning."

"Do not distress yourself. My maid will fix it. She is a genius with needle and thread."

#

Heavy bluish-grey clouds hung over Pemberley the next morning. The butler entered the breakfast room with a note for Mr Darcy. He cursed under his breath as he read it, but Elizabeth heard.

"I must go to Edensor. There is news about Sir Lawrence's successor that I need to address," he explained as he glanced at the window.

"It seems likely it will rain," Elizabeth remarked.

"Yes, and very soon. I hope I can get there before it begins."

"Are you not taking the carriage?"

"No, it is much faster to ride. I shall take the shortcut through the heathland. The road goes via Lambton."

He still looked tired, even though he had spent the previous day at home.

"Although I shall miss you dreadfully, I hope you will not risk your health returning if those clouds do deliver what they are threatening to. They look suspiciously dark, and I would not be surprised should a thunderstorm erupt."

"Let us hope not," Mr Darcy said with feeling and rose to order his horse saddled.

# Chapter 3 A Gallant or a Gentleman

Elizabeth had not heard Mr Darcy return from Edensor, and for that, she was grateful. She had experienced many thunderstorms in her life, and she was not fearful, but most ended in less than fifteen minutes. She kept waiting for the rolling thunder and lightning strikes to pass, but the storm continued in an endless blaze of flashes and claps. It was eerie how long it remained hovering above Pemberley's chimneys, and she could not help but feel a little uneasy. She lost count of how many lightning strikes hit the garden.

A flash lit up her chamber, and she leapt back from the window. A small fire caught in the grass and was doused in the deluge that followed. The heavy drops drumming on the windowpanes synchronised with the rhythm of her heart. Elizabeth prayed that Mr Darcy had stayed at Edensor and was not lying injured somewhere out in the rain. It was past midnight, and darkness had fallen hours ago, but Elizabeth could not sleep.

There was a quiet knock on her door. Elizabeth secured her robe tightly around her body and opened it. In the hall stood a trembling Jane, who had been afraid of thunder since lightning had struck the tree near their bedroom. A branch had broken off and smashed one of the panes. Elizabeth had been too young to remember and was usually the one who comforted her sister when a storm raged.

"Can I stay with you?" Jane begged.

Elizabeth opened the door fully to allow her sister to enter. "Of course."

They padded to the bed and hid under the covers.

"Has Mr Darcy returned?" Jane enquired.

"Not that I am aware of."

"I hope he is not caught in the storm."

"No, I do not believe so. Mr Darcy is much too sensible to risk his health when there is perfectly safe accommodation to be had."

"I am sure you are right." Jane yawned.

"How is Mr Bingley?"

"Very well..." Jane continued to expound happily on her favourite topic—her handsome and amiable betrothed—while the tempest raged over Pemberley for more than two hours before it finally passed on.

"Listen, the thunder has finally relented. We should sleep. You do not want to greet Mr Bingley on the morrow with shadows below your eyes."

Jane did not reply; her breath had evened out, but Elizabeth was not so fortunate. She could not be completely sure Mr Darcy had not braved the storm...

#

Elizabeth entered the breakfast room the next morning and was relieved to see Mr Darcy sitting amidst her family.

"Pray, tell me you did not ride through the storm!"

Mr Darcy smiled, but it did not reach his eyes.

"Good morning, Miss Elizabeth, and no, I did not. I took your advice and waited until it abated."

"Thank you." She smiled and allowed him to fetch her a plate of food.

The storm dominated the conversation, and Mr Darcy

informed them that he must ride out to appraise the damage. They should not expect him to be back before dinner, at the earliest.

Elizabeth watched from the window and saw an informally attired Mr Darcy enter the courtyard to collect tools and supplies. He took the working horses with him to pull logs from fallen trees back to the estate, which would serve as firewood once it had dried.

Mrs Reynolds was busy ordering food for the extra workers who had been called in to help. Elizabeth wondered what Mr Darcy expected of her. Should she aid Mrs Reynolds or pay her respects to the workers? If she had been at Longbourn, there would have been no doubt. Elizabeth decided she should contribute what she could and not be so missish. She helped Mrs Reynolds fill the baskets and walked out into the garden to greet the men who were repairing the damage. Mr Darcy's two greyhounds, Lord and Lady, had taken a liking to her and accompanied her wherever she went.

She rounded the southern corner of the house and saw a group of people approaching on the road from the north. They were making a racket, smacking sticks on pots and pans or banging lids together. It was a custom she was not familiar with, and she began walking towards them to learn what their purpose might be.

Lord and Lady whined, and she grabbed both by their collars to keep them from running away.

From the opposite direction, Mr Darcy came riding on his magnificent steed. He cut a fine seat, and she could not help but admire him. His mount seemed less impressed by the cacophony; it began to stamp and buck. Elizabeth watched from a distance as Mr Darcy struggled to keep all its hoofs on the ground, finally choosing to dismount and throw the reins to a nearby worker, who led the distraught horse away from the fray.

Elizabeth was still too far away to hear what the throng

shouted, but a maid she had previously encountered in Lambton broke away from the group and came running towards her. To her astonishment, a quarrel seemed to have arisen between Mr Darcy and the men. Loud, indiscernible shouts reached her across the lawn, whilst her betrothed pointed in the direction from whence the troublemakers had come. It was obvious he was trying to chase them off his land, but they paid him no heed. *Surely they could not blame the master of Pemberley for the storm?*

The maid reached Elizabeth and halted in front of her, heaving for breath.

"Please, madam, stay here. Go no farther."

It was a preposterous demand when Mr Darcy was clearly in danger from miscreants from the village.

"Whyever not?" Elizabeth exclaimed incredulously.

"We're playing the charivari[1] to the master of Pemberley."

"I am unfamiliar with the charivari, and no piece of music will ever stop me from supporting Mr Darcy. I dare say this noise is an insult to music in general."

"It might be called skimmington or stang riding in your home parish," the ill-mannered maid continued, undaunted by Elizabeth's churlish reply.

"I have never heard of either!" Elizabeth cried, her patience exhausted by the gibberish the servant spouted.

The maid sighed.

"Mr Darcy was caught in a delicate situation, embracing my mistress last night. This might be acceptable and even respected behaviour in London—I've heard them called gallants[2], as if it was something to admire—but this is Derbyshire. We don't tolerate adultery, Miss Bennet. Sir Lawrence might be dead, but he's not even buried. He's lying in the very same house where the sordid affair unfolded. The master of Edensor was much respected in the village as a benevolent man who was very kind to the poor."

It could not be true! Mr Darcy, who adhered strictly to every propriety, would not act so distinctly against his character.

"There must be a misunderstanding. I assure you, Mr Darcy would never—"

"I saw it with my own eyes, miss," the maid interrupted her, raising her chin in defiance.

The accusation rendered Elizabeth speechless. She did not believe her own ears, and now, she could not believe her own eyes either.

The men grabbed Mr Darcy by his arms and lifted his legs off the ground. He did not stand a chance of freeing himself from the strength of four or five men, though he made valiant attempts by thrashing and kicking. Pemberley's workers came running to his aid but were too far away to stop the event. Four burly men carried Mr Darcy to the lake, and after a couple of lofty swings, they threw him into the cold, murky water.

"This is ridiculous!" Elizabeth muttered through gritted teeth. Lord and Lady growled their support but remained close to her sides.

The rapscallions spat on the ground to show their contempt and retreated to whence they had come using the shortcut through the heathland leading to Edensor House.

"This is how we treat profligates in Derbyshire, Miss Elizabeth. With a dip in the lake to show our disdain and derision."

Elizabeth closed her mouth and tore her eyes away from the maid to look at Mr Darcy. He had made it to the bank, and the gardeners were helping him onto dry land.

"Madam, do not feel alarmed. This unfortunate event by no means reflects on our favourable impression of you."

Elizabeth had heard enough. She would not believe a maid so wholly unconnected to her who was employed by a lady she had no reason to trust. She turned her back on the stunned servant and ran to help her betrothed. Lord and Lady barked and followed. Mr Darcy was walking briskly towards the main entrance, dripping as he went. She reached him at the foot of the steps.

"Mr Darcy—"

"Not now, Miss Elizabeth." He dismissed her and left her rooted to the bottom step.

He had made it abundantly clear that he would not allow her to share his burden, and he had not deemed it necessary to contradict the claim of the rabble, but what vexed her the most was that the maid had observed her rejection. She would hasten back to her mistress and report the incident.

A ghost ran an icy hand down her spine, and she shuddered. She was not cold but needed a long and strenuous walk to gather her thoughts. She set out on a path leading in the opposite direction to the maid and her mob.

The obscene accusations could not be true. Mr Darcy was such a proper man with an inherent sense of propriety. Although he might allow acts of overfamiliarity upon his person by forward females like Lady Baslow and Miss Bingley, it was out of politeness that he did not rebuff them. Of that she was certain because he had not taken advantage of her, despite their status as a betrothed couple. He had not even requested the right to use her Christian name but had once let it slip that Lady Baslow's first name was Celia. Which was not so strange when she considered that they had been intimately acquainted since childhood.

The only liberty Mr Darcy had ever taken with her person was when he had held her hands and bestowed a chaste kiss—which was rather decorous for an affianced couple. He had offered her his arm and bowed over her hand on several occasions, but he had never kissed it. It was not his rakishness that troubled her but rather his lack of it.

She was concerned that Mr Darcy, with his excellent and gentlemanly behaviour, was a cold man. The thought had settled as a gnawing doubt in her mind. The fervent declaration of love in his proposal had given her the sense of a passionate nature hidden below his austere mien, but she had seen nothing of it since they had arrived at Pemberley. Had she been mistaken? Elizabeth prayed she had not. She wanted a marriage of devotion —ardour even—and she coveted a tactile relationship. Nothing scandalous, but a kiss on the hand, a warm embrace, or to curl up in his lap on a frigid winter evening. As much as she yearned to give small, affectionate touches, like patting his arm or holding his hand, her instincts told her that he would not appreciate such gestures, and that was what worried her the most. Would he ever demonstrate his admiration, or was he a man of words only?

If she was to be completely honest with herself, it was not enough. A jolt of pain hit her chest at his lack of tenderness. How could she believe he loved her when he did not need intimacy?

Was he too bound by decorum and duty? Would her life be limited to tedious days, waiting futilely for her husband to come home, with nothing to do? Of course, when the children arrived, she would have occupation, but how could they possibly be conceived with the staid Mr Darcy?

Elizabeth tried to conjure the image of an unclothed Mr Darcy in her mind, but he simply would not shed his coat and cravat for a moment of fancy. Was that a premonition of her future as his wife?

A chuckle escaped when she imagined what he would say if he knew about her musings. He would surely be shocked or appalled.

Elizabeth reined in her thoughts. These doubts, as common as they might be for a bride, served no purpose. Her rational thoughts were quieted by the cravings of her heart, which had decided that Mr Darcy was what it wanted, and nothing could ever change that fact.

Her circuit around the garden ended, and she entered the house to brush the dust off her hems.

"Miss Elizabeth!"

Elizabeth stifled a sigh and turned to Mr Bingley, who beckoned her into a parlour. Within, all her sisters sported stunned expressions and were holding hands whilst they huddled together on the sofa.

"I have heard about the atrocious accusations levelled at Darcy and the mob's undignified behaviour. How people who have known him for most of their lives can believe such a glaring falsehood is unfathomable. I have been his friend for a decade, and not once have I witnessed him act with anything but the utmost attention to propriety!" Mr Bingley blustered, then spluttered and coloured. "That is to say, he does occasionally speak out of turn, and he has a satirically bent mind that might offend, with no malicious intent, of course, on particular occasions with nothing to do..."

Mr Bingley must have remembered the insult Mr Darcy had spoken at the Meryton assembly, but she very much doubted his remarks had been sarcastic. No, he had been in earnest on that occasion. It was fortunate that first impressions could be improved...

"Thank you, Mr Bingley. I am certain Mr Darcy appreciates your staunch defence of his character. I dare say we shall not become the objects of any of his sarcastic remarks because I have never encountered anyone with so much to occupy his time."

"Lizzy, you cannot jest at such a moment, and I would be much relieved if you took a footman with you on your next stroll in the garden. I do not think it is safe to walk alone when a gang dared to enter Pemberley's park in broad daylight. Who knows what is lurking behind the bushes," Jane admonished with concern.

"I am hardly their target, Jane."

"Neither should Mr Darcy have been. These deranged people are not to be trusted."

"Do you think Lady Baslow is safe at Edensor?" Kitty worried. "She is so very pretty and elegant. I hope she will not be attacked like Mr Darcy was. Her dress would be utterly ruined."

"I hope she is well protected, and I believe her reputation will suffer more than her attire," Elizabeth remarked before turning to Mary. "Have you any instructive excerpts from Fordyce for me, Mary?"

"This is a most unfortunate affair and will be much talked about. But we must stem the tide of malice and pour into your wounded bosom the balm of sisterly consolation."

"Thank you, Mary. Do you know where Mama and Papa are hiding?"

"Mama suffered a fit of nerves, and Father has escorted her to her room. I am afraid she witnessed the entire spectacle and is now convinced that every resident of Pemberley is in peril," Kitty informed her. "Do you believe we are safe, Lizzy?"

"Yes, the thought of any threats made towards us Bennets is ridiculous. One of the attackers told me so herself. I am quite convinced. I should tell Mama. She need not fret for her own safety."

Elizabeth, with the intention of alleviating her mother's distress before she refreshed herself, walked into the hall just in time to see a dry and immaculately dressed Mr Darcy disappear into his study. He did not see her, which was just as well. She had no idea what to say to him that would not further embarrass them both. Her mother was much easier to assuage. She told her that the incident was a mistake and that a maid from the group had assured her that their favourable impression of her had not suffered. Her family must be included in this, and it would be best to pretend that it had never happened.

"I should wager a small fortune that Sir Lawrence's servants have been neglected in his will and are persecuting the messenger since the perpetrator is dead," Mr Bennet suggested. "For this purpose alone, I have not written a will myself. That way, no one need quarrel about my meagre possessions when I am gone."

Her father thought the whole turmoil a great lark, and Elizabeth could not help but think that her youngest sister had inherited one trait from her father. She never took anything seriously, and neither did he. Her mother huffed, but she was not aware of the calamitous effects of the absence of a will. Only Elizabeth was privy to the particulars, and she dearly hoped her father was jesting.

# Chapter 4 The Crooked Shapes of Dread

"Colonel Fitzwilliam!" Elizabeth exclaimed. She dipped into a quick curtsey after she remembered her manners. "What a pleasure to see you again."

"Miss Elizabeth!" he replied in equal astonishment. "I must beg you to pardon me for entering unannounced. I was not aware that Darcy had company."

"Of course, you could not have known. It was an impromptu decision made after he received the news about Sir Lawrence's death."

The colonel looked even more bewildered.

"I am so sorry. Did you not know? How inconsiderate of me to blurt it out so unfeelingly."

The colonel raised his hand to stop her apology.

"Think nothing of it. I heard the sad news about Sir Lawrence, though we were not close. It is nature's course to find eternal repose, and he was an old and feeble man."

Elizabeth eased and smiled. He must be here to offer his felicitations before their wedding.

"I hope your leave will extend to our wedding."

"May I offer you my sincerest congratulations?"

"You may." Elizabeth chuckled. It was the first time anyone

had asked whether she would accept felicitations. He must have noticed the disgruntlement between them at Rosings and feared she had been forced to accept.

"I wish you a long and happy marriage. And would you be so kind as to introduce me to your family? I have long wished to know those you spoke so warmly about in Kent."

"It would be my pleasure, Colonel."

Elizabeth introduced the good-natured colonel, and the merry exchange that followed did much to cheer the rest of her family.

#

Darcy paused his incessant pacing at the knock on his door and bade whomever was waiting to enter, hoping it was Elizabeth yet dreading the necessary conversation. What could he say to her but plead his innocence? Whether she would believe him after the performance by the lake was another matter.

Anger still simmered in his veins at the brutish treatment he had suffered at the hands of his neighbours, but he had to quell his vexation before speaking to Elizabeth. His relief was palpable when it was his cousin who entered, and he collapsed into his chair.

"Darcy, I suspected I would find you hiding in your study. The parlour seems a little too crowded for your taste at the moment."

The colonel grabbed a chair and positioned himself in front of Darcy.

"The Bennets are pleasant, if a little boisterous," Darcy admitted.

"I remember a time when you did not think so highly of them," the colonel reminded him.

"Yes, but I have since been chastised for my improper pride and disdain for the feelings of others."

"I would have liked to have been present on that occasion."

"You would have enjoyed it, I am sure. Especially since I did not."

"But you managed to become engaged?"

"Yes, I am betrothed to Miss Elizabeth Bennet," Darcy admitted with a measure of pride for accomplishing the difficult feat. "But you already knew that."

"I did not."

"But surely you must have received my letter?"

"I assure you, I did not, but I managed to conceal that fact when I greeted your intended."

Darcy searched through his papers and found the stack of letters informing his family of his engagement under a pile of bills from the butcher. He groaned and rubbed his hand over his face.

"Are you for Matlock soon?"

"Yes, and I do not mind delivering your letter to my parents and the viscount."

"Thank you. It has been a difficult couple of days, but I am happy Elizabeth finally consented to be my wife."

"Finally? I thought you did not even like each other. I was obviously mistaken. But it sounds like an interesting story—you must tell me about it later. What is this I hear about a contest to Sir Lawrence's will? My mother is rankled someone would dare defy the dear old man's last wishes."

"Sir Lawrence has two cousins, each descended from one of his father's twin brothers. The twins are dead, and their eldest grandsons are battling for the Edensor estate. John Baslow is the grandson of the first-born twin, while Robert Baslow is the grandson of the second."

"It sounds indisputable to me."

"One would think so, but Robert Baslow claims that the church register is wrong and that his grandfather was the first to be born."

"Does his claim hold any bearing?"

"I doubt it. None who were present at the birth or the christening are still alive. But he may delay the execution of the will for years if he chooses to take the dispute to the House of Lords."

"And will he?"

"I am trying to dissuade him. Whether I shall succeed remains to be seen..."

"And how is the fair widow faring?"

Darcy's head snapped up, and he studied his cousin. What did Richard know about his embarrassing display with Baslow's servants and tenants? He must have scowled because the colonel raised his hands in mock surrender.

"As well as can be expected," he finally replied.

"Then she is not bereft."

"That is cruel, Richard. We live in the age of reason, and Sir Lawrence is enjoying eternity in peace with his loving god. Such a fate is not an occasion for mourning but rejoicing. Besides, expressing deep grief in public would be inappropriate. Lady Baslow is a member of polite society. A calm and collected manner is expected, and certainly no displays of strong emotions."

"She has no strong emotions to display. She married a good man, but he was in his dotage even then. We both know she chose him for his wealth and consequence. You of all people should know. He essentially stole your betrothed from under your nose."

"We were not engaged. I had yet to reach my majority at the time."

"No, not formally. But everyone knew you were attached and

destined for each other. It was unusually cunning of him to make his move whilst you were attending your last year at Cambridge. I doubt he would have managed it once you had finished."

Darcy could not protest. *Had Miss Conksbury of Haddon Grove not been married when I returned, I would have proposed. How different my life would have been if it had been so. I would have had a partner when my father died and the responsibilities of a grand estate and grieving sister weighed heavily upon my shoulders. I would never have met Elizabeth. Or I would have, married with a brood of children at home. Would she still have caught my attention?*

"Your dreamy expression worries me. Are you having second thoughts about the little minx from Hertfordshire? I admit I was surprised to hear of your engagement. She is nothing like Celia. I would say she is the exact opposite. In looks *and* in disposition."

"Of course not! I admit to being a little confused, that is all. Old memories are haunting me. Do you find it strange that Lady Baslow is not mentioned in the will? She keeps the fortune she brought to the union, which is secured through her marriage settlement, but he left her nothing else. Not the right to live out her days at Edensor, no stipend, nothing."

"Not particularly. There was some tittle tattle back when they wed, claiming that she had forced his hand. It was mostly disregarded considering the prize she is and how fortunate he was to secure her. But the will might blow new life into that old rumour. Do you believe it was a coincidence that *you* were appointed executor of his will?"

"I was not, per se. It was my father who was assigned executor. I simply inherited the task."

"It has been five years since your father died—plenty of time for Sir Lawrence to change the executor of his will. Perhaps it was his way of pardoning himself for stealing your lady."

"We shall never know, and no apology was necessary. He had as much right to marry where he pleased as I. She accepted him of her own free will, and that is all."

Darcy rose, poured his cousin a glass of port, and filled one for himself too. They sat in silence, nursing their tumblers.

To be honest, he had questioned Celia's decision at the time. Her marked attentions towards him, Darcy, had been unmistakable. She had even declared herself to him in an unguarded moment. They had held hands without gloves, discussed their future, and shared fervent kisses.

"Hypothetically, is it possible to love two women?" Darcy regretted the enquiry the moment the words left his mouth. It might give Richard the wrong impression. He was not *that* confused.

"No, I should say not. Either one or both would not be love. You may have infatuations, but true and abiding love comes only once. That you can even ask such a question makes me worried that your recent commitment might have been hasty."

Darcy laughed mirthlessly. "It was the work of a year. If you call that hasty, I plead guilty. She rejected me the first time, in Kent. And very thoroughly too. Miss Elizabeth has a keen wit and is not afraid to use it."

*You are the last man in the world...*

"So that was what brought you so low after Easter."

"It was."

"How did you change her mind?"

"By divine intervention allowing me to correct a misunderstanding of sorts, combined with the goodness of her heart. By grace, she forgave me my transgressions. I can only hope she will continue to do so in the future."

"Do you need forgiveness?"

"I do not know... I was retained at Edensor last night. God, has it only been a day? A thunderstorm struck, and in the dead of night, a bolt of lightning hit the house near Lady Baslow's window. There was a loud crack. She screamed, and I ran to her aid, believing she had injured herself. When I entered her chamber, she was shaking so badly that I had no choice but to embrace her to calm her hysterics. Her maid and the butler discovered us thus engaged. And this afternoon, a group of Edensor's tenants and servants came playing rough music and threw me into the lake. Given what they accused me of, they believe I did more than embrace her. As if I would disrespect Sir Lawrence before he was cold in his grave! Preposterous!"

"Does Miss Elizabeth know?"

"Yes, she was there to witness the heinous act. But I do not believe she heard their accusations because she was, fortunately, too far away. She was playing with my dogs near the house. That she came running to my aid, as I was returning to the house, also indicates that she is unaware of the nature of the display."

"Did she not speak of it?"

"I was too embarrassed to talk to her. What must she think of me?"

"Very little if you do not tell her the truth."

"Will she believe me?"

"Probably. She is a rational being and not prone to hysterics."

Darcy was not so certain. She had believed him capable of depriving Wickham of a rightful inheritance and forcing him into a state of poverty with no more inducement than petty jealousy.

"By the bye, I have an invitation for you from Mother. She has requested your presence at her musical soiree on the morrow. She begs you to pardon her for the late notice, but she was not aware you had returned until yesterday."

Darcy sighed. Another social engagement was the last thing he needed, especially with the sordid rumours flying about.

"Must I?"

"Do you want to rouse my mother's ire?"

"No."

"Then yes. You must."

He supposed he had to... It was fortunate that, at least, the mourning widow would not be present to feed the gossip.

#

Darcy was most pleased. It turned out that an engagement away from Pemberley was just what was needed. An evening to put the Edensor troubles out of their minds and to enjoy each other's company unencumbered. He entered Matlock's ballroom with a smiling Miss Elizabeth on his arm. It had been arranged as a concert hall for the occasion, with chairs facing a temporary stage where the musicians had yet to take their seats. They were early, judging by the small number of people present.

The hosts came to greet them as their guests of honour with fervent felicitations. Miss Elizabeth was accepted into the family with no further ado. The earl whisked her in one direction, and Lady Matlock pulled Darcy in another. Under protest, he was dragged to a quiet corner, and he was fairly certain he knew why.

"Richard told me about your little dip in the lake."

"He should not have."

"Of course he should. You cannot redeem yourself without the support of your family. I have arranged everything because I know your disposition and your penchant for eschewing unpleasant situations. Hiding from a circumstance such as this will fuel the fire, not extinguish it. Therefore, I have persuaded Lady Baslow to attend, despite her being in mourning."

"She is here?" he cried incredulously.

"Lower your voice, Darcy. Yes, she is, and it is vital that she is seen speaking to Miss Elizabeth as if nothing were amiss. It is very convenient that you have recently become engaged."

"Thank you," he replied with as much sarcasm as he could muster.

Darcy turned and caught sight of Miss Elizabeth, on his uncle's arm, conversing with Lady Baslow.

"Be at ease, Darcy. Richard has spoken very highly of your betrothed. Her vivacious nature is just what will quell the gossip. When people see that she does not shun Lady Baslow but treats her as a friend, they will understand that there is nothing to the rumours."

"I would have appreciated being informed in advance as to your purpose for the evening."

"We both know that you would not have come. You simply must trust me in this, Darcy. I have navigated the treacherous waters of superior society for decades, and I know how to act in these situations. I pride myself in having often succeeded in averting repercussions from scandals. Besides, I have your best interests at heart, and this is the only method to prove that the tattlers are in error."

He tried to gauge Miss Elizabeth's response to the ambush, but she had her back turned. The one facing him was Lady Baslow, who acknowledged him with a nod. He wished she had not and considered whether he should single her out by returning the greeting or chance to overlook it.

"Stop staring at Lady Baslow, or even I shall become convinced that the rumours are true," Lady Matlock admonished. "Come, let us join the ladies."

Darcy obediently followed his aunt and halted awkwardly when he arrived. Miss Elizabeth's hand rested on the earl's arm, and he could not very well demand his uncle relinquish her. He wanted Miss Elizabeth to become acquainted with his family, and he could not fault the Matlocks' warm welcome of his betrothed. The introduction had gone much better than he had dared hope.

"Mr Darcy, what a pleasure to see you," Lady Baslow greeted him, latching her hand around his arm. "I hoped you would come to Edensor today because I have excellent news to relate. I received a note from my father. They have left Birmingham and should arrive soon."

He stared into her eyes and tried not to frown. If that little speech was supposed to quell the rumours, Lady Baslow was not as astute as he had thought.

Lord Matlock said something to Miss Elizabeth that he did not catch, but she delivered her reply in her usual arch manner.

"Is not general incivility the very essence of love?"

Lord Matlock barked a laugh, which was a rarity Darcy had seldom experienced.

In his distraction, Darcy failed to notice that the rest of the Bennets had joined their little party, but a shrill voice notified him of the fact.

"Lady Baslow, what a pleasure to see you again so soon. What a remarkable dress you are wearing. So particularly fine. The silk is exquisite and so becoming on you. I had never thought the day would come that I would encounter someone whose beauty rivals my Jane's... Not that Elizabeth is plain. She is very pretty. Mr Darcy certainly thinks so, or he would not have condescended to ask for her hand." Mrs Bennet drew a gulp of air before she continued. "My brother is a purveyor of fabrics, and I would like to know from whence your silk came and order some for my Jane's bridal clothes."

"I do not know, Mrs Bennet. I ordered the dress from a seamstress in Bond Street. You may enquire at Madame Celeste's regarding where she purchases her silks."

Lady Baslow was at least polite in her reply, but her measured tone of voice revealed her contempt. Miss Elizabeth's smile became forced, and she glanced at her father for support. Mr Bennet raised an eyebrow. Miss Elizabeth visibly stiffened and looked away. Darcy wished she had turned to him. Not that he had the authority nor the knowledge to subdue Mrs Bennet's overenthusiastic effusions. But he knew exactly how to curb her snubs towards her daughter. Only his aversion to making a scene prohibited him from speaking his mind on this occasion.

Lady Baslow saved the group from the awkwardness that had descended by enquiring after his cousin Viscount Crawford, and for that he was grateful.

"Lord Matlock, it has been too long since we were all together at Pemberley, Matlock, or Haddon Grove. We must not let it be so in the future. I have yet to greet the viscount. Is he at home?"

Lady Matlock answered as to her son's whereabouts, but Darcy paid them no mind. Richard approached, and he was frowning at him. Probably because he had the wrong lady on his arm. He shrugged to convey it was not his doing.

The colonel soon had other matters on his mind than Darcy's current predicament. The persistent Mrs Bennet forwarded her two remaining daughters to his cousin's notice. She squeezed herself in between them, and Darcy stepped back to avoid a collision. It was Richard's turn to squirm, and Darcy would be lying if he did not admit to taking pleasure in watching the spectacle. It was not so easy to reject a lady without giving offence.

The musicians had arrived and were tuning their instruments, guests were mingling, and with his attention directed at Richard, Elizabeth had been whisked away. He looked about the room and found her seated in the front row between the earl and the countess. The viscount was with them, and no other seats in her vicinity were unoccupied. He hastened to secure the chair directly behind her and belatedly remembered the lady still clinging to his arm. He would have preferred to have seen Miss Elizabeth's face to read her expression when the music began. Her emotions were displayed on her countenance, and it was always a delight to study. He would have relished being in her presence to offer her his handkerchief when the music moved her to tears and have the honour of escorting her to the refreshment table when the concerto ended. He had to detach himself from Lady Baslow, or this evening would cause further damage to his reputation. He leant in while the commotion of guests finding their seats would cover his words.

"Our purpose in coming here tonight was to refute the atrocious rumours about a liaison. I suggest we separate after the music has ended."

"I see your point, Mr Darcy," Lady Baslow agreed as she lost her grip on the opera glasses she was holding.

They were sliding down her skirt, but his quick response launched him forwards, and he grabbed them before they shattered on the floor. He righted himself, handed the glasses back to Lady Baslow, and turned in time to see Miss Elizabeth's head twist away.

He waited impatiently for her to look at him again, paying scant attention to the music, but an enraptured Miss Elizabeth was listening intently to the opera singer. She had a lovely voice, so he could not fault her taste, but no hoping or silent pleas on his part made her turn to him.

The musicians finished their performance. He applauded politely and tried to move from his seat, but an elderly lady beside him was struggling to rise. He offered her his arm, and with Lady Baslow supporting her on the other side, they managed to aid the lady to a sofa by the wall.

"Lady Baslow, it is a pleasure to see you. I only wish the circumstances were happier."

Darcy could not have been more pleased by Viscount Crawford's timely interruption.

"Thank you, Viscount Crawford."

"May I offer you refreshments? My mother sets an eclectic table, but I am sure I can ferret out the edible parts."

Lady Baslow curtseyed and strolled away on the arm of the viscount. Darcy exhaled in relief and searched the room for his betrothed. He did not immediately see her because Richard's wide shoulders obstructed his view. He was coming his way with an unmistakable expression.

"What in the blazes are you doing, Darcy? How do you suppose we shall stop the rumours with you stuck to the *bereft* widow's side for the entire evening?"

The sarcasm in Richard's voice did not escape Darcy, but he was not at fault in this predicament.

"Whose arts were at work here, I cannot say, but it was certainly not by *my* design."

"I am sorry. I must be mistaken. I took you for a grown man and not a child without a mind of his own."

Darcy tried to quash his ire, turned away, and briefly caught Miss Elizabeth's gaze upon him. They looked into each other's eyes. An eerie sensation fluttered through his chest. He somehow got the impression that her eyes saw nothing at all but were blindly staring into the air, and that he had randomly happened to be in her line of sight. She averted her gaze and hastened in the opposite direction. She was either avoiding him or suffered an urgent need to refresh herself before supper.

He followed her graceful movements until she disappeared behind a monstrous potted plant, then he reverted his attention back to his dolt of a cousin. At this moment he resented his whole family and would honestly prefer an evening in the sole company of the Bennets.

"What was I supposed to do? It was *your* mother who led me straight into a disadvantage with Miss Elizabeth."

"My mother led you to your betrothed. It was you who preferred another lady."

"Miss Elizabeth was captured in your father's grip."

"And you could not request an exchange with my mother?"

"Do not be so obtuse. That would not be the polite thing to do."

"No? If not perfectly decorous, it would have been the honourable approach and would certainly have appeased your betrothed's concerns."

"I shall warn you but once…"

Darcy glared at his cousin, who stared back at him in disgust.

"Very well, suit yourself. You are on your own for the rest of the evening and may ruin your future in any way you like."

"Thank you," he hissed and watched his cousin stride away.

Darcy found Mr Bennet nearby, and he asked whether he knew where to find Miss Elizabeth. Mr Bennet did not, and Darcy continued to search for her until he spotted her seated at a supper table, surrounded by her sisters. She looked resplendent, in earnest conversation with Miss Catherine. He had not thought the two would have much in common, but when he contemplated Miss Catherine's behaviour since Miss Lydia had left the family, he had to admit that she was a sweet girl and mostly well-behaved. Miss Mary was too awed in his presence to speak, but Miss Catherine occasionally paid a polite compliment to his estate or commented on the weather.

He took a seat as close to Elizabeth as he could find and asked whether he could fetch her some food. She declined, undoubtedly because she already had a full plate in front of her.

The food was clearly not to her liking because she had hardly touched it. It spurred a memory from one evening at Netherfield, where she had professed that she preferred a plain dish over a ragout. She would not find anything plain at his aunt's table. Lady Matlock liked to impress. He took a bite of his aunt's renowned pastry, the puits d'amour—the well of love—how ironic…

When those in his party had put down their knives and forks, he wasted no time in ordering their carriages. No one could fault him due to the long journey they had to get home to Pemberley.

He offered Elizabeth his arm and sought out their hosts to express a gratitude he did not feel and bid them a relieved farewell.

*How could I have imagined that my aunt would let us leave without stirring the pot?*

"Lady Baslow's conveyance has left. I took the liberty of offering her a place in your carriage so that the young ladies, who are soon to be neighbours, could become better acquainted."

Lady Matlock spoke loud enough for everyone to hear, so he had better quash that notion before he was committed.

"That is not possible."

"Dare I ask why? There is certainly room with only two in the carriage, and you need a chaperon."

His mind conjured the pleasant image from their journey thither. He had spent the carriage ride staring at Elizabeth, who had worn a slight smile as she gazed out at the passing scenery with only a sleeping Mrs Annesley to accompany them.

"Mr and Mrs Bennet are occupying the other two seats. Mrs Bennet has expressed a wish to try my particular upholstery and the new springs, as they are contemplating refurbishing their own."

He glanced at Mr and Mrs Bennet. It was not a lie, although the specific time had not yet been agreed upon. Unfortunately, that did not deter his aunt, who raised her voice above Mrs Bennet's clamorous delight.

"Very well. I suppose Lady Baslow can ride with the young girls."

He gave his aunt a hard look that she disregarded. They were soon ensconced in their carriages. Mrs Bennet's praise of the superior carriage was effusive, and an awkward silence descended upon the occupants.

Miss Elizabeth looked tired, and there was not a trace of a smile gracing her plump lips. She appeared deep in thought, judging by her serious expression. He was accustomed to studying her delight, and he kept surveying her handsome features, observing her serious countenance. He was startled when she turned to him and asked him an odd question.

"I have been contemplating a conundrum, and I cannot decide... Would you say propriety or honour is most important?"

He had a feeling he had participated in this conversation before. It reminded him of something Richard had mentioned previously, but in this instance, he knew the answer.

"I dare say you cannot have one without the other, so they are of equal significance."

Elizabeth tilted her head and regarded him earnestly.

"I would think there are small nuances that separate them. The meaning of the words are not the same."

"No. I meant that they go hand in hand, even though they are not exactly the same. You do not act with honour beyond the boundaries of propriety, and you cannot dishonour someone and act with decorum. Do you disagree?"

"No. Never mind me, Mr Darcy. My father can attest that I often get these silly, random thoughts when I am fatigued."

He wanted to make amends for the terrible evening that had sapped her of her vivacity, but he could not do so in the presence of her parents. Or could he give her some relief by a small gesture such as recognising her family? His relations had certainly not presented themselves in a good light this evening, and he still needed to atone for his abominable speech at the Hunsford parsonage.

"You may address me by my Christian name when it is just family, Elizabeth."

"You have not given me leave to do so, sir."

Could it be true? He tried to remember, quite certain that she must be mistaken, but he could not recall having offered her the use of his first name.

"Then please forgive my oversight. It must have escaped my mind. You may all call me Fitzwilliam, or Darcy if you prefer."

Elizabeth nodded her acquiescence.

Mr Bennet's eyes flickered between them. Mrs Bennet had fallen asleep, leaning upon her daughter who brushed away some wayward strands from her mother's face and kissed her hair. What would he not do to swap places with Mrs Bennet? Nothing sprung to mind that did not breach propriety.

After a brief stop to return Lady Baslow to Edensor, he was finally at home. He helped Elizabeth alight from the carriage, and she immediately sought out her sisters, who were generous in their praise of Lady Baslow. To his astonishment, Georgiana greeted them in the entrance hall. He thought she would have retired hours ago, and a pang of dread gripped his heart. For a moment, he imagined all sorts of disasters that could have befallen his sister. His troubled mind was assuaged by Georgiana's enquiries about the musical part of the evening. It appeared that the opera singer, whose name he had quite forgotten, was a favourite of his sister's, and she would not relent until all the particulars had been thoroughly examined. It was not his opinion she wanted though but that of the Bennet sisters. When had she become so at ease with Miss Mary and Miss Catherine? They were all addressing each other by their Christian names, and he had not noticed.

Darcy remained until the topic was exhausted; he wanted a word with Elizabeth. Should he apologise for the turn of the evening? He had yet to relate his history with Lady Baslow, which was even more important now after his involuntary dip in the lake. Elizabeth would better understand why the local people had drawn the hasty and erroneous conclusion once she had been made aware of their youthful romance. Their attachment had been commonly known, which was probably why everyone had believed the worst after the storm, he reasoned.

The girls were bidding each other good night; the moment was upon him, but it was a long story to tell, and Elizabeth had expressed that she was weary in the carriage.

"Elizabeth? May I escort you up the stairs?"

"You may," she allowed and rested her hand on his offered arm.

"I have not thanked you for the service you have done for my sister. She has not been so happy and at ease since... Well, you are aware..."

"Georgiana is a dear, sweet girl. I assure you that there is no reason to thank me. It is my pleasure to soon call her sister."

They had reached the landing and would have to part as their bed chambers lay in opposite directions. Yet again, he found himself tongue-tied and awkward. To imagine Elizabeth readying herself for bed was wreaking havoc with his faculties.

"Good night, Elizabeth."

He bowed low over her hand and contemplated kissing it. Only one thing often led to another, and the urge to tug her into his embrace was a hazard he could not risk.

"Good night, Mr Darcy."

Even the small, insignificant platitude soothed his soul. Her voice was like velvet to his ears, and the corners of his mouth twitched. She turned and walked away from him. Soon, he would be allowed to follow.

# Chapter 5 Veni Vidi Vici

"Lady Baslow to see you, Miss Elizabeth."

The lady herself followed directly after the butler.

Why had she come? There had been no more words spoken about the sordid affair with Mr Darcy, but her coming here would surely fuel the tattle.

"You find me all alone this afternoon, Lady Baslow. Mr Darcy has gone on an errand to the village, and the rest of my family is resting."

Mr Darcy and his men had worked tirelessly for days in the aftermath of the destructive thunderstorm, and he had decided to treat them to a night of food and drink at the Rose and Crown. The master was not participating himself but had gone to make a speech to express his gratitude before letting his tenants and servants celebrate undisturbed.

"I came to see you, Miss Elizabeth. We had such a marvellous time together at the Matlocks' musicale. It really has been too long since we were all together. I imagine we shall make up for lost time when my parents and brother arrive."

"Mrs Maria Dickons is a lovely soprano. I saw her once as a child at Vauxhall Gardens," Elizabeth replied, avoiding the unpleasant topic of last evening. Her sentiments differed vastly from Lady Baslow's.

"You were fortunate to reside so close to London. We Derbyshire children were left at home while our parents enjoyed

47

the Season in town, usually tucked away at one of the estates to take advantage of each other's masters. Georgiana was not born until we were twelve—by we I mean my brother Cornelius, me, and Fitzwilliam. Colonel Fitzwilliam is two years older, and Viscount Crawford is four. Oh, the mischief we made... It was very convenient to be the only girl because our tutors never blamed me for any of the trouble we caused," Lady Baslow related with a slight smile.

"It sounds like an ideal childhood."

"It was, it certainly was... Of course, we all grew up, and the boys were sent to school, and I was finally allowed to go to London for the benefit of the superior masters. We met occasionally in town and at Christmas parties, but it was the long summers I cherished the most. You know, there was a wager in the books at White's about whom I was going to marry out of the three boys. It was not a competition, really, because everyone knew it was going to be me and Fitzwilliam. He proposed every year from when he was five years old. I always replied that he had to wait for his majority and an allowance that could support a family. But he was so sweet, kneeling with a bouquet of flowers he got into trouble for stealing from his mother's rose garden."

"What an adorable tale and such happy memories. I can just picture a serious little boy, begging his childhood friend to marry him."

And rather different from his adult proposals, Elizabeth imagined, or Lady Baslow would not have let him approach her a second time.

"Darcy was not a serious child. He was as merry as the rest of us. He lost his gaiety when he was about twenty."

"What happened?"

Elizabeth wondered whether it could have been after the death of his mother. Something he had said had made her believe they had been quite close. But the answer made her wish she had never enquired.

"I married another man, and he was crushed. For a time, I worried he would drink himself to death or get thrown from his horse on one of his reckless and irresponsible rides. He ranted and raved at me, of course. We had an understanding that I would wait for him until he reached his majority, but he was still a boy, and Sir Lawrence was a grown man.

"We were all so worried about him, and then his parents died so unexpectedly, within a year of each other. Lady Anne was four-and-forty, much too old for childbearing, and neither the mother nor the child survived. Mr Darcy took the blame upon himself and followed his wife to the grave not a year later. The doctor said he died of a broken heart..."

"Pray, how long did this game of proposals continue?"

"Every fourth of August for fifteen years."

Was that not the date she had visited Pemberley with her aunt and uncle? Elizabeth was certain that it was. Could that be the reason he had travelled ahead of his party? To grieve a bygone love lost, in peace. Haunted by pleasant memories, could he have made a rash decision to pursue her, Elizabeth, to rid himself of his loss?

"Had I known he would take it so hard, I may have acted differently. You are the first lady he has shown even a remote interest in. I am so glad he has found you, and so vastly different you are from the one who disappointed him. I shall go as far as to call us complete opposites. I am a selfish creature, whilst you are so compassionate and generous, but I must confess— a bit naïve... But so was I at your age. I hope that I have learnt from my mistakes, and one should always beg for forgiveness when one has sinned. Which is why I must beg your tolerance and clemency for a moment of ill-advised passion. I swear it was not by design but due to extraordinary circumstances that lowered our guard so abominably. I have always been fearful of thunderstorms, but this one seemed supernatural in the way it lingered and raged. I was so very frightened, and Darcy was an old friend whose embrace I had known since childhood. Of course, he is a grown man now and very much improved in figure. He was a late bloomer and so adorably awkward, but I am glad he has outgrown the quirks of his youth...

"I was witless with fear and fell deeper into his embrace rather than pull away—as I should have. I cannot explain the madness that followed. Cupid must have fired a dozen arrows and compelled my pulse to beat in the rhythm of love. The ardour proved impossible to resist. I was senselessly heady and enslaved by the powerful magic of his persuasion. How was a mere mortal like me to subdue such a fatal attraction after he had confessed his most ardent regrets? I could have as easily vanquished my soul as conquered the yearnings. No, I was consumed by Darcy's divine fervency."

Lady Baslow brushed some imaginary fluff from her skirt. A stunned Elizabeth could not speak but studied her opponent's calm and collected comportment. It was difficult to imagine the lady affected by any form of emotion—a trait she shared with Mr Darcy. Could it be true?

"I woke up at dawn. We had forgotten to close the curtains, and I shrieked because the first thing I noticed was a hideous scar on his buttocks. It had healed in a distorted fashion, and my scream woke him. When he turned, I had to laugh because of his heart-shaped chest hair. Is it not adorable? God must have made him in the image of a lover.

"But unfortunately, my cries alarmed my maid, who hastened to my room. Due to her concern for my wellbeing, she forgot to knock and wait to be admitted. Of course, my butler had discovered us the previous evening and caused us to jump apart. So, you see, it cannot be concealed fr—"

Jane entered the room and interrupted Lady Baslow's confession mid-sentence with a brilliant smile.

"Lady Baslow, it is a pleasure to see you." Jane curtseyed, turned towards Elizabeth, and frowned.

Elizabeth worried that her anguish was discernible on her face and tried to smile to placate her sister.

"Have you not rested, Lizzy? You look frightfully pale. If you have one of your headaches, I must warn you that our mother and sisters will join us soon. Mama will be so glad to see Lady Baslow, and so will Mary and Kitty. But their ebullience might not be the best remedy for a migraine."

Jane turned away from her to address the widow.

"You made quite an impression upon our younger sisters. They admire you very much," Jane explained.

Elizabeth was not in any condition to endure company. Especially not such a hateful object who brought nothing but disappointed hopes.

Pain, despair, and jealousy crowded in her heart and swelled until it was nigh on bursting. The violence of her emotions robbed her of her breath and every rational thought. Lady Baslow's admissions had guided her through a labyrinth of doubt to an open field of certainty, but a landslide had ripped the ground from beneath her feet. She rose to escape the confining company, and her sight clouded into blackness.

Jane was shaking her whilst muttering unintelligible nonsense. It took her a while to notice that the solid surface beneath her was the floor.

"Are you able to rise?" Jane enquired.

"Of course," she replied without thought, but the world spun as soon as she lifted her head. "Or not. Give me a moment, and I am certain I shall be well."

"You are not well, Elizabeth."

"Perhaps a glass of wine would not go amiss," a measured voice spoke from above.

The owner of the voice must be an angel. She was even fairer than Jane with an incandescent halo of golden hair. Tall and resplendent, she loomed above Elizabeth.

That two such ethereal beauties existed in the world was unfathomable. Had she not seen it with her own eyes, she might have thought she had died and gone to heaven.

Sudden memories assaulted her senses, and her wayward thoughts sobered. The dizziness disappeared, and she managed to rise from the floor and haul herself onto the sofa. Jane offered to fetch the aforementioned glass of wine and hastened from the room, leaving her to a miserable fate.

Elizabeth had never cured a headache with wine in her life but chose not to oppose the idea. It was clear that Lady Baslow had not finished, and she might as well hear her last confessions. The widow reached out, as though to lay a comforting hand on Elizabeth's arm, but she recoiled.

"You have my deepest sympathy, Miss Elizabeth. I am so sorry you are injured by our news and must be suffering vastly. I grieve to be the bearer of such dreadful tidings, but I could not leave you in ignorance. It will soon become known to all, and it is better to be prepared than caught unawares. If you need any further details, I am happy to oblige."

Elizabeth decided to put her off as civilly as her anxiety gave her leave. "Lady Baslow, I want nothing further from you. I must beg you to leave as expeditiously as possible."

"Miss Elizabeth!" Mr Darcy advanced rapidly into the room and came to a stop before her. His concern was unmistakable, lodged in the crevice between his brows. Jane must have told him about her ridiculous display, and contrition grew beneath her breast.

In a deep voice, he whispered for her ear alone, "How can you throw a grieving widow from my house? Have some compassion!"

Elizabeth bowed her head to conceal the tempest that rolled

through her in wave upon wave of unmitigated rage. She rose to leave before she could say something stupid. "Pray excuse me. I am not feeling well."

She brushed past the colonel, hardly cognisant of anything around her, and fled the room. Fortunately, Jane was coming down the hall with a glass of wine in her hand. "Should you not be lying down?" she admonished.

"Pray, if you would escort me to my room, I promise to do exactly what you ask of me."

Jane looked at her quizzically, and Elizabeth tried to conceal her anger. Whether Jane understood or not, she acquiesced without further enquiries.

She reached her room, tore off her gloves, tossed them into a corner, and flung herself onto the bed just in time to bury her head beneath a pillow. The turmoil turned into tears and allowed for more rational consideration.

Jane busied herself unbuttoning Elizabeth's dress and loosening her stays, muttering to herself that they must have been tied too tight and that was the reason for her indisposition.

"What has upset you, Elizabeth? Do you have a migraine?"

Jane only used her full name when she was deeply concerned. Elizabeth knew she owed her sister an explanation, but she could not manage it at present.

"I shall tell you but, please, not tonight. You are right, I do have a fierce headache. The pain flashes hard and hot in my head. I need to rest," she mumbled into the pillow.

Jane patted her shoulder, and her sister's weight lifted off the bed. "I have left a glass of wine on your bedside table. Perhaps I should fetch you a glass of water instead?"

Elizabeth shook her head and proved that she did have a headache. The motion made her wince. The door closed, and the silence left behind advanced upon her. The quietude brought her no peace of mind, only emptiness. Neither her scruples nor her vanity were strong enough to withstand the shock to her pride. *No! Let me rather die than beg for his constancy.*

Frightened by her own thoughts, she flung the covers off and jumped to the floor. Pacing back and forth, her need to escape her engagement was foremost in her mind. But her mother would never allow it, and her father would be too entertained to act.

Oh, why had she interrupted Mr Darcy when he had wanted to tell her about his previous history with Lady Baslow? It would have been better to face the truth prepared rather than unawares. She had felt skinless against Lady Baslow's confession, but then, she had never imagined the lady's shared past with Mr Darcy had been so consequential.

It was impossible to compose herself enough to rest. She tossed and turned until dawn broke. In her breast beat a hollow shell that once had been a complete heart. Veni Vidi Vici—he came, he saw, he conquered. She had danced on roses and was left with thorns in her feet.

#

After a short respite in Morpheus's arms, Elizabeth awoke to a maid stoking her fire. She contemplated forgoing breakfast, but that would only lead to questions from her mother that she was not prepared to answer. She was late going down; her family was already seated, and so was Mr Darcy. He stood and bowed at her entrance but did not meet her eyes.

"May I prepare a plate for you?" he enquired.

"I thank you, no. A cup of tea will suffice at present." Elizabeth made the tea herself. Mr Darcy resumed his seat and picked up the newspaper. The atmosphere was tense and uncomfortable; even her family was quiet.

"May I have a moment of your time, once you have finished your tea?" her father enquired.

"Certainly," Elizabeth replied after taking a sip. It tasted bland. "If you have finished your meal, I see no reason to delay," she added.

"Then let us adjourn to the library."

Elizabeth smiled; her father was easy to predict. They strolled in silence until the library door closed behind them, then he guided her to a corner and gestured for her to sit. He did not take the opposite chair but paced restlessly in front of her.

"There is no polite way for me to broach this subject, so I shall not attempt it. Are you with child, Elizabeth?"

Elizabeth was shocked.

"Certainly not! How can you even accuse me of such a thing?"

"You have never fainted in your life! Spells of dizziness are an early sign of pregnancy. Combined with your waning appetite, pale complexion, and the awkward conversation in the carriage between you and Mr Darcy, it is a fair question."

"But a child? How little you know me if that is your conclusion. Let me ease your concerns. I am not with child. It is in every way impossible. And yes, I know how they are created."

# Chapter 6 Happiness is Seldom of Long Continuance

"Lord Matlock, Lady Matlock, and Viscount Crawford will join us this evening. I have just been informed that the Conksburys arrived last night. I shall read the will on the morrow, and Sir Lawrence's funeral will be held the following day," Darcy announced in the parlour before he ducked behind his newspaper.

The atmosphere had lost the ease from their first week at Pemberley. Mrs Bennet still chattered, Miss Bennet still smiled, and Mr Bingley looked more moon-eyed than ever. It was an indefinable shift, but he observed that Miss Elizabeth had begun to avoid her father, which was very strange indeed. He had always regarded their relationship as particularly close.

That she eschewed his own company was certainly more understandable. He needed to explain yesterday's events to her and beg her forgiveness, preferably when she was not entertaining his cousin. If he could manage a moment of privacy...

The butler entered with a note for him on a silver salver. He unfolded the unsealed piece of paper with an inward sigh. On the Pilsley tenant farm, a tree had fallen and hit the house, and the damage was substantial. Darcy had thought all the repairs had been completed. No one had noticed that the tree had been struck in the storm, and a gust of wind had finished it off.

His steward wanted him to come and determine whether the house was repairable or needed to be rebuilt. He should take a carpenter who could estimate the cost of both outcomes. He preferred to use Beeley in Lambton and hoped he was free.

"Richard, would you accompany me to see Pilsley? A tree has fallen through the roof of his house, and I need to appraise the damage," he blurted out before he had even raised his eyes from the note.

Richard had been speaking to Elizabeth, whom he had interrupted mid-sentence. Would he ever cease to offend her, or was he forever doomed to err where she was concerned? She made him anxious—through no fault of her own. It was he who turned into a bumbling fool whenever she was around. He had hoped time and familiarity would conquer the affliction, but judging by his latest efforts, it had grown worse.

"Heavens! Were there any injuries?" Miss Elizabeth enquired.

Her face was a picture of concern. She had such a compassionate heart.

"No, by divine intervention the family was spared, but the house is in a miserable condition. It is uncertain whether it is beyond repair. I beg you to pardon me for interrupting your conversation, but I thought the colonel might be interested in seeing it. Richard?"

"Yes, I shall accompany you."

He needed Richard's advice on another matter, and the long ride to his most remote tenant farm would provide him with ample opportunity.

"Good. If you have finished eating?"

Richard nodded and rose from his chair. Darcy stood up, and they went to change into their riding clothes. When he returned to the entrance hall and ordered his greatcoat and hat, Miss Elizabeth emerged from the shadows of the statue of Venus.

"Pardon me for interrupting you again, but how is the family faring? Have they a roof over their heads?"

"Yes, according to the note, they have moved into the hayloft."

"If there is anything I can do?"

"No, they are well taken care of."

It was the wrong thing to say, but he could not take it back. It was like he had snuffed out the light in her eyes. She gave him a forced smile and wished them a safe journey.

"I owe you an apology for drawing a hasty and erroneous conclusion last evening. I must beg your forgiveness and pray that your health has recovered."

She was regarding him with an inscrutable expression; it was impossible to deduce her frame of mind.

"We are both prone to hasty and unfounded presumptions. That, I can easily forgive." She smiled whilst mischief danced in her eyes. Or was it contempt?

Richard called from the courtyard; the saddled horses were stomping impatiently. All he could do was to leave unsatisfied. With a final bow to Miss Elizabeth, he donned his greatcoat and hat and strode to his waiting mount. They rode in silence until they were out of earshot of the men working in his gardens.

"I need your advice on another matter," Darcy addressed his cousin. "I have a conundrum to sort out. After my dealings with Lady Baslow and the events in the aftermath…I am loath to return to Edensor House. Well, the funeral is no issue, but I must read the will now that all the beneficiaries have arrived. I wonder whether I should ask someone else to do it?"

"No, absolutely not. That would only confirm your guilt. I say you should return to Edensor House with your head held high and prove them wrong."

"Yes, that is sound. Thank you, Richard."

"And while you are asking for my advice, I am going to

offer you some that is unsolicited. Miss Elizabeth is a vivacious creature, and she needs occupation to thrive. Why did you not give her a task to help the Pilsleys? Or were you too concerned with appearing the great master?"

Perhaps he had not mended his pride as much as he had thought...

"You may not believe it, but I have trouble thinking clearly where Miss Elizabeth is concerned. If I do not have a speech prepared, I tend to say nothing at all or blurt out something absurd or abominable."

"I have no problem believing you, and you are fortunate that she did not berate you last night. Anger was clearly written on her face, and I am curious what you could have said to her to make her flee in a rage."

"I might have castigated her for throwing Lady Baslow out of my house and urged her to have some compassion."

"Hell and damnation, Darcy! For a sensible man, you are extraordinarily dull-witted in your dealings with women."

He could not but agree with that sentiment.

"It is just that I have never heard her be cruel to anyone before. And to choose the grieving widow of a titled gentleman seemed so...unnecessary. When we were at Netherfield, she met that harridan Miss Bingley's frequent barbs with sweet archness."

"She might have a greater incentive in this case. She could be blaming Lady Baslow for the lake incident."

"I need to inform Elizabeth about my current and former dealings with the widow. I have just begged for her forgiveness. She must be getting tired of accepting apologies from me...and I need to make up for my inattention for the last fortnight."

"I think you are intimidated by your betrothed, and you are avoiding her company for fear of being perpetually outwitted. Perhaps some exercise will restore your sense?" Richard grinned and kicked the flanks of his mount.

It took Darcy a few seconds to absorb his cousin's words and to spur forward his own horse. Richard arrived at the tenant's farm before him, and he would have to endure his gloating for the rest of the day.

Beeley was there with Darcy's steward, Mr MacGregor, and after a thorough investigation, the decision was taken to rebuild. The work would begin immediately. Winter would soon be upon them, and the hayloft was unsuitable accommodation.

#

Elizabeth encountered Mrs Reynolds in the hall after breakfast.

"Mrs Reynolds, I understand that the Pilsley farm suffered considerable damage last night, and I wondered whether I could be of service?"

"Oh no, miss. Mr Darcy has everything well in hand."

"But…I heard that they had to take shelter in their hayloft. Perhaps we should send them warm blankets to stave off the chill?"

"The master has already requested the delivery of blankets, warm clothing, and food. He will also arrange for them to stay at a nearby neighbour's farm, knowing full well that Pilsley will decline. His farm is on the outskirts of the Pemberley estate and far from his closest neighbour's house. I suppose he will want to remain to rebuild. Mr Darcy truly is the best landlord and the best master that ever lived."

Elizabeth thought he might be too generous towards one neighbour in particular, but she kept that thought to herself.

"You have painted him in a very favourable light."

"But of course. I have never had a cross word from him, and I have known him since he was four years old."

*'She is tolerable but not handsome enough to tempt me.'* Elizabeth chased away her uncharitable thoughts and smiled at Mrs

Reynolds.

"There are very few people of whom so much can be said. You are lucky in having such a master."

Mrs Reynolds smiled.

"Are not we both? I dare say we could go through the entire world and not find any better. But then I have always observed that they who are good-natured as children are good-natured when they grow up. Mr Darcy was the sweetest-tempered, most generous-hearted boy in the world."

'Have some compassion!' Elizabeth remembered his words from last evening, and the muscles in her cheeks ached from forcing her smile. Mrs Reynolds continued her speech, but Elizabeth was not truly listening to her words.

"—and so very handsome. There is a likeness of him as a boy in the gallery. Do you remember where it is, or would you like me to escort you?"

"Oh yes, I remember it well. Please, do not let me detain you any longer, Mrs Reynolds. I shall manage to find the gallery on my own."

Elizabeth continued to the stairs but encountered Miss Darcy's lady's maid at the top.

"Marriott, do you need any help mending Miss Darcy's riding habit?"

"Oh no, miss. The tear was ever so small, and I finished it days ago."

"Good, thank you."

She continued down the hall to the picture gallery, which was lined with Mr Darcy's ancestors. The Darcys had once been titled, but the earldom had been lost because there was no male heir, and the current Mr Darcy's line had inherited through the bachelor earl's sister. Elizabeth wondered why the earl had not married when he had such splendour to offer his offspring...

That must be why the current Mr Darcy had proposed to her. A sturdy country miss to carry his children when his true love was unattainable.

Elizabeth saw nothing of Mr Darcy until supper. She did not mind in the least and wondered whether she needed to be present when the Matlocks arrived. Since the master was away, the library was a safe choice and a great comfort. She found a novel written by a lady and curled up in a chair by the window. Deprived of sleep from the previous night, she could not stay awake.

#

"Lizzy, I thought I would find you here. I only wish I had thought of it sooner."

Her father was shaking her with a firm grip on her shoulder. Elizabeth tried to bat him away, but he persisted, and she reluctantly opened her eyes. A quick glance out of the window revealed that it was already dark.

"Heavens, how late is it?"

"It is a quarter to seven. Supper will be served in an hour. The Matlocks have arrived, and we have been looking for you. You should greet your new relations."

Elizabeth looked down at herself. She was wearing an old walking dress, wrinkled beyond redemption.

"I must change."

"Then make haste. It does not do to let an earl wait."

Elizabeth hurried up the stairs and rang the bell for her maid. She arranged her hair as best she could with so little time, and she arrived in the parlour a little flustered. She drew a deep fortifying breath before she entered the fray.

To her consternation, no one noticed her entrance. An unfamiliar officer was quarrelling with Lady Baslow—a very unwelcome addition to their party. Why had she come? To gloat?

"Why did you leave Robert at home? He could be packing your effects and changing the locks as we speak. And I doubt it would take long since the furnishings belong to the estate." That the gentleman was behaving uncharitably towards Lady Baslow aroused Elizabeth's curious nature.

"He is not!" a second unknown gentleman cried as he brushed past Elizabeth, who had halted just inside the door.

"Robert!" Lady Baslow exclaimed.

"I could not let that snake John have the ear of the executor of the will alone. Heaven knows what he might say to try to convince Mr Darcy."

"It is Sir John now, Robert."

"You cannot claim the title before the funeral!"

"Gentlemen!" Mr Darcy stepped between the two, who stood toe to toe, glaring at each other. "I have no authority over the contents of the will, nor the result. I simply have to read it. You may both petition the Lord Chancellor for a writ of summons to the House of Lords for the next Session."

The Earl of Matlock stepped forwards. Elizabeth had not even noticed he was there.

"Why do we not enjoy our supper and discuss business after the ladies have withdrawn."

The gentlemen all nodded in deference. The earl set his eyes on Elizabeth.

"Find Mrs Reynolds and ask what the delay is about."

Elizabeth curtseyed, turned, and walked out of the door. The earl either had not recognised her and mistaken her for a maid, or perhaps he did not bother with pleasantries since he was a peer and could behave as he liked. Hurried footsteps followed her, and she did not need to turn round to know it was Mr Darcy.

"Miss Elizabeth!"

She stopped, faced him, and cut him off before he could utter another word.

"Go back to your guests and try to stop them from killing each other. I shall find Mrs Reynolds and order the additional three places at the table."

She did not wait for a reply before she continued down the hall in search of the housekeeper.

Elizabeth found Mrs Reynolds, and the table was set for the additional guests. She procrastinated until dinner was announced. Mr Darcy was looking for her and approached in long strides. He offered her his arm, and she had no choice but to take it. Together they entered the dining room. Mr Darcy escorted her to the head of the table and helped her into her seat. It was the first time she had held the position of mistress. Miss Darcy had previously sat at the top of the table when they dined, and she glanced at Mr Darcy's sister. She was smiling shyly at her and did not look surprised. Mr Darcy must have asked her permission for the change in the arrangements. He lingered, resting his hands on the back of her chair. Heat radiated to the exposed skin on her shoulders where his fingers touched her ever so lightly. Every muscle in her body became taut, but Mr Darcy remained until everyone was seated.

"May I introduce my betrothed to those of you who have not yet had the pleasure. Miss Elizabeth Bennet of Longbourn in Hertfordshire and I are engaged to be married on the eleventh of November."

Elizabeth dared not meet the eyes of the Matlocks, and she bowed her head. Neither could she gainsay Mr Darcy and reveal before his relations something she had yet to inform him of: there was not going to be a wedding. At least not one between herself and Mr Darcy. On that subject she was quite decided, and she would apprise him at the first opportunity.

Congratulations and well wishes assaulted her, and she lifted her head to acknowledge the felicitations. To be deceitful did not sit well with her, and she knew her mien was too serious for the occasion.

Mr Darcy patted her shoulder and strode to his seat at the opposite end of the table. He was smiling, which was a rare treat, and she struggled to tear her gaze away. Colonel Fitzwilliam was looking at her with a strange expression. He was, perhaps, too perceptive for his own good.

Lord Matlock, to her right, addressed her, and she thought no more about the colonel. The earl was inquisitive, and she answered his questions to the detriment of the meal. She was hungry but noticed that Lady Baslow was shuffling food around her plate, bringing only dainty morsels to her mouth. It reminded her of Miss Bingley, who was also in the habit of playing with her food rather than eating it. Elizabeth filled her spoon with the delicious turtle soup.

Midway through the meal, Lord Matlock turned to his other dinner companion, Miss Darcy. Elizabeth decided that he must be of a curious mind because he continued his questioning, which was now on the subject of Georgiana's education. The viscount, on her left, was not loquacious, and they only exchanged polite observations. His attention was fixed on the bereaved widow, and Elizabeth wondered whether Mr Darcy might have competition for the fair lady's hand. She waited for the final guest to put down his fork and rose.

"Ladies, if you would follow me."

And with that, she left the gentlemen to their port, cigars, and possibly a heated debate.

In the drawing room, Elizabeth poured a glass of sherry for the ladies and made sure Jane was the last to receive one. It was not in disrespect of her eldest sister but to remain in her comforting company once her duty was done.

"What a tumultuous day we have had." Jane sighed.

"Yes, I find it intriguing how the prospect of an inheritance changes one's character. People may act in ways you could not have foreseen."

Her own father sprung to mind. Mr Bennet, with his strange combination of quick-wit, sarcasm, reserve, and caprice, had not grabbed the opportunity to forward his family's standing in society, as most fathers with five unmarried daughters would. Mr Bingley would be confounded—if her father ever decided to accept his fate. Uncle Henry had offered to advance him one of his subsidiary titles, but her father had yet to reply. There would come a day when he had no choice, but until that day arrived, Elizabeth would keep his confidence.

Elizabeth left her sister's side and approached Lady Matlock, who was speaking to Miss Darcy. She curtseyed low and rose with a smile stuck on her face.

The countess was the same as she had been at Matlock— very eager to further the acquaintance between Elizabeth and Lady Baslow. Elizabeth was tired of putting on an act and guided the conversation to a topic she could have no part in— memories of time spent in each other's company. Her mind was then free to wander until her mother called for her attention. The commotion before supper had unsettled Mrs Bennet, and Elizabeth had never been more grateful for her mama's fluttering nerves, gladly offering to tend her as she wished to retire.

She escorted Mrs Bennet to her chamber and eschewed calling for a maid. She sat her down before the dressing table and began to remove the pins from her hair. Her mother grabbed her hand and stroked it.

"Something is not right in this house. I can feel it."

Elizabeth embraced her mother and gave her a long hug. She was going to bring her a great disappointment.

"It is the lack of cracks in the wall. I have noticed the paper seems to be intact in every room too, but it is not a home, not like

Longbourn."

"You will make it a home, Lizzy."

She did not reply but continued her task.

"You know, it is not inappropriate to show a little affection when one is betrothed. Nothing scandalous mind you, but neither your father nor I would begrudge you a stolen kiss..."

Elizabeth thought of the swift kiss they had shared, but Mr Darcy seemed disinclined to repeat it; he had made no further attempts.

# Chapter 7 The Last Honour

Mr Darcy was occupied at Edensor with the reading of the will. Lady Baslow's relations, the Conksburys, had finally arrived, and the funeral was to be held on the morrow. Elizabeth did her best to entertain Mr Darcy's Matlock relations while he was away. She had just convinced Miss Darcy to play the pianoforte when a carriage entered the courtyard.

"Who can it be?" she muttered to no one in particular.

The carriage was unfamiliar, but the visitors alighting from the conveyance were not.

"It seems we are to have some additional guests joining our party," she notified a footman nearby. "Please direct them to this parlour."

"Who is it?" the earl enquired.

"It is Mr and Mrs Hurst and Miss Bingley."

"They have been visiting my aunt in Scarborough and are breaking their journey here on their way to Netherfield and our wedding," Mr Bingley explained as he smiled nauseatingly at Jane.

Elizabeth hoped that Mr Bingley's comment meant that the guests were expected and that rooms had been made up. She knew she had better ask Mrs Reynolds so as to be certain. She had not heard anything about their imminent arrival, but she had spent much of her time absorbed in her thoughts and might have been wool-gathering at a critical moment. No one else appeared surprised by their arrival.

"Yes, I am looking forward to reacquainting myself with them," Jane replied.

Elizabeth's sentiments on the matter differed vastly from her sister's. She had no stomach for the supercilious sisters when she was barely holding on to her sanity.

The ladies and the gentlemen were shown into the parlour. They appeared to be acquainted with the Matlocks and did not ask for an introduction but greeted them with deference. Neither did they appear resentful when they greeted Jane, whom they addressed with more warmth than Elizabeth had expected. Mr Bingley must have taken them to task, which looked promising for her sister's future felicity.

"Miss Eliza, what are you doing here?" Miss Bingley blurted out.

"I am a guest, Miss Bingley."

"She is engaged to marry my brother." Miss Darcy beamed.

"We are to marry in a joint ceremony with Mr Darcy and Miss Elizabeth. I am certain that I mentioned it in my letter, Caroline," Mr Bingley informed his sister uneasily.

Several emotions washed over Miss Bingley's face until she settled on a smile.

"You really must do something about that dreadful handwriting of yours, Charles. I could not make it out from the letter you sent me. You must pardon my ignorance, Miss Eliza. May I wish you joy."

Elizabeth did not know what to make of Miss Bingley. Perhaps she was so fond of Pemberley that she would do anything to secure an invitation in the future. Or she was so in awe of the Matlocks that she dared not do anything that might offend.

Elizabeth sighed in relief at Miss Bingley's improved behaviour and nodded her acceptance. She moved away to let the Bingleys talk about the state of their northern relations, then slipped out of the room and found Mrs Reynolds, who confirmed that the Hursts and Miss Bingley were expected and that every preparation had been made before their arrival.

#

Darcy watched Miss Elizabeth converse with Richard about a piece of music Georgiana had just played. In that moment, she appeared to be her usual self, but towards him she was formal. The ease she had displayed throughout their acquaintance was gone.

Miss Bingley joined them, and after a short conversation, Miss Elizabeth withdrew to observe rather than participate. She circled the room to make sure nothing was wanting and that everyone was engaged in conversation. He should tell her he was pleased and not only ponder the thought. He met her halfway, in an unobstructed corner.

"Hosting parties comes so naturally to you. It appears like you are already mistress of Pemberley."

Miss Elizabeth stiffened and did not at all paint the picture of someone who had just received a compliment, and he was at a loss as to why.

His butler ended his musings by announcing the arrival of the Conksburys. Cornelius and he were particularly close, and after introducing Miss Elizabeth, they greeted each other as dear friends with the usual banter.

"I never thought you would ever convince a lady of breeding to marry you. You are so dull I would not think you would attract anyone with sense."

"I have yet to say, *I will*, in a church," Miss Elizabeth quipped with a smile.

"I shall do my best to convince you," Darcy retorted, which returned the sparkles to her eyes.

"I shall take that as a challenge and only add that you should be aware of my competitive nature by now."

"I remember that I once before mentioned your great enjoyment in occasionally professing opinions that are not your own."

Miss Elizabeth laughed heartily.

"And I should know you well enough not to contest your excellent memory," she admitted.

They had drawn the attention of the room, but he was transfixed by Miss Elizabeth's radiant expression. She looked like she knew something he did not, and he searched the windows to her soul to see what the underlying meaning of her words could be.

"I dare say that your betrothed is nothing like I imagined her to be. I had not supposed that you would brave a witty wife but rather pictured you with someone taciturn and cross. I predict that we are going to become the best of friends, Miss Elizabeth. There is something oddly familiar about you. Have we met before?"

"I very much doubt it. My father hates town and goes but rarely. We occasionally visit our relations, but I would be surprised if we frequented the same circles. I have an uncle, Mr Gardiner, who resides in Gracechurch Street, and Uncle Henry, the M—"

Miss Bingley had sidled up unnoticed and interrupted Miss Elizabeth mid-sentence.

"Your uncle lives close to his warehouses, I believe. In Cheapside..."

The gentlemen paid no attention to Miss Bingley's comment, and Mr Cornelius Conksbury begged Elizabeth for an introduction to her family. At her assent, he offered his arm and whisked her away.

"Pray, do you have any unmarried sisters?" was the last Darcy heard before the introductions to the Bennets commenced.

"I see that you have made amends with Miss Elizabeth. What a transformation. She is almost back to her old self."

Richard had crept up on him with his usual stealth.

"I have done nothing at all. Miss Elizabeth is simply marvellous."

"About that there can be no doubt."

"Mr Darcy!" Mr Conksbury approached. "I would like a word in private."

Darcy was expecting him. He had not looked pleased about his daughter's meagre mention in Sir Lawrence's will.

"Let us adjourn to my study."

#

Elizabeth watched Mr Darcy walk away with Mr Conksbury, leaving her to entertain the rest of his inquisitive party. They wanted to know when and where she had met Mr Darcy—a story she had related many times before. He had been visiting his friend at a neighbouring estate. No, it had not been *love at first sight*. They had been together in company in Kent and Derbyshire before reuniting in Meryton, where Mr Darcy had proposed and she had accepted.

"Really? I thought your understanding was of a longer duration, but I must applaud your persistent pursuit, Miss Elizabeth," Mrs Conksbury commented. "Few would bother to travel the entire country, even though Darcy is so rich."

"I am sure I would deserve such praise had I known Mr Darcy would be present at either location," Elizabeth replied blankly.

"It must have been fate," Mr Cornelius Conksbury offered graciously to make up for his mother's insolence.

"Have you told the Conksburys about the insult he gave you when you were first introduced? My brother was appalled..."

Miss Bingley chirped in.

"Oh, do tell, Miss Bingley," Lady Baslow begged.

"I do not know whether I can do it justice, but if my memory serves me right, it was something along the lines of"—Miss Bingley looked up at the ceiling as if the words might be found above—"she a beauty! I should as soon call her mother a wit. No. That was not the first. Pray, have patience with me. I have it on the tip of my tongue..."

Elizabeth wondered when Mr Darcy had disparaged her mother so cruelly. Could Miss Bingley have spoken an outright falsehood? She had not thought her perfidious when they were last together at Netherfield, where there was always a sliver of truth to her barbs. The silence was deafening. Elizabeth could bear it no longer and said with a voice deprived of emotion, "She is tolerable but not handsome enough to tempt me. I am in no humour at present to give consequence to young ladies who are slighted by other men."

With her humiliation thus complete, she left the company with a curtsey and engaged a giggling Georgiana in conversation.

"How can you keep such a serious countenance while you jest? You must teach me!"

Elizabeth smiled and pretended not to overhear the tittering females laughing behind her back. The countess, Mrs Bennet, and Jane were the only ladies who had not joined the merriment. Even the earl and viscount chuckled at her expense.

When she retired for the night, Jane asked for a word, and Elizabeth followed her to her chamber. Jane wasted no time addressing what had her concerned.

"You are not happy, Elizabeth."

It was unusual for Jane to speak so candidly. Perhaps she believed Elizabeth would prevaricate, but Jane knew her so well it would be impossible.

"I admit that this visit to Pemberley has been somewhat of a disappointment. I had not realised how occupied Mr Darcy would be and how little I would see him. The house, of course, is splendid, and the grounds no less so. But..."

"Lady Baslow..." Jane paused and looked contemplative. "You do not care for her."

"No, I admit that I do not. She was Mr Darcy's first love, and it unsettles me that he spends so much time with her."

"I thought that you might have drawn a hasty conclusion where that lady is concerned. She may not behave entirely as a widow ought, but you have nothing to fear. Mr Darcy looks at you like you are the brightest star in the sky. Charles was quite appalled when his trusted friend was thrown into the pond. He is confident about Mr Darcy's honour. He would never do what they have accused him of."

Elizabeth hid her face in her hands to hide the tears she could not stem. Jane embraced her and whispered words intended to comfort. Why did she not confide the entire sordid tale to her sister?

Because Jane would never conceal such a secret from their parents. Elizabeth's spirit was too frail, and she could not withstand her mother's lamentations any more than she could stomach her father's sarcastic remarks.

She could not forget the quip he had made at Jane's expense after Mr Bingley had left so unexpectedly. She had laughed then, in her ignorance.

No, it was best to wait until she had put sufficient miles between herself and Pemberley. She just knew that Mr Darcy would not travel south with them. Something would arise, invented or real, that obligated him to remain at Pemberley, and he would promise to travel to Hertfordshire once his business was concluded. Then something or other would prevent him from keeping his word. The wedding would be postponed indefinitely, until someday no one remembered that she had once been engaged to be married.

Or worse—he would sacrifice his happiness and marry her despite his inclinations. They would live side by side without affection, and she knew very well the end of that tale. She would manage his house whilst his emotions were engaged elsewhere, and that was what she feared the most. To be with a shadow of the man she loved, bearing witness to his betrayal, and ending her life as a bitter, jealous old crone.

No! It was insupportable. She would release him from their engagement on the day they departed. She had not the courage to do so sooner because she was not strong enough to withstand any form of persuasion if he begged her to reconsider. Love still beat in her breast, and time and distance were the cure. Decided in her resolution, she fought the inconceivable torment with the full strength of her stubbornness. It was for the best for everyone involved. She straightened her spine and escaped Jane's comforting embrace.

"Thank you, Jane. I am just overwrought. The strain of Sir Lawrence's death, the damage from the storm, and the daunting task of becoming mistress of such a vast estate has made me silly, indeed. I shall wake on the morrow and think no more about it. I am quite decided."

Elizabeth bid Jane good night and left her sister's room quietly so as not to disturb her family in the nearby chambers. A board squeaked, but it was not the one she had trodden on. The squeak had come from farther away, and a frisson ran down her spine. She froze in place and listened. Footsteps were approaching down the hall, and she stepped back into the shadows. The clack of a boot against the wooden floor made her heart pound in her chest. In the dim light, Mr Darcy passed without noticing her and continued down the stairs. Was he going out? Did he have a rendezvous with the beautiful widow? Her throat narrowed and her chest constricted, making it a struggle to draw breath.

She managed to reach her bed and fell upon it fully clothed. Was she having an apoplexy? She was exhausted and had not the strength to rise to pull the bell. She closed her eyes.

#

The gentlemen would attend the church service and committal, whilst the ladies would join Lady Baslow at Edensor House for the final preparations. As an outstanding member of superior society, Sir Lawrence was honoured with an elaborate night-time burial with a large procession from his home to St John's church in Lambton. In addition to his tenants and servants, Mr Darcy had hired a large party of men from all levels of society. It would not do for the renowned baronet to be escorted by a handful of servants. He had mentioned as much in his will and had set aside funds for this specific purpose. Mr Darcy had done as instructed but not without concern for the excessive number of followers. It was not uncommon for some of those in the procession to be inebriated and boisterous, which was the reason fashionable ladies avoided the event.

Elizabeth was not supposed to participate as she had no connection to the Baslows, but Lady Matlock had received a desperate missive from the widow. She had not managed to assemble the tokens to be handed out to the participants in the procession, and she needed every free hand to help. The request for the Bennet and Bingley sisters' presence could hardly be denied. All the ladies at Pemberley settled into the carriages and travelled the long route to the neighbouring house.

Edensor was a handsome house the size of Longbourn, or perhaps a little larger. Elizabeth shuddered and chased away the image of Lady Baslow in the arms of Mr Darcy. Despite her foreboding imaginings, her curiosity compelled her to enter.

The butler greeted the guests. It must have been he who had discovered her betrothed in the arms of another woman. Elizabeth's heart fluttered in her chest and not in a pleasant manner. The rhythmic beat quivered unsteadily, and her mind fought an upwards battle for consciousness. Elizabeth claimed a chair immediately after she entered the parlour where the affected widow was receiving condolences. Mrs Conksbury commented upon her rudeness for not condoling with Lady Baslow forthwith, but Elizabeth's faintness had not relented, and she remained seated until her unsteady pulse quieted. Once a modicum of calm had been restored, Lady Matlock whisked her away to a drawing room which smelt strongly of rosemary.

"I am a little disappointed that Lady Baslow has only arranged for tied rosemary twigs. It is the simplest gift she could have offered, but even worse, none of them are ready. We have more than two hundred bouquets to tie with ribbon, so there is no reason to tarry, ladies.

"I dare say Sir Lawrence's immaculate reputation warranted gloves, hatbands, or handkerchiefs at the very least, but it is too late now. I assume it is the covetous, quarrelling cousins who have limited dear Celia's spending. Very well. We shall manage."

She shooed them to the table, and they began tying black ribbons to the abundance of rosemary twigs.

Lady Matlock sidled up to Elizabeth and spoke quietly in her ear.

"I expect you to make a greater effort to befriend Lady Baslow than what I have witnessed so far. It is vital to quell the ghastly accusations against an honourable gentleman who, may I remind you, is your betrothed."

"Yes…" Elizabeth's stomach churned, and the floor swayed beneath her feet.

"You are dreadfully pale, Miss Elizabeth," Lady Matlock cried with concern.

"I am not feeling well."

"Should I summon the apothecary, or perhaps a physician?"

"Oh no. Please, do not. It is just a slight indisposition and will soon pass. I would be loath to make a spectacle at Sir Lawrence's funeral."

"Very well," Lady Matlock said and left her to her task.

The door opened, and Lady Baslow entered with Mr Darcy in tow.

"Oh! I had no idea the room was occupied." Lady Baslow tittered. "What a picturesque prospect you girls make amongst the rosemary. Darcy! I have a special token of remembrance for you."

She handed him a silk-wrapped box tied with a black ribbon.

"Open it."

Elizabeth watched clandestinely while Mr Darcy opened the box to reveal an elaborate gold ring with a locket.

"It has diamonds and emeralds. See?"

Lady Baslow stood far too close to Mr Darcy to show him the gems.

"And a lock of Sir Lawrence's hair. Should this not be reserved for one of his descendants?" Mr Darcy enquired, seemingly ill at ease.

"I have made one for John and Robert too. This is yours. It would please me if you used it."

Mr Darcy put the ring on his finger. It was ridiculously big, even on Mr Darcy's large hand, and Elizabeth smiled at the consternation the stoic man must feel at wearing such an ostentatious item. He who tried to avoid those weaknesses that exposed a strong mind to ridicule. Mr Darcy met her eyes. Did he remember their battle of wits at Netherfield and shared the same thought?

The Baslow cousins entered and received their rings with locks of hair. Elizabeth did not fail to notice that theirs were not as ostentatious as Mr Darcy's. Lord Matlock received a box of cigars, Lady Matlock a brooch, whilst the colonel and viscount were each given a bottle of Sir Lawrence's finest port.

#

The large contingent of funeral attendants arrived and appeared to have been paid in advance, judging by their inebriated state. Despite the solemnity of the occasion, crude and vulgar remarks were made even to the ladies handing out their mourning gifts. Darcy tried to settle the masses, but he was only the one against in excess of two hundred men. Soon his attention was solely on deterring Lady Baslow from attending the funeral herself by explaining the perils of such an endeavour. But the lady's mind was decided, and her carriage was ready. He had no choice but to watch her leave, since both Mr John Baslow and his cousin approved. He was to follow the hearse and wished to get the procession going before any more of the ladies decided to attend.

#

The cavalcade attracted large crowds along the route to the church, shouting lewd and uncouth remarks. Darcy kept a watchful eye on the throng, unaware that next to the church, by the place of interment, a handful of pickpockets were waiting for the procession to arrive. They chose the most expensive-looking equipage and ripped the escutcheon off its sideband before boarding the carriage.

A lady screamed over the din. Darcy was carrying the coffin and had to proceed into the church. He met Richard's eyes, and by the look of concern on his face, he had heard it too. They hastened their steps and prayed that Sir Lawrence would forgive the jostling caused by their hurried manoeuvring.

Darcy, Richard, and the viscount ran out of the church in time to see three ruffians alight from Lady Baslow's carriage. The rascals immediately set off at a run when they discovered the approaching gentlemen. He and Richard gave chase whilst Crawford stayed to see to the widow's comfort.

Darcy's legs pounded on the ground beneath him, and he was gaining on the thief when his opponent stumbled in the darkness and fell flat on his face. Darcy was upon him in an instant. He grabbed the miscreant by the collar and hauled him to his feet.

Darcy thrust his hand into the man's pocket and pulled out Lady Baslow's diamond necklace. The scoundrel tried to wrench himself out of his grip, and Darcy called out for someone, anyone, whether it was a tenant or servant, to help retain the thief. A couple of men responded to his cries for help and led the rogue away. Darcy rested his hands on his knees to catch his breath and was relieved to discover that Richard had caught one of the others. But the third was still on the loose and nowhere to be seen.

By the carriage, he found the coachman with a severe head injury. He had been hit with something blunt  whilst trying to protect his mistress. Another funeral attendant had been trampled by one of the frightened horses and suffered a broken leg. In the chaos that followed, the crowd turned upon the church and tried to enter by breaking the beautiful stained-glass windows. He could have cried for the meaningless destruction had he not been so enraged. When had his friendly, peaceful neighbourhood turned into this anarchistic disorder?

It could not be denied that he owned much of the blame himself. It was he who had hired the attendants and, perhaps, spent too little time in the area for the last eight years. He would correct that mistake immediately and find the underlying cause of this decay in decency.

*Elizabeth!*

The image of her being whisked away in the melee appeared unbidden in his mind. He had been so occupied with the procession that he could not say with any certainty whether she had stayed at Edensor. He mumbled a fervent prayer that she had not foolishly accompanied Lady Baslow to the funeral. Miss

Elizabeth's compassionate heart could be prevailed upon to do the most reckless, unwise...

And he had accused her of lacking compassion. It was clear who was the fool. He should not have joined the ladies so soon after the quarrel at the Rose and Crown but taken a few moments to calm himself. Or not have let the allegations levelled against his character vex him so much, but it was no use. He could not let it stand that he would act in such a despicable manner as to seduce a widow even before her husband was in his grave. They should have believed him; he was unfailingly honest.

When he had entered the parlour and heard Miss Elizabeth tell Lady Baslow to leave in an abrupt manner, Lady Matlock's words had resonated in his mind. *'Let people see that Miss Elizabeth does not shun Lady Baslow but treats her as a friend. Then they will understand that there is nothing to the rumours.'* He had snapped at the one person the least deserving of his ire—Elizabeth.

In his vexation with himself, he tore open the door to the carriage and frightened Lady Baslow out of his cousin's comforting embrace. Her neck was bleeding from where the necklace had been torn.

"Did Miss Elizabeth accompany you?" he barked more brusquely than the situation warranted.

"I am too fraught to even think," Lady Baslow lamented. "They stole my most valuable diamond necklace. It has priceless sentimental value, and my diamond wedding ring is gone too," she sobbed.

"Just answer my question," he barked impatiently.

"Have some sympathy, Darcy. Can you not see that the lady is overwrought?"

He paid the protective viscount no mind and bore his penetrating gaze into Lady Baslow's light orbs.

"Very well. Miss Elizabeth refused to escort me. Now you

have it! She claimed to have no connection to the Baslows and refuted any need I might have for *my* comfort. She could not be persuaded."

Darcy looked upon the starlit sky and thanked the Lord for that mercy before he assured Lady Baslow that both her necklace and her ring had been recovered. Two of the thieves had been apprehended, but her escutcheon had not been found, yet.

"This is ridiculous!" Richard had joined them but was regarding the savages. "We must try to calm down the barbarians and continue the service. The vicar has blocked the door so we cannot enter."

"But I must attend!" Lady Baslow cried. "I do not care about the wagging tongues."

"The vicar will not allow any daughter of Eve to be present," Richard explained.

"He informed me that only John and Robert Baslow would be allowed at the grave-side for the burial," Darcy reasoned with the widow.

She resigned, just as the crowd discovered that entering the church was a futile endeavour and dispersed into the night.

The wounded men were taken with the injured widow to Edensor to be attended by the apothecary. The ladies had remained at Edensor. With all the men occupied with the funeral procession, there were none left to escort them home.

Lady Baslow was leaning heavily upon Darcy and the viscount as they helped her into the house. Lady Matlock, Mrs Conksbury, and the Bennet ladies immediately surmised something was amiss and gathered around the widow.

"Dearest Celia, what on earth has happened?" his aunt enquired before they had found the lady a chair.

"I was attacked by ruffians who ripped the diamonds from my neck and tore off my precious wedding ring. It must have been the Irish, because they moved like rodents," Lady Baslow informed them in a calm and collected manner that belied her frightening experience.

"Did you notice a particular accent?" Darcy enquired whilst guiding the lady to a chair and urging her to sit. She had seemed unsteady, and it was best she was seated in case she should faint.

"I cannot recall exactly, but I believe so."

Elizabeth had retreated into the background to allow the other ladies more room. Darcy did not tarry long before he was by her side, but she did not seem to notice, transfixed as she was on Lady Baslow. The lady was untying her bonnet, and she threw it haphazardly towards a table. It glided across and landed with a soft thud on the floor. The viscount guarded the back of her chair, whilst Lady Matlock fussed over the victim.

"Miss Elizabeth, may Lady Baslow borrow your fichu?"

His aunt had not given up thrusting the two into each other's company, but Elizabeth was behaving quite the opposite to what was her habit. He had never observed her shunning anyone's company; not even his formidable aunt Lady Catherine had intimidated his fearless betrothed. But it had become obvious that she deliberately avoided Lady Baslow. He hoped no one noticed, or tongues would surely wag.

"Certainly."

Elizabeth unfastened the item and handed it to him. In his surprise, he took it without thought. He gave the fichu to his aunt, who made repairs to Lady Baslow's dress, and he retreated with due haste. He blamed the darkness for not noticing the tear in her apparel sooner.

The widow was soon whisked away for her injuries to be tended by her mother and his aunt, and Darcy returned home with the Bennet ladies, while the Matlocks chose to stay to protect Lady Baslow.

# Chapter 8 Immersed in Sin's Obscurity

The Bennets had been at Pemberley for three weeks, and their return to Longbourn could no longer be delayed. There were preparations for the weddings that could only be managed in Meryton. Mr Bennet had informed the party that they would leave the next day and urged them to finish their packing.

"Miss Elizabeth, would you take a stroll in the garden with me?" Mr Darcy enquired of his betrothed.

"It would be my pleasure," Elizabeth replied; though in truth, she dreaded the conversation.

They dressed for the cool autumn air and left for the formal gardens. The October roses and Michaelmas daisies were still in bloom, even on the first of November.

Mr Darcy cleared his throat, but Elizabeth did nothing to help him on. This was a conversation he would have to carry himself.

"I regret that my departure will be delayed due to the hearing." The thieves faced the noose, and Mr Darcy was an important witness. He was obliged to remain and attend court. "But I am hopeful it will be no more than a week before I join you in Meryton."

"I am certain that the evening before the wedding would suffice, if you are to stand up with Mr Bingley."

Mr Darcy halted abruptly, and so did Elizabeth, who was holding his arm.

"Explain yourself, madam. I am not certain I understand you

correctly."

Elizabeth released his arm and turned to face him. She would leave him in no doubt of *her* emotions. A direct approach was less hurtful than to shift between happiness and the despair of indifference.

"The banns have not been read. I have spent three consecutive Sundays in Pemberley's chapel, and not once has my name, or yours, been called. Our wedding cannot proceed. Which makes perfect sense, considering the circumstances."

Mr Darcy's expression would have been comical for a person whose first object in life was a joke, but Elizabeth saw no humour in their predicament. He let his hand rub over his face and exhaled. Elizabeth kept her face rigid and her back straight. She would not be overcome by the battle between her heart and mind. Every muscle in her body was strung to the limit, but it would be over soon, and she could go back to who she once had been—Elizabeth Bennet of Longbourn in Hertfordshire—no longer Mr Darcy's betrothed.

"I could buy a licence. It should not take more than a week."

"What would be the point of that, Mr Darcy? I believe we both know where we stand, and a marriage between us would be insupportable. But I do have a favour to beg of you. Do not tell my family. Jane would be crushed, and I am loath to ruin what will be the happiest day of her life. I shall inform my father once we have returned home. I suggest you concoct an excuse to further delay your travel to Meryton. I shall play the compliant betrothed and claim our union is postponed until you have finished your business. Perhaps if we delay long enough, people will forget an engagement ever existed."

"Elizabeth, my feelings and wishes have not changed."

Elizabeth's heart thundered in her breast, but she held his gaze, determined not to give in to romantic nonsense. "But mine have."

All colour drained from his face. "I love you," he blurted out with frustration clouding his countenance.

Elizabeth contemplated whether she should reveal all or let him reach his own conclusions.

"Not as fervently as you love Celia," she stated firmly.

She had said all she wanted to, and her composure was slipping. She dipped into a curtsey.

"Goodbye, Mr Darcy."

Elizabeth turned and walked sedately towards the house.

"This is not over," he called after her.

"Yes, it is," she muttered to herself.

She chose the shortest route to her chamber and bolted the door. No one missed her until dinner, which she chose to take on a tray in her room. She had sent a note to her father claiming a headache and informing him of Mr Darcy's prolonged duty to Sir Lawrence's estate. By now, everyone knew about the uproar at the funeral and the associated court case. The investigation to find the last criminal continued in full force. Mr Darcy, as one of the prime witnesses, could not be spared.

#

"It is rather quiet without the Bennets," Richard claimed, jolting Darcy out of his reverie.

It was mid-morning, and the Bennets had left at dawn.

"Yes, I have noticed," Darcy replied as wryly as the obvious statement deserved.

"Miss Elizabeth looked downtrodden when she departed. I surmise you did not get a chance to speak to her?"

"No, I did. It just did not proceed as I had planned." Darcy pondered how much to disclose. Richard was one of his closest confidants, and he was not opposed to revealing his flaws exactly, but her rejection was still raw.

"She wishes to end our engagement..." he admitted. The revelation lifted some of the burden off his shoulders.

"Why would she do that? It makes no sense."

"She believes that I love Celia. More than herself, I might add."

"Do you?"

His ire was instant and violent. If he had not struggled so to breathe, he would have knocked Richard out cold. But his anger soon turned in the right direction—inwards—at himself. How had he made such a muddle of his affairs? Did he even know his own mind?

He laced his fingers behind his head and pulled it down.

"Darcy! I have never seen you so distraught. Is there anything I can do? You know I shall always support you, whatever you decide to do."

Could he reveal his innermost thoughts? The dirty little secrets churning in his mind day and night, robbing him of his sleep, peace, and pleasure.

"They are so very different," he finally acknowledged.

"Miss Elizabeth and Celia?"

"Yes."

"What attracts you to Celia?"

How could Richard even ask? Although he was no longer enamoured with Lady Baslow, her attractions were glaringly obvious. She had impeccable manners, extraordinary beauty, came from a good family, and owned a significant fortune. His parents had both approved of her. His mother had even abandoned her desire for him to marry her niece, Lady Catherine's daughter Anne, when their attachment had become known. He liked her family; her brother he considered the closest of his friends. Their friendship had withstood the test when Celia had chosen someone else to marry—a choice that still hurt him to this day. He had never fully acknowledged to anyone just how crushed he had been, and he had embarked upon his grand tour with fervour, wishing to be as far away from Derbyshire as he could manage—for as long as it took to forget her.

His year-long absence had not worked as well as he had hoped. The trip had been pleasant enough, and interesting. For long moments, admiring a particular work of art or strolling through a street of architectural delights, he had managed to forget her entirely. He had returned to Pemberley in tolerably good spirits. But seeing Lady Baslow and Sir Lawrence, sitting together in church, had reopened the wound. He could not believe she had chosen that feeble old man over him. Sir Lawrence was kind, and generous to a fault, but she was a celestial being, destined for a much greater purpose than to nurse a square-toed old cuff[3]. Had Darcy's station been higher, she would not have abandoned him. If he had not been two months short of his majority... And although his allowance was substantial, it was not enough to buy, or even lease, a comfortable home. They would have had to live with his parents at Pemberley until he came into his inheritance. An event that had come decades before anyone had expected; his parents had been young and healthy, but fate had robbed him of both within the year.

"I suppose Celia is someone I expected to marry. She is beautiful and well-mannered with desirable connections and fortune. My parents approved of our union. Mother, in particular, doted upon her—"

"Who did not?" Richard interrupted. "The angelic twins with snow white curls and pale blue eyes. They were her angels. I suppose she longed for a daughter with her fair looks, and she doted just as fiercely upon Georgiana when she was born." He looked Darcy in the eye. "And what attracts you to Elizabeth?"

It was her eyes he had noticed first.

"Elizabeth... At first, I noticed her eyes and their expression. It was much later that I discovered their unusual colour. A deep green emerald—I have never seen the like. I soon realised that she was uncommonly clever and sagacious. She fended off Miss Bingley's barbs with sweet archness and never retaliated in a demeaning or cruel manner. Yet she won every battle of wits. Do you remember our exchange whilst she played the pianoforte at Rosings?"

"Yes, though not word for word. She accused you of overlooking young ladies in want of a partner at a ball."

Darcy chuckled at the memory. "It was more than that. I snubbed her before we had even been introduced. Bingley forced me to attend an assembly on the very day I arrived. I was travel worn and in a dreadful mood. It was too soon after Georgiana's foiled elopement with Wickham, and I was guilt ridden for leaving her in London. Bingley was pestering me to dance and singled out Elizabeth as a particularly desirable partner. In my foul humour, I called her looks tolerable but not handsome enough to tempt me."

"Hell and damnation. I had no idea!"

"I tried to excuse my abominable behaviour by admitting to my deficiencies in dealing with strangers. I wondered whether she believed me, because she continued by pointing out my good sense and education."

"You may add a forgiving nature to her virtues. Most ladies tend to take umbrage when a gentleman disparages her looks, and they can hold on to their grudge for decades."

"Exactly! She is more than I deserve, but I shall devote a lifetime to atoning for my indiscretions. Once you have earned her good opinion, it is yours forever. She is fiercely loyal. Her compassion is relentlessly bestowed when one she loves is sick or injured—a ministering angel in the diligence with which she nursed her sister back to health at Netherfield." His thoughts flew unbidden to Wickham. "Even a fleeting friend she protects with all her might. Yet she is mostly light and joyous. Her liveliness bounces her back to good humour and affects everyone around her. She has an extraordinary capacity for bringing joy into other people's lives. Elizabeth is who *I* want to marry."

"Then why did you leave her in doubt of your affection?"

"I did not! I told her I loved her, but she threw it back in my face. Not that she denied loving me—she simply stated that I loved Celia more. What was I supposed to do?" He had raised his voice, but it could not be helped.

"Did you not object to her claim? You are supposed to tell her she is wrong!"

His cousin threw his hands in the air, obviously thinking he was a fool. But Richard had not been there, not seen what he had seen, nor observed the injuries he had inflicted.

"How could I when my words no longer mattered? She was on the verge of losing her composure completely. I saw tears well in her eyes and her lips quiver. I could offer nothing to comfort her."

"So, you let her escape to her room to cry in solitude?" Richard spat, clearly aghast at his inertia.

"I could not take her into my arms and prove my devotion, could I?"

"Yet, you embraced Celia..."

"That was different, and you know it. Celia is a widow and does not have the same need to protect her reputation as a maiden. And you know how Celia is—she is an affectionate person."

"Elizabeth is not affectionate?"

"She is but she cannot— She is so innocent. I mean she has her reputation and that of her sisters to protect. It would be entirely up to me to stop before it went too far, and I do not trust myself to that extent," Darcy admitted with his head bent and heat rising in his cheeks. He was exceedingly uncomfortable discussing such a private matter, even with his cousin. And the thought of holding Elizabeth flush against his body made his blood stir. "I would never dishonour Elizabeth by acting inappropriately."

"Because you respect her more?"

The thought had not crossed his mind, but he knew Richard was right.

"I have wondered why you let Celia behave so overtly familiar with you," Richard continued.

"She did nothing inappropriate. She may have patted my arm or leant a little too close on occasion..."

"In the presence of Elizabeth?"

"Perhaps. I do not recall."

"Well, I do. I watched your betrothed try to hide her distress, but her countenance is easily read if you pay attention. I imagine her watching your ease with Celia must have made her immensely uncomfortable. But it is more damaging that you never showed her any affection. You never singled her out in company or demonstrated your preference. You could have kissed her hand, at the very least. You were engaged to be married..."

"I have held her hands."

"When?"

"We walked to the hunting tower, on the morning before the storm."

He smiled at the memory. She was so sweet and inexperienced. Celia would never have joined him on a walk in the park. She shunned daylight—always had because it would ruin her complexion. Elizabeth felt no such impediments against the sun and relished being out of doors as much as he did.

"I even kissed her lips. A chaste kiss, mind you. I would not scare her with my ardour. I should not have done it because I am fairly certain it was her first. I should have behaved more like

91

a gentleman and waited until we were married. Another thing she accused me of in Kent was not behaving in a gentlemanlike manner. Her mind is bright yet so very innocent where carnal pleasures are concerned."

"Does that put you off?"

"Not at all, but it makes me cautious not to move forwards too quickly."

"You have loved Celia for as long as I can remember, but you love her as if she were a heavenly creature of the angelic race, not a mortal human of this shadowy world below. The truth of our shared youth is long since lost to the injury of time. Does the reality of Lady Baslow fulfil your expectations?"

"No..."

He had painted her image in the purity of youth and innocence, which they had both shed during the last eight years. From afar, she was a beauteous star upon the heavenly dome, but upon closer inspection, she behaved in a detached and selfish manner. A sad imitation of his first love. Elizabeth burnt with lustrous light, but it was genuine and came from within rather than an outward reflection.

The spell broke and collapsed slack and lifeless to the ground. Strife struck him like clashing swords in a fight. Why did he revere his duties above all else? Disillusioned, he was no longer so certain he was on the right path.

Richard was shifting in his seat and jolted him from his reveries. He obviously had something on his mind.

"Out with it," Darcy demanded.

"I thought it best you hear it from me, or at least one of the family. Crawford is contemplating offering for Lady Baslow. He has always liked her—more than liked her, but she only had eyes for you. Crawford claims that Celia's virtue is still intact. That Sir Lawrence's old age made him incapable of consummating their marriage."

"Yes, she told me as much," Darcy agreed.

"And you did not find that tidbit inappropriate?" Richard exclaimed incredulously.

It was definitely not proper, even though she was a widow.

"Yes," Darcy admitted. "It was most improper, but she had just been frightened out of her wits by the thunderstorm and could not have been conscious of what she was rambling about."

"Do you believe it?"

"I have not considered the matter, as it is none of my business."

But if he were to contemplate it, he was inclined towards disbelief. Her air was not one of innocence. Not compared with the ladies he knew for certain were untouched. Elizabeth's blushing cheeks, wide eyes, and delighted smile after he had kissed her sprung to mind. She had been utterly flustered when she had accidentally touched his knee at the hunting tower, and the blush had made her skin glow in the morning light. He had removed himself with haste because his mind had swiftly imagined her hand moving up his thigh, and the heightened colour of her cheeks would fit perfectly with the afterglow of carnal pleasure.

Darcy entertained the thought of Celia married to his cousin. Would it injure him? He let his mind wander down the path of marriage to his first love, but his imagination would not produce her image. In her stead, Elizabeth strolled in his garden, read in his study, comforted a child in his nursery, and reclined in his bed. He must have groaned aloud because Richard was excusing his brother's behaviour. He held up his hand to stop him. He imagined Celia on the viscount's arm, and it did not affect him as much as he would have thought. She would always have a place in his heart, but he was not in love with her...

"If he succeeds, I shall wish him the best."

"May the best man win!"

"No, there will be no competition…"

#

The journey home to Longbourn was long but uneventful. Leaving Mr Darcy and Pemberley had brought only relief; it was Georgiana Elizabeth's heart struggled to part with. To depart with Miss Darcy uninformed about the broken engagement wreaked havoc with her conscience.

Jane repeatedly engaged her in merry wedding conversations and expounded upon their future felicity once the deed was done. Elizabeth forced herself to maintain her cheerful disposition, but it was draining her spirit. At home she could escape the cheerfulness and wedding planning simply by walking out of the door. The much-needed reprieves would be short but necessary once they returned to Longbourn.

A week before the blessed event, Mr Darcy returned to Netherfield. It made her stomach coil into a knot when her father mentioned it, but she kept the smile on her face. Elizabeth had yet to inform him about the broken engagement. She had hoped Mr Darcy would have delayed his return, but with no such luck, she did not know what to tell her father. Well, at least not something he would accept. Perhaps Mr Darcy could be persuaded to delay the announcement of their separation until after Jane's wedding. What would happen next, she cared not.

Mr Darcy arrived with Mr Bingley in the afternoon. Her mother had invited them to dine, and it was of the utmost importance that she managed to speak to Mr Darcy before the Lucases and Gouldings arrived. They needed to prepare an excuse as to why there would be only one wedding.

The carriage arrived but only Mr Bingley joined the ladies in the parlour. Mr Darcy must have gone directly to her father's study without the simple courtesy of greeting the ladies of the house. Twenty minutes passed before Mrs Hill called Elizabeth from the room. The housekeeper escorted her to the entrance hall and dressed her in her warm cloak, tied her bonnet, and handed

Elizabeth her gloves.

"Mr Darcy is waiting for you in the wilderness."

Elizabeth breathed deeply, straightened her back, and expelled all emotions before she strolled towards him. He was pacing back and forth, running a stray hand through his hair every time he turned. The dry leaves crunched under her feet, and Mr Darcy stilled his restless movements.

"Mr Darcy." Elizabeth greeted him and curtseyed.

He appeared lost and stood gazing into her eyes for an uncomfortably long moment.

"I have contemplated what to say to you when we met again, but I am no poet. I can only promise you that I am prepared to make amends. I know my faults and can only beg for the forgiveness I do not deserve."

"There is nothing to atone for. I am not a vindictive person, and why would I wallow in what would best be forgotten?" Elizabeth enquired.

"I am immensely relieved to hear it. I have bought a common licence and—"

"That will not be necessary," Elizabeth interrupted. "I have no intention of marrying you. We need to devise an excuse as to why the wedding will not take place but leave enough room for the interpretation that it will proceed in the future. I shall not allow our separation to ruin my sister's wedding. I assume you are willing to offer the same courtesy to your friend."

"Elizabeth, the marriage settlement is signed. There is no escape, and neither do I want one. I understand that it will take time for you to forgive me, and I intend to afford you however long it takes. If it is unwanted advances that intimidate you, you need have no fear I shall importune you until you are ready to receive me."

"Mr Darcy, I have two guardians of my honour—virtue and

pride. Of those, you are only a threat to my pride. I shall not marry you!"

Mr Darcy scowled at her; his anger could no longer be concealed. His finely chiselled nostrils quivered, and his lips were pressed into a thin, scarlet line. It was a blessing to Elizabeth, whose own ire matched his.

"Can you not see? We have no choice!" he delivered in his usual condescending manner.

"There is always a choice. I suggest we discuss it with my father. He will find an escape."

"Very well," Mr Darcy gritted out between clenched teeth.

They strode into the house and knocked on Mr Bennet's door. He bade them enter and make themselves comfortable.

"What brings you young people to my sanctuary on this blessed day?" he droned.

"I have rescinded my acceptance of Mr Darcy's proposal," Elizabeth informed her father.

"Have you now?" Mr Bennet replied measuredly.

"A lady is entitled to change her mind…"

"And what is your stance, Mr Darcy?"

"I have reminded Miss Elizabeth that the settlement papers are signed and that the wedding will proceed as planned. It is too late to change her mind."

"You are, of course, correct, if not particularly wise, Mr Darcy. I once thought better of you than I do now. Wickham is now my favourite son, but I like you just as well as Mr Bingley."

"Papa! Do be serious. Toss the marriage settlement into the fire, and we can all return to our lives."

Mr Bennet sobered his mirth and looked at her pensively.

"You have made your point, Elizabeth. Your message is clear and noted by your betrothed. But burning one copy of the settlement does not change the fact that you must marry Mr Darcy. Your betrothed, my attorney, and his, all have a copy. Your engagement is widely known. Imagine the effect it would have on Mary and Kitty if it became known that you had jilted a most eligible gentleman. Not to forget the repercussions on your reputation. You will be shunned by every honourable gentleman as the most determined flirt."

"But...I cannot!"

"Whyever not? He is rich, to be sure. I dare say you will have more fine clothes and well-sprung carriages than Jane."

"Please, do not make me say it," Elizabeth whispered, looking pleadingly at her father.

"I do not understand you, child. I did warn you that you, with your lively talents, would neither be happy nor respectable with a man you did not esteem. But you claimed you loved this man —even absolved him of improper pride and pronounced him amiable."

How earnestly she wished she had been more reasonable whilst asserting her former opinions and more moderate in her declaration of love! A rush of emotions surged through her blood, and her rage could no longer be contained. Weeks of restraint broke, and she rose from her chair and looked her father in the eyes.

"You do not know me at all if you can question *my* respectability. Especially when Mr Darcy has demonstrated so indisputably that he has none."

"Excuse me. Of what do you accuse *me*?" Mr Darcy countered and rose to gain the upper hand.

But Elizabeth could not be cowed by the stronger sex, despite his impressive height.

"How can you even ask? Your liaison with Lady Baslow is widely known, but far be it from me to shun an unpleasant topic. I shall remind you of the thunderstorm when you were discovered in Lady Baslow's embrace—in her bed chamber!"

"I was comforting a lady who was terrified! Lightning had struck just beyond her window, and she screamed for help. What was I to do but to comfort a childhood friend?"

"By her account, you were more than friends," Elizabeth retorted. "Then, now, and forever."

Mr Darcy looked shocked. He could not have expected her to be so well informed about his intention to continue the affair after the marriage vows had been spoken.

"It is true that we once formed an understanding of sorts, but we were young and foolish. Whatever had been our understanding in our youth was broken eight years ago when she married Sir Lawrence."

"How convenient that she is now free to choose whomever she pleases. Though I am not entirely certain whether she has set her cap at you or the viscount. May the best man win..."

It had not escaped her that the viscount was doing everything in his power to win the favour of the widow, or that she received his overtures with pleasure yet only pursued Mr Darcy. She could not determine whether she entertained the viscount to induce Mr Darcy's jealousy or because of genuine affection.

"I am not in a contest to win Lady Baslow, and I have certainly not had a liaison with any lady."

Elizabeth had had many grievances with Mr Darcy during their acquaintance, but until this very moment, she had not believed him to be a liar. And however insincere he may choose to be, she would be frank.

"Lady Baslow told me so herself. I assume you remember the evening you berated me for asking her to leave. I had just fainted at her graphic narrative of the previous night's events. When I awoke, she would not let the matter rest, and I could no longer bear to listen. Do you want me to relate the sordid details, or are your memories sufficient to sustain you until your next rendezvous?"

"It is a despicable lie," Mr Darcy barked.

She might have believed him had he not looked so utterly guilty.

"I disagree. Her renditions of your"—Elizabeth waved her hand over his body—"features were too specific not to be true. Do you, or do you not, have heart-shaped chest hair, and do you have a scar on your left buttock?"

Her blunt speech made heat creep from her chest to her face, and she glanced at her father. She imagined her cheeks were as red as Mr Darcy's.

"I do, but she did not have to undress me to find that out. It is commonly known that I had an accident that left me with a scar, and the other feature you mentioned has been the source of my cousins' mirth for more than a decade."

"Whether this is true or not holds no bearing." Mr Bennet interrupted the squabbling lovers. "To break the contract would cost me twenty thousand pounds I do not have. Should I get a loan, it would send your mother and sisters into poverty until Uncle Henry dies. Not even that might save us. Only the Lord knows how much the excessive renovations of his house have cost him, but it must be substantial. You do not wish to be the cause of your family's suffering, Elizabeth. You *must* marry."

"Twenty thousand pounds! I do not understand," she whispered. Great Uncle Henry was wealthy, but even if he could raise such a sum, she would never ask it of him. No, there had to be another way.

"It is standard procedure to name a sum for breach of contract. I copied that part from my mother's settlement. Never had I imagined that I would need it..." Mr Darcy muttered under his breath.

"We could delay it indefinitely. Give me a year, and I shall find a way out of this quagmire," Elizabeth begged her father.

"I shall grant you three months, at the most, to accustom yourself to your fate," Mr Bennet allowed.

"You cannot expect Mr Darcy to travel in the dead of winter?" Elizabeth knew she was grasping at straws, but she was unwilling to surrender.

"I can, but if that time comes and the roads prove to be utterly impassable, I suppose March will do as well as February. But what shall we tell our neighbours?" Mr Bennet asked.

Mr Darcy remained silent with an inscrutable expression.

"Pemberley is a vast estate," Elizabeth blurted. "Tell them I need more time to learn to manage it."

Elizabeth would gladly take the blame if it would postpone her marriage. Three months would have to suffice. If she acted quickly, it might be done. She could not marry Mr Darcy if she could not be found...

"No one would believe it," her father countered. "You are too clever."

Elizabeth huffed; she had become impervious to flattery after she had been deceived by Mr Wickham's pretty but insincere puffery.

"We may say that I cannot remain while the banns are read because of the imminent trial of the thieves. That should make a probable excuse to delay our wedding until spring." Mr Darcy broke his silence with a solution to their conundrum.

"Thank you," Elizabeth responded sincerely. It was the most sense her betrothed had uttered since he arrived. A glance in his direction revealed a serious Mr Darcy, his expression devoid of any emotion.

"Good. With that settled, we should join our party. Dinner must be imminent." Mr Bennet herded them to the parlour where Elizabeth had no trouble appearing cheerful and delighted. Her father announced the delay to their nuptials, and everyone expressed their consternation at such untimely misfortune. The conversation continued on to complaints against the judicial system in general.

Jane was the only one who expressed any deeper distress, but Elizabeth put her at ease.

"I am not concerned, but then I have had time to adapt. I have suspected this delay since we were at Pemberley. I shall celebrate you and Mr Bingley as prodigiously as if it were my own wedding, and I expect you to do the same for me at mine."

"You have been very sly and reserved with me, for you have told me nothing about it. But how will you occupy your time? Mr Bingley is taking me on a bridal trip for a month, then we are to visit his relations, and Mr Darcy has business in the North."

"Perhaps I shall indulge my mother and order a ridiculous number of dresses. Derbyshire is colder than Hertfordshire—I might need them."

"As long as you are not unhappy. You have not seemed yourself of late."

Elizabeth gathered her sister's hands and looked her in the eye.

"I am happy, Jane. In fact, you may smile, but I shall laugh." *All the way to Ireland*, she thought, but that tidbit she kept to herself. "You know that matters are quite settled between us, and I have no cause to repine. I admit that I was a little miserable when he first broke the news to me, but you know my disposition. I cannot bear to be brought low, and what cannot be helped must be endured."

#

Elizabeth put on a brave face when her mother escorted her through the neighbourhood on Mr Darcy's arm. She was diligently avoiding even a moment alone with him because she did not trust herself to that extent. If he gathered her into his arms and swore his eternal love, her heart might override her sense.

Mr Darcy was even quieter than was his wont, but at least he did not appear overbearing to her neighbours.

#

Jane's wedding day dawned bright and cheerful, as it should. The bride looked splendid, and the groom was overjoyed.

Mr Darcy stood opposite Elizabeth at the altar, with a contemplative mien gracing his handsome face. He escorted her out of the church after the deed was done and handed her into the carriage.

Breakfast was a boisterous but a happy event. Elizabeth kept her composure until the carriage carrying Jane and Mr Bingley to their secret location had disappeared round the bend. When she turned to enter the house, Mr Darcy detained her.

"If you wish it, I could stay at Netherfield until the wedding," he offered with his head bowed to the ground.

Seeing Mr Darcy with his regrets on display tugged at her heartstrings, but she did have some pride left to bolster her resolve.

"I would rather you did not. Return to Pemberley. Time and distance will heal the wounds."

Mr Darcy lifted his eyes from the ground, and his stormy blue orbs bore into her. The depth of his gaze made goose-flesh erupt down her legs.

"I intend to prove myself, my love for you, and my constancy," Mr Darcy swore.

Elizabeth's barely held composure slipped. She looked away whilst embracing herself. Did it truly matter whether he had lain with Lady Baslow or not? She shut her eyes to break the spell Mr Darcy had cast on her and inhaled deeply through her nose. For three weeks she had been a guest in his home, and in those weeks, he had made her feel wanted but one morning. He had had business to address, but during what little time they had spent together, he had been distant and aloof. She instinctively knew that he had contemplated a future with Lady Baslow. Probably compared the two of them—a contest she could not win. She might be comely but could not hold a candle to the beguiling Lady Baslow. The widow was everything Elizabeth was not.

Mr Darcy touched her arm and brought her out of her miserable thoughts.

"If you happen to marry Lady Baslow while you are away, I shall not hold it against you."

"I have no wish to marry Lady Baslow."

A mirthless laugh escaped her. "I find that hard to believe. The lady is ethereally beautiful, particularly acquainted with you, very accomplished, in possession of a significant fortune, and has no connections you need be embarrassed to acknowledge."

"I love *you*—most ardently."

"Yet, I cannot compete, can I? You were distant and aloof from the moment we arrived at Pemberley. I was treated like an insignificant guest, like an intruder in what was supposed to be my future home. It brought to my attention the disparity in our dispositions. I value loyalty highly, and your words matter but little..."

"I..." Mr Darcy began, but she stepped back and held up her hand to stop whatever he was going to say.

"It does not matter, but before we part, I want you to know that I would never have dishonoured you in the way my father implied. I did not contemplate his words when he first spoke them, on the day we became betrothed. I was too inclined to be happy about our understanding to hear it.

"I am not one of those young ladies who would risk her marriage by dallying with a dashing gentleman. I am not impressed by wealth, consequence, or a handsome face. I was once susceptible to flattery, but no more...

"Until we meet again, I shall think of you with fondness for the days we spent in Hertfordshire, and even Kent. I do cherish the memory of our little picnic at the hunting tower. It was my first kiss, you know. A lady never forgets such a treasure... I wish you health and happiness, Mr Darcy."

And on that pleasant note, she quit his company. It was important to end their acquaintance on amicable terms. She hoped that would enable them to think about each other without animosity and to forget about the last few weeks.

Elizabeth walked to her room and could not refrain from peeking out of the window. Mr Darcy was still there, staring at the closed door. He glanced up, and she stepped back into the shadows. Finally, he turned and fetched his horse. He swung himself up into the saddle and kicked his mount into a gallop. The dust cloud he left behind took minutes to settle. By the morrow, he would be gone, she was certain of it, and by the next day, so would she.

# Chapter 9 Counselled by Despondency

Elizabeth's escape did not come about as quickly as she had hoped. She needed an excuse to go to London without anyone wanting to escort her, and trips to the dressmaker would not be unattended.

"Mr and Mrs Collins to see you, ma'am."

The future heir to Longbourn and his wife had come for the wedding or, more likely, to escape the wrath of his patroness. Mr Darcy's aunt Lady Catherine de Bourgh vehemently opposed his engagement to Elizabeth Bennet, simply because she was not her own daughter.

The Collinses were staying at Lucas Lodge, and her family would become suspicious if she wished to leave while her friend was still in the neighbourhood. But their friendship had suffered since Charlotte had married Mr Collins. Firstly, because she rarely escaped her husband's presence—unless he was occupied with his garden or Lady Catherine de Bourgh—and he was not what she deemed good company. And secondly, Elizabeth could not deny that despite not regretting her rejection of Mr Collins's proposal, her friend had secured him through a deceitful method. It had put a strain on their relationship that Elizabeth suspected was a permanent fixture. She no longer trusted Charlotte completely, as she had done in the past, and she had never had more need of a confidante.

Elizabeth pondered whether she was being fair to her old friend or if her recent disappointment with a certain gentleman had corrupted her perception of everyone else. Her view of her most beloved father had suffered at the altar of her corruption. Jane, she still held in the highest regard—she and *Mórai*, of course. Her paternal grandmother was the one person she trusted implicitly.

Mr and Mrs Collins entered the drawing room, and after being served a cup of tea, they directed their attention to Elizabeth.

"Mrs Collins and I are most satisfied. Yes, dear cousin. And most obliged by your wise decision not to run hastily into a marriage unsanctioned by the illustrious Mr Darcy's family. You know Lady Catherine is not in favour of the match and has gone as far as calling it a disgrace. Despite the Bennet line being respectable, there is no comparison to the ancient and noble line from which the de Bourghs descend. I am confident that by the time spring is upon us, you will have reached the most desirable conclusion for everyone involved and decided upon releasing Mr Darcy from his promise to you."

It was disconcerting how similar her mind was to Mr Collins's. It was a novel feeling, and she smiled, wishing she could be present when Mr Collins was informed about Uncle Henry's title.

"I am glad to have been of service to my father's second cousin."

"And heir to Longbourn," Mr Collins added.

"Presumably..." Elizabeth said, knowing full well the implication.

"Mr Collins, the wedding has simply been postponed, since Mr Darcy is a busy man." Mrs Bennet tried to insert herself into the conversation, but no one paid her any heed.

"I think it is safe to say that your mother will not produce a son, at her age..."

Elizabeth was speechless, and so was her mother. Charlotte saved them from further embarrassment by calling the visit to an end.

After sending off the Collinses, Elizabeth contemplated whether she should write to her grandmother and notify *Móraí* of her intention to visit, but fearing what would happen if her reply fell into the wrong hands, and knowing her mother's curious nature, she dared not risk it.

Instead, she moped, which was not an act; she simply saw no reason to conceal her misery. The scheme had worked well for Jane, who had been sent to the Gardiners' to mend her broken heart. With any luck, Elizabeth would soon receive the same leniency.

#

Sleep alluded Elizabeth most nights. She spent them reading for the brief moments her mind could centre on the pages, then it wandered off down treacherous paths, prompted by a word or sentence that reminded her of Mr Darcy. The fatigue was ever present, but the moments of sleepiness were too brief for her to settle into bed. By the time she was under the covers, a thought chased sleep away, and she tossed and turned until she rose again in agitation.

Two weeks flew by, but no chance of escape presented itself. The Collinses returned to Kent. Life at Longbourn was a series of unremarkable events that made no difference to her disposition but for the letter she received from Mr Darcy. It was only one sheet, and she debated whether she should toss it into the fire or read it. She could not decide and so hid it inside a book.

In a month, the Gardiners were expected to visit, and she hoped for an invitation to join them in town in the new year. That hope dwindled into nothing when word reached them that the Gardiners would not be celebrating Christmas at Longbourn after all. They had taken Mr Darcy's invitation to spend the yuletide at Pemberley to heart and had arranged for a northern journey. They would not go to Pemberley, of course, with the wedding delayed, but would visit their relations whom they had neglected after Lydia's folly had terminated their previous journey too early.

Elizabeth's reserves were drained, and a visit from Sir William did not help matters. He droned on and on about his invitation to St James's for a party. Mrs Bennet could hardly contain her envy, and the call was feeling most uncomfortable when Mrs Hill interrupted the awkwardness by delivering the post.

"This has come for you, Miss Elizabeth. The stationery is exceedingly fine, and the seal looks like it is from someone important, so I thought it best to hand it to you at once."

Elizabeth took the missive from the silver salver and was relieved that the feminine hand on the envelope was not Mr Darcy's. Neither the seal nor the handwriting looked familiar, and she tore it open, rather curious as to who the sender might be.

"What is it, Lizzy? Who is it from?" her mother wanted to know, her pique with Sir William quite forgotten.

"Lady Matlock has invited me to town for a musical soirée she is having at Matlock House in London on Saturday. Heavens, that is only six days hence. She apologises that her nephew will not be present as he is still busy with the trial. She would like to get to know me better and noticed my enjoyment at her last event." This proved that Lady Matlock knew her but little if she believed Elizabeth had felt any pleasure during that evening. Though she had to admit that the opera singer did have a lovely voice and had enthralled her enough to allow her short reprieves from the flirting behind her.

"A musical soirée in town would set me up nicely," Mrs Bennet proclaimed. "It may not be St James's, but an earl is not to be dismissed."

"I am afraid that the invitation only includes me," Elizabeth stated.

"I never heard such nonsense. An unmarried lady cannot travel to town alone without her family."

"Her ladyship is offering to host me in Grosvenor Square. I would hardly be sleeping in the streets."

"How are you going to get there? You cannot take the post!"

"Jane did, when she visited Uncle last year."

"She was not betrothed to one of the most illustrious gentlemen in the country!"

*Neither am I*, she wanted to say but bit her tongue at the last moment.

"I may have a solution to your problem. I am, as you know, going to town, and I would be happy to convey Miss Eliza to Matlock House. Grosvenor Square is not an inconvenient distance from St James's," Sir William generously offered.

"I am not certain your father will approve," Mrs Bennet protested, but not even she believed that.

Mr Bennet did not object and approved Elizabeth's visit to the Matlocks'.

As soon as Sir William left, Elizabeth sat down at the writing desk to compose her reply.

*Dear Lady Matlock*

*I am sorry to send my regrets, but a prior engagement prohibits me from attending your musical soirée. Do pardon me, madam, and do not believe me insensible to the condescension conferred upon me.*

*Your humble servant,*

*Elizabeth Bennet*

"Lizzy! We must visit my sister and tell her about Lady Matlock's invitation. Come along."

"Yes, Mama."

Elizabeth finished her letter in a hurry, sanded it, and wrote the name and address on the envelope. She must post it immediately before she lost her nerve.

#

Darcy sighed and raked his hand through his hair for the third time in ten minutes. Ten days had passed since he had left Hertfordshire and his heart behind. Three arduous months she had requested they wait, but the worst was that he was no closer to discovering how to rectify her erroneous conclusions. Though, if he was perfectly honest with himself, albeit founded on mistaken assumptions, she was not entirely wrong, and that was gnawing on his conscience—depriving him of his ability to sleep.

He had wavered, if not for long, when Lady Baslow had again become an eligible choice—not so much as to change his mind, but he had experienced moments of doubt brought about by memories of a youthful romance, much of which was a figment of his imagination. It had to be, or Celia could not have married Sir Lawrence. He supposed her betrayal was as much his own fault because he had flaunted certain rules of propriety at the time. A kiss behind the stables, in the orchard, and everywhere else in between. Every opportunity they had to steal a moment of privacy had been used similarly. It was a miracle they had never been discovered, though it was not by divine intervention. The Lord must have had much more pressing matters to attend to than their youthful antics.

Sequestered as they had been in each other's company for much of their formative years, it was almost unavoidable to let their beguiling childish fancies run away with them; painted in the colours of paradise but unfounded in reality. No, love, he had discovered, was equal measures of pain and pleasure. He had learnt his lesson and had stood firmly in his principles ever since.

With two months and two weeks until he would see Elizabeth again, he needed occupation. There was no more he could do at the Edensor estate. Not until the conundrum of who was the heir had been decided. John and Robert Baslow both claimed the baronetcy and had written to the Lord Chancellor. Who would succeed Sir Lawrence was out of his hands; the House of Lords would decide who had the greater claim. In the meantime, the bickering cousins resided at Edensor with the baronet's widow and relieved him of the responsibilities of the affairs of that estate.

Lady Baslow should be preparing to remove with the Conksburys to Haddon Grove, taking with her what she had brought to the marriage, but she had chosen to remain at Edensor. With the execution of the will postponed, she was also delaying fulfilling her part. They were in limbo until the House of Lords had decided upon who was the rightful heir. Which reminded him, he should invite the Conksburys for dinner before they departed. As close friends of his parents', they expected nothing less, and it had the additional benefit of sparing them an evening in company with the quarrelling cousins. The opportunity to speak more to Lady Baslow's brother, Mr Cornelius Conksbury, had not presented itself since the funeral. He would like to enquire whether he had a docile mare for sale that would suit Miss Elizabeth. It had not escaped him that Elizabeth was no horsewoman; even on the short ride between Pemberley and Edensor, her shortcomings had been obvious. She needed a compliant horse to overcome her fear.

The Conksburys, and even Lady Baslow, were the least of his problems. They would all sort themselves out with time. Elizabeth was another matter entirely. Her accusations were flawed, but he still needed to investigate how she had come to believe he had offered more than a comforting embrace to Lady Baslow. Yet, he could not believe that Lady Baslow would have invented such a tale. There must have been a misunderstanding of sorts that could be rectified. Could Lady Baslow have related his bodily features as a jest, and could Elizabeth have, wrongfully, connected it to the events of the thunderstorm? But Darcy could not imagine the proper Lady Baslow making such a sordid joke to a maiden. Yet Elizabeth had claimed that she had, and she was honest to a fault.

*Dear Lord, how have I managed to muddle everything up? Where have I erred?*

He had laboured tirelessly to fulfil his duties to Sir Lawrence. Then the storm had hit, and he had worked even harder to be ready to depart for his wedding, but misfortune seemed to come in threes. The uproar at the funeral had been the last in a series of unfortunate events. Forced to admit defeat, he had remained at Pemberley when his party had left for Hertfordshire.

His dreams for a future filled with pleasure and happiness had evaporated somewhere amidst the disasters. He must woo Miss Elizabeth all over again. No, not woo but grovel at her feet and beg her forgiveness. It was going to be an uphill battle because courting a woman was clearly not something he excelled at.

The pain in Elizabeth's eyes haunted him day and night. But it hurt him equally that she could believe such an obvious lie about him. He might have been confused for a short while, but he would never act as despicably as her accusations claimed. That was how Wickham behaved—not he.

'*Never shirk your duties, abide by the law, adhere to the strictures of polite society, and you will live a comfortable life,*' his father had taught him from an early age. At present, despite adhering to the great man's advice, he did not feel it was helping.

Should he write her a letter? That had worked to his advantage before; it might do so again and would allow him to consider his words. But even the written word failed him, and he ended up sanding an honest but pitifully brief note.

What he feared the most, as he endeavoured to prevail upon Elizabeth to abandon her absurd new scheme, was finding her insurmountably decided.

#

Elizabeth's apprehension grew the closer they came to Grosvenor Square. Her stomach roiled, whilst she fought to give the appearance of delightful anticipation. Sir William and Lady Lucas would wish to escort her, and she had to discourage them from entering Matlock House. The carriage rolled to a halt in front of the red brick building, seven windows wide, cramped between Darcy House and the de Bourgh House. The three Fitzwilliam homes spanned one entire side of the square.

"Let me hand you out, Miss Elizabeth," the master of Lucas Lodge offered gallantly.

"There is no need for you to escort me, Sir William. You have not been introduced, and Lady Matlock adheres strictly to the rules of etiquette. She would not look favourably upon a breach of propriety. Allow me to present your card on this occasion, and I shall speak on your behalf. I am certain Lady Matlock will offer you an audience when you return to fetch me."

It was not a lie, although she suspected his perception of her words differed vastly from her intent. But it was not likely that Lady Matlock would see an unknown gentleman who had come to call upon her ladyship.

With Sir William's effusive gratitude for her intercepting his great *faux pas* droning on in the background, Elizabeth prayed she would not encounter any of the residents and that her precarious scheme would prove effective.

She alighted from the carriage and knocked on the door. As predicted, it was opened by a butler. With a final wave to Sir William and Lady Lucas, she waited for the raps on the carriage roof and watched it lurch into traffic before she entered the house. The door closed behind her, and she gave the butler her card.

"Mrs Phillips to see Lady Catherine de Bourgh," she announced in an assertive voice. She had managed to pilfer one of her aunt's cards during one of her many visits.

"I beg your pardon, madam, but this is Matlock House. The de Bourgh residence is the yellow building to the left."

"Oh. How embarrassing! I have only visited Lady Catherine at Rosings Park. I am dreadfully sorry to have inconvenienced you."

She turned to leave, but the butler detained her.

"Lady Catherine is not in residence, madam."

Elizabeth faced the butler, trying to quash her rising apprehension and calm her racing heart.

"That is unfortunate indeed. Lady Metcalf was certain she had caught a glimpse of her on Bond Street yesterday. I suppose she could have been mistaken. Are you quite sure?"

"Yes. Allow me to find you a room to await the return of your carriage."

That would not do at all. The longer she stayed under the Matlocks' roof, the greater was the threat of being discovered.

"You are ever so kind, sir, but I only sent my carriage to circle the square. One of my horses is barely broken in and tends to get restless when forced to stand still. It will come back round in no time at all. Thank you for your excellent service."

This time, the butler opened the door, and she escaped the house for the freedom of choice. She picked up the  box the driver had left on the steps, glanced at the white Darcy House, and turned in the opposite direction. She wanted to put distance between herself and Grosvenor Square before she hired a hack to take her to the employment office.

#

The Conksburys arrived, and Darcy greeted them in the blue parlour. He had not included Lady Baslow in his invitation, but she had come regardless.

He was anticipating hearing what news Cornelius had brought from town and hastened to speak to his friend.

"Darcy, I thought you would hie off to Hertfordshire as soon as your business at Edensor was concluded and that you had no time to entertain old friends."

"Yes, well... There was a problem with the reading of the banns."

"Her father cannot have objected, or he would surely have said something sooner." Cornelius raised his voice and drew the attention of the rest of the room. "Or has Rosings' old dragon been spitting fire?" He wiggled his eyebrows. He was intimately familiar with Lady Catherine de Bourgh's quirks and her fancy for Darcy to marry her daughter.

"No, it was an absent-minded groom who forgot to request the reading from Reverend Peterson."

"It is not like you to forget such important matters, but the delay should only be a couple of weeks. Yet, I did not hear them read this Sunday."

"No. There is no rush. They must be read no longer than three months before the wedding, and it has been postponed."

"Indefinitely?"

"No, only until spring. I had to return to Pemberley to negotiate how to proceed in the interim, before completing the execution of Sir Lawrence's will. Then there is the trial over the thefts at the funeral. It is impossible to predict how long the court will detain me. Miss Elizabeth is concerned about me travelling during the harsh winter months and preferred to postpone the wedding."

Cornelius bent towards him and whispered in his ear, "Is she having second thoughts?"

Darcy did not reply, but none was needed. Cornelius knew him too well to be fooled by any prevarication.

"Does a certain dip in the lake have a bearing on her decision? Because if it does, I shall gladly correct her mistake."

Darcy flinched when Lady Baslow grabbed his arm and inserted herself into the private conversation.

"Miss Elizabeth is full young and excessively ambitious. Until she lowers her expectations, I very much doubt that she will find contentment in any situation. Is it not time to move on to someone of maturity and refinement?"

The room was quiet, waiting eagerly for his reply, as if they were expecting him to degrade Miss Elizabeth. He regarded his first love and studied her expression. His mind cleared away the memories of the angelic girl, who had changed and distorted into an unrecognisable grown lady. He lifted his eyes to regard his oldest friend. Cornelius was frowning. Mrs Conksbury was eagerly watching the scene with her glass of sherry raised halfway to her mouth, whilst her husband feigned indifference. Returning his eyes to Lady Baslow, he could detect an unbecoming smugness in the set of her mouth.

"You do not know Miss Elizabeth well. Because if you did, you would understand that she is a vivacious lady with a lively mind who finds pleasure in many things. As for her ambitions, they do not tend towards an advantageous marriage, or she would have accepted my first proposal."

The Conksburys gasped in unison. He should not have revealed so much, despite their longstanding connection. Mrs Conksbury thrived on gossiping with her friends, and her children enjoyed teasing him. But he was weary, and he would not allow anyone to tarnish Elizabeth's name, not even Celia. Especially not Lady Baslow. Elizabeth must have spoken the truth; there was no misunderstanding. How helpless had the widow truly been since Sir Lawrence's passing? In retrospect, it was questionable whether she was quite as incapable as the image she had presented. Was it all a ruse to ensnare him?

Did she love him still?

His heart pounded in a wild rhythm until he remembered her chosen method. If given the choice between injuring Miss Elizabeth and disappointing Lady Baslow, he need not ponder. Disabusing Lady Baslow of all thoughts of a union between them must be his priority. But before he managed to do so, the door opened, and his butler entered; supper was served.

"Now that you are all alone with nothing to do, why not celebrate Christmas at Haddon Grove?" Mrs Conksbury suggested as soon as they were seated. "Celia is in mourning, so it will just be the family and no elaborate parties." She laughed.

Was she implying that his usual reserve was a joke?

"I shall not be alone," he hastened to reply. "I plan to bring Georgiana home very soon."

"Dear Georgiana." Lady Baslow simpered. "You must bring your sister, of course. We quite dote upon her, do we not, Mother?"

"Oh yes." Mrs Conksbury smiled and clapped her hands together. "You are both most welcome." She stole a glance at Cornelius.

Darcy felt like he was back at Netherfield in the autumn of 1811, where matchmaking had been Miss Bingley's primary object. Not only his own marital prospects had been in her sights, he had since learnt. Miss Elizabeth had revealed the contents of Miss Bingley's parting letter to Miss Bennet. Her scheme, naming Georgiana as Bingley's future spouse, had spurred him to revile the lady until she harboured no more illusions as to his own or his sister's future felicity. His experience with Wickham must, partially, have taken the blame for his loss of control at that pitiful moment. He had regretted his harsh words but not the sentiments behind them nor the impromptu visit to Scarborough Miss Bingley, immediately thereafter, had embarked upon. She had not suffered any lasting effects of his reprimand, because her behaviour had not improved.

"I shall interpret your silence as acceptance. Those who remain silent assent," Mrs Conksbury chirped.

"I regret that I must decline. I have business to conclude before I bring back my bride to Pemberley. Not only do I plan for a long absence to go on a bridal trip, which needs planning, but the master's and mistress's chambers, among other rooms, are in dire need of decorating."

"We could help you," Lady Baslow suggested. "Decorating needs a female touch. Do you not agree?"

"Exactly. I am counting on Georgiana's excellent eye for fashion *and* practicality. I dare say that between the two of us, we shall manage."

"But surely, decorating a couple of rooms will not occupy all your time. You simply must have dinner with us and spend a night or two," Mrs Conksbury entreated him.

She would not let a dead horse lie, so he decided to change the subject. There was nothing that could tempt him to spend another night under the same roof as Lady Baslow.

"As I said, it will not be possible. Cornelius, I need a docile mare for my bride. Do you still have the small white one?"

"Yes, but docile does not cover it. She is meek enough for an inexperienced child," Cornelius replied.

"Miss Elizabeth is no horsewoman," Lady Baslow interjected. "She can barely stay in the saddle at a walk."

"I am immensely looking forward to teaching her to ride," Darcy countered.

There was to be no separation of the sexes with such a small party, but Darcy spoke to Cornelius to the detriment of everyone else. He had not been in town since spring and wanted to know whether his friend had heard about any new investments to consider. The gentlemen's talk of business could be of no interest to the ladies, but he was out of charity with them both.

#

Elizabeth entered the employment office and requested a list of suitable companions. One name stood out as most promising.

She was a gently bred widow of six and forty—Mrs Clodagh Finnegan. Elizabeth pointed at the name to show the clerk.

"I wonder whether this lady might be amenable to immediate employment?"

"Most likely, she is Irish…"

Although the comment irked her, Elizabeth pretended not to hear the derogatory remark. It was best not to make too great a nuisance of herself and attract unwanted attention.

"How soon can she be here?"

"I did not know you meant it quite so literally. She lives not too far away, but the traffic is heavy at this time of day. I suggest I send a hack to fetch her tomorrow morning. If you return at nine, I am sure I can present her to you."

"I have no pressing engagements. I shall wait while you send the hack."

"That would be most irregular, Miss Conyngham."

"Yes, but not impossible." Elizabeth sat down on a chair and pulled her book from her basket.

# Chapter 10 The Gentle Trace of Grief

*Virtute non astutia*—by courage, not by craft—was the Conynghams' family motto, but Elizabeth needed both to succeed. By chance, whilst waiting for Mrs Finnegan at the employment office, she overheard an intriguing conversation. A ship named the Vermont was destined for New York but would stop to retrieve more passengers in Dublin. It was a long way from her destination of Limerick, but at least she would be on Irish soil, and from there she would hire a hack. Mrs Finnegan agreed to the sea voyage, and they spoke to one of the crew to add their names to the passenger list.

"Miss Eilís Conyngham and Mrs Clodagh Finnegan," she answered when the clerk requested their names. She thought herself very clever to use Eilís—the Irish equivalent for Elizabeth and her grandmother's family name—on her escape. She was not of a mind to be found, so she dared not use Elizabeth Bennet...

The clerk wrote their names on the list as though there was nothing untoward and gave them directions to where the Vermont was docked. Elizabeth released a sigh of relief when they left the coffee-house where the clerk had set up a table.

"'Twill be a cold voyage, miss. Be sure you have warm clothes and extra blankets," Mrs Finnegan admonished, reminding her of Mrs Hill back home, and a pang of guilt hit her full force. Her family, with the exception of Mary, would worry about her. She had needed to inform someone of her whereabouts, and Mary had been the natural preference. Was she behaving utterly selfishly? Yes, but she had no choice.

Mrs Finnegan's prediction proved correct. The voyage was excessively cold, with no fire to warm oneself upon, but Elizabeth hardly felt the chill. Her mind shifted between exaltation at her escape and guilt-ridden despair for leaving behind everyone she held dear. Mr Darcy was not included in her loved ones. Her anger towards that man had not abated. It was despicable that he would not let the matter of their marriage rest when he clearly loved another woman.

They arrived in Dublin on a chilly winter morning. The city had lost its status as capital in 1801, under the Irish Act of Union, and had suffered a decade of financial decline. The absence of hundreds of peers and MPs, and their thousands of servants, had led to many of the great houses becoming redundant and had turned elegant neighbourhoods into slums.

Elizabeth chose not to stay, as they had hours of daylight left, and she hired a private coach to convey them to Limerick. It was not as fast as the post but more comfortable for two ladies travelling on their own. Yet she could not be at ease until she had spoken to her grandmother, and her anxiety increased as the time neared. Long days in the carriage and sleepless nights at unfamiliar inns left much time to ponder her decision.

In addition, the significant expenses had depleted most of her funds. It was her entire life savings, and she had even pawned her necklace. By the time she arrived in Limerick, she was dependent upon her grandmother's benevolence and worried that *Mórai* would refuse the necessary secrecy, promptly writing a letter to inform her father of her whereabouts. Mr Bennet was her son and most likely held her loyalty.

It was with a tremulous heart that she lifted the knocker on the door and gave it three sharp raps.

"Are you absolutely sure this is your grandmother's house?" Mrs Finnegan seemed unconvinced, but Elizabeth was certain. The house was impressive, albeit not the size of Pemberley. It was a newer building. A necessity the peers in Limerick had been forced into after the siege in 1691, when the English had burnt all their castles to the ground. The initial rebuild had been a modest house that Uncle Henry had spent the last thirty years improving and expanding.

"Áth Dara is picturesque with its steep gabled roofs, is it not? The pointed arches and lacy tracery work remind me of a chateau. My grandmother's brother, the Marquis of Limerick—"

"Heaven forfend!" Mrs Finnegan exclaimed, but Elizabeth continued unabated.

"—has done much to the old and smaller house he inherited. He has spent the last thirty years transforming it in the model of great houses and churches he has visited on the continent. Is it not splendid?"

"Yes, I dare say it is," Mrs Finnegan agreed as the butler opened the door.

"Miss Elizabeth Bennet to see Mrs Bennet."

The butler looked like he was about to have an apoplexy, but he recovered quickly and accepted her card.

"And this is Mrs Clodagh Finnegan." Elizabeth introduced her companion.

"Was Mrs Bennet aware that you were coming, miss?"

"No."

"Then you better come with me."

The butler guided them up the stairs and through a long, well-lit hall. He knocked on a door, and the lady inside bade him enter.

"Miss Elizabeth Bennet and Mrs Clodagh Finnegan to see you, madam."

"It cannot be!" Mrs Bennet exclaimed.

Elizabeth stepped into the room and curtseyed before her paternal grandmother, who rose to kiss both her cheeks before enveloping her in a fierce embrace.

"I beg you to excuse my coming here without an invitation."

"Of course you need no invitation to visit, and the marquis will be delighted to see you once he returns from his business. Will you introduce me to your friend?" she graciously offered whilst studying her granddaughter intently.

"This is Mrs Clodagh Finnegan. She has been my companion since I arrived in London. We voyaged to Dublin on the Vermont and hired a hackney to convey us hither. I hope you will allow us to stay. I shall explain later."

"Pery! Escort Mrs Finnegan to the Casamari chamber, and have her luggage taken up. I am sure she is eager to refresh herself after the long journey. And prepare the Notre-Dame chamber for my granddaughter."

The butler bowed and led Mrs Finnegan away.

"Close the door please, Eilís." Eilís had been Grandmother Bennet's preferred soubriquet for her second-eldest granddaughter since she had discovered that it irked the girls' mother.

"The last I heard from you, you were engaged to be married to the dashing Darcy heir. But your face does not glow with happiness, so I presume something has happened. Pray, come and sit by me and tell your *Mhórai* everything."

"Thank you." She sat down beside her grandmother on the sofa. "Are you acquainted with Mr Darcy?"

"We have never been formally introduced, but we have attended the same events in town. With his handsome features and noble mien, he is a difficult gentleman to overlook. Though I suspect he is dead to gaiety. He is staid and taciturn—quite the opposite to what I imagined would attract *you,* my dear."

Elizabeth nodded.

"True, on both accounts. At first, I did not like him at all, but he improved upon further acquaintance. We became engaged, and my limited experience with gentlemen in general must be my excuse for that impolitic decision. I must admit that he is the reason for my journey hither. He and my dear father, who must own his part in my current predicament. Mr Darcy proposed, and I accepted, but that was before the woman he loves was widowed. Certain events brought the two much into each other's company—and in the biblical sense during a thunderstorm. I decided it was best to end the engagement. Unfortunately, the settlement papers had already been signed. My father must pay Mr Darcy twenty thousand pounds for breach of promise if I do not marry him."

"I take it that Mr Darcy will not release you from your contract?"

"You would be correct."

"Why would he not?"

"He is an honourable gentleman who does not go back on his word. I chose to release him because it is the right thing to do. I would not force a man to marry me against his inclination just to uphold some exaggerated sense of duty. When he and my father refused to release me, it occurred to me that Mr Darcy cannot marry a bride he cannot find."

Elizabeth felt a rush of emotions just speaking about the gentleman she had once loved, though it was ridiculous to believe she had purged him entirely from her heart. If only she found it an insipid or indifferent subject; but the coldness in her words were contradicted by the fire still burning within.

"Does your mother know about your broken engagement?"

"No, she and my father believe that the wedding has only been postponed for three months. I begged for a year, but Father would only allow a quarter of the time because he worried for my and my sisters' reputation. As compensation for the sacrifice I would make by marrying Mr Darcy, and my recent doldrums,

Father sent me to visit Lady Matlock. I had received an invitation to one her renowned musical soirées, and my father regarded my acceptance as a sign of my defeat. I was fortunate to be conveyed to town by our neighbour Sir William and his wife. I entered Matlock House and requested to see Lady Catherine de Bourgh. The butler naturally assumed that I had entered the wrong house and allowed me my escape. I hired Mrs Finnegan at the employment office and have come to you with an outrageous request."

Elizabeth struggled to continue, to speak the words aloud, and she looked imploringly at her grandmother. Tears welled in her eyes, but she blinked them away. This was not a moment for weakness.

"And pray, what is your request, *a leanbh*—my child?"

"To let me stay with you for all eternity, or until Mr Darcy marries. And to conceal my whereabouts from my parents."

"This may come as a surprise to you, but I am rather old. For all eternity may not be as long as you think."

"I shall not give such an evident falsehood a second thought." Elizabeth refused to give way to sorrow and preferred to think of her grandmother as immortal.

"You are a dear, even when you are dissembling. Who knows you are here?"

"Only Mrs Finnegan and Mary," Elizabeth admitted with chagrin. "I have told Mary everything and Mrs Finnegan nothing at all."

Elizabeth had needed a confidante, someone who would be able to find her should Mr Darcy demand compensation for his missing bride, and had told Mary everything she held against her betrothed. Mary had been even angrier than Elizabeth and had promised not to divulge her whereabouts unless it was strictly necessary. Mary relished being of use and could be trusted. It was a shame Elizabeth had not realised that sooner.

"Is Mrs Finnegan trustworthy?" her grandmother mused.

"I believe so." Elizabeth had no reason to doubt Mrs Finnegan. She had been an invaluable aid during her journey and had not asked any intrusive questions.

"Perhaps it is best that she remains here until you are certain."

Her grandmother allowing Mrs Finnegan to stay made hope swell in Elizabeth's chest.

"*A Mhórai*, are you saying you will have me?"

"Always, *a leanbh*, always. I shall do my utmost to console you and not breathe a word to my son where you are hiding. Not because I do not trust *him*, but I would be a fool indeed if I ever gave credit to his *wife*…"

"Thank you! I am forever in your debt and shall strive to make as little nuisance of myself as possible."

Elizabeth threw her arms around her grandmother's neck and sobbed in relief.

"There, there, my child. You must be over-wrought indeed if you believe you could ever be a nuisance to anyone. You are the most delightful company, my dear. Dry your tears, *a leanbh*, and we shall get you settled."

The ladies walked to Elizabeth's appointed chamber, where a maid was busy unpacking her apparel.

"Pray, is this all the clothing you have?"

Elizabeth smiled ruefully.

"Not all I own but all I have brought with me. I could not very well pack my entire wardrobe for a three-day visit to town, but I shall manage."

"Nonsense! We shall visit the seamstress as soon as I can get an appointment. This will simply not do for a relation of the marquis. Half of these"—Mrs Bennet pointed at her meagre selection—"are Jane's old gowns, and her colours do not suit you. No, let me have the pleasure of thwarting your mother in this. *She* never appreciated your lovely auburn hair. It should be complemented by wearing richer colours that will also bring out the lovely colour of your eyes. Maroon and bronze would look particularly attractive."

Elizabeth knew it was a futile endeavour to protest, so instead she voiced her deeply felt gratitude.

#

Some passions are quiet, whilst some are tightly knitted. Elizabeth suffered from the latter, and the more she fought it, the tauter it became. Rejected by the man to whom she rightfully belonged, a path to recovery must be set upon, and occupation was her chosen remedy. If only she could bury the last year of her life in oblivion. But she was plagued by one sole haunting dream.

Elizabeth felt wretched when she should be rejoicing in her narrow escape. It confounded her that she seemed unable to return to her former buoyant nature.

She was looking through fashion pages and should be relishing the pleasure of ordering a new wardrobe for herself, but she could not help but feel that the beautiful dresses would be redundant. She had no one to impress and did not lament that fact. With her heart irrevocably lost, beaux and marriage were not in her future.

Three young ladies entered the establishment and drew her attention from the illustrations. The seamstress's assistant tended to them and their specific requests. The ladies moved into the back room whilst Elizabeth began selecting fabrics, and when they returned, they were wearing nuns' habits.

Elizabeth could not help but study their cornets. The large, white, heavily starched headgear obstructed their peripheral vision, and they had to turn their heads to look anywhere but straight ahead.

The tall one, who was obviously more senior, curtseyed to Elizabeth, who blushed at being caught staring.

"May God be with you," one of the sisters blessed her.

"Thank you," Elizabeth replied.

"Introduce us," Mrs Bennet demanded of the seamstress, who immediately complied.

The ladies presented themselves as Sisters of Charity of the Presentation of the Blessed Virgin Mary—Honora, Catherine, and Erin. Sister Honora was the tallest and the leader.

"I have not seen you in Limerick before," Mrs Bennet mused.

"No, we have just come from Dublin to open a school for the poor, a shelter for women, and a respite for the sick," Sister Honora replied. "God came to me in my dreams and showed me women and children stretching out their hands in need. I felt a persistent calling to devote myself to the service of the poor, the sick, and the uneducated. Especially those who suffer from the debilitating ignorance of God's consoling love. I am determined to alleviate their distress, to educate, and to nurse in the name of the Almighty."

"How admirable of you," Elizabeth spoke in earnest awe.

The nun smiled. "We are trying to establish ourselves in the community and would welcome anyone who would like to observe how we work."

"We would like that very much. Where are you situated?" Elizabeth asked.

"We have rented a house on Shannon Road, by the Athlunkart Appleyard. If you visit us in the day, you can meet the children."

"I would like that very much," Elizabeth said with a glance at her grandmother, who smiled and nodded.

"I admit that you have caught my interest too, and if it is convenient, we shall visit you Monday next. This week is rather busy. I hope you do not mind the wait, *Eilís*?"

"No, I am at your disposal."

"Nonsense, dear, but we have tasks to accomplish before we can be at leisure. Sisters, we shall see you next week."

The nuns curtseyed and left Elizabeth to finish her shopping. Her measurements were taken before they proceeded to the cobbler to order new shoes.

As the week continued, Elizabeth's spirits did not lift, despite the abundance of new additions to her wardrobe.

"I have received a letter from your father."

Her grandmother jolted her out of her unpleasant memories with this most unwelcome news. Elizabeth sat quietly, waiting with bated breath to hear whether her grandmother would keep her word.

"He is dreadfully worried about you and has been searching for you all over London. He seems to believe that you might have gone north because he has scouts looking for you on the Great North Road."

"That is strange..."

"No, he firmly believes that you love Mr Darcy very much."

"I do not deny it." Elizabeth had no concerns admitting the truth.

"Is there truly no hope for the two of you to reconcile?"

Elizabeth looked out of the window; a blue mist crept amongst the shivering, barren trees. At a distance, the light from a lone farm shone. A swinked shepherd was driving his bleating flock to the stream. If only it were that simple. To forgive and forget...

"I might have forgiven him for his unfaithfulness if he had been a flirt, but he is not. He never even kissed my hand. Once, in private, he pecked my lips and held my hands. Throughout the rest of our acquaintance, he has behaved with impeccable manners. I confess I was concerned he was a cold man, aloof even. But the night of the thunderstorm proved that he is a man of passion. I am simply not the object of his fervency, and I cannot bear the thought of watching him bestow his ardour on someone else."

"But why would he choose you, propose to you, and declare his love?" her grandmother cried.

"I do not know. But I suppose the fact that the object of his affections was already married had some bearing on his decision."

"By your own admittance, he overcame several obstacles to love you, including his own pride and prejudice."

Elizabeth could not account for it and did not try.

"Dare I ask where these questions tend?"

"To help me understand what you are so adamant to escape."

"He has expressed his love in words but never in his actions."

"Was not saving Lydia from her folly of eloping with Mr Wickham, and covering the expenses of their marriage, a form of action? And proposing despite his concerns about your family? I dare say whoever is prepared to accept your mother into his life must be deeply attached."

Elizabeth chuckled mirthlessly and mumbled, "Unfathomable!"

Her grandmother was an excellent opponent in a debate, but it only confused Elizabeth.

"I acknowledge that his gestures were of consequence, but at what cost? If I add it up, it amounts to not much at all. I am simply not whom he wants for a wife, and I no longer wish to marry him. Mr Darcy may not have changed in essentials, but I have. His transgressions are greater than my will to forgive. I never want to see him again. Ever!"

Elizabeth's passionate admissions had left her drained. Her grandmother said nothing for several minutes, and her stomach churned until she was ready to cast up her accounts.

"I shall not tell your father that you are *here*," her dear grandmother allowed. "But I shall tell him not to be concerned. He has an industrious daughter. Very much like her *Mhórai*, and you will not be discovered until you wish it."

"Thank you. But what will Uncle Henry say?"

"Leave the marquis to me. He is uncommonly sensible for a man."

# Chapter 11 To Wither Away Agony

The churning in her breast did not abate. Elizabeth needed something so engrossing it would take her mind away from her concerns.

She sat down at the pianoforte and played Beethoven's Piano Sonata No. 14—a piece so sad each note broke her heart.

"Elizabeth!" her grandmother exclaimed. "Would you please play something more cheerful?"

"I could, but would you not rather visit the Presentation Sisters? It was good of them to invite us, and I am intrigued by their work. Especially their education of young girls."

Piety comforted her sister Mary. Were they more alike than she had thought?

Elizabeth and her grandmother took the carriage to visit the nuns and filled the back with crates of supplies Mrs Bennet thought might be useful. The sisters had a small grange with a vegetable garden to support them but not much else. The cottage itself was modest. The parlour functioned as a schoolroom and was currently occupied by seven young girls who were learning their Catechism.

"Please, do not let us disturb you. We are quite happy to observe," Mrs Bennet announced, and they sat down at the back until the lesson concluded.

The students ate a luncheon at the Grange, and Elizabeth suspected that for at least one of the students, it was her only meal of the day.

Sister Honora gave them a quick tour of the downstairs but would not take them upstairs where the sick were treated.

"Do not worry on my account," Elizabeth declared. "I have a particularly hardy constitution. I am never ill."

"I would not advise it, regardless," Sister Honora replied.

"But who are tending them whilst you and Sister Catherine are occupied with your students and Sister Erin is working in the kitchen?"

Sister Honora flushed. "We are a little short of hands, but once the students return home, we tend to the sick. At present, we do not have that many patients, so it is manageable."

"But winter is upon us. I suppose there will be an increase in patients once the cold sets in?" Elizabeth voiced her concern.

"Yes, I fear you are correct, but we shall manage."

After luncheon, the girls were taught the practical art of sewing, which would serve them well when they later applied for work. Elizabeth helped a little girl with her cross stitch before they departed for Áth Dara with much to occupy their minds.

At supper that evening, Elizabeth begged permission from her grandmother to offer to aid the sisters. Not in the material sense but with her time and knowledge—to educate and comfort. Her voluntary aid in the schoolroom would free a sister to tend the sick. Neither the marquis nor his sister opposed the idea. The following day, Elizabeth's offer was received with gratitude, and she immediately began instructing the young girls.

Elizabeth worked tirelessly from dawn to dusk, helping the nuns care for the poor. She shifted between vigils through the evening for a poor soul's last hours, listening to their regrets, to days instructing the girls who flocked to the only education in the area.

At the end of the previous century, the repeal of the penal

legislation had enabled nuns to set up schools. But they were too few and their accommodations too small for board. Fortunately, Canon Law allowed the superior sister the privilege of trade, administration, and financial freedom usually reserved for men. Sister Honora came from a wealthy landowning family and had left the protection of her brother to fund the school. She had been educated in Belgium from the tender age of ten but had finished in the Presentation Sisters' convent on St. George's Hill in Dublin. She had adopted the rules of that order, including the education of the poor. An inheritance from an uncle provided sister Honora with the capital needed, as neither marriage nor spinsterhood enticed the zestful young woman. Elizabeth's mother would have called her a bluestocking for her lack of marital ambition.

Exposed to the rhythm of religious life—prayer, daily mass, novenas, and the celebration of feast days—Elizabeth found purpose if not happiness. The nuns were excellent company; not a word ever passed between them about eligible gentlemen. It was liberating to leave every consideration of marriage behind, especially since she was never going to enter that state.

\#

Darcy rifled through the post on his desk with an ever-present dull headache thrumming at his temples. He fought off the nausea and a slight dizziness to search for an envelope written in a feminine hand, but there was no reply from Elizabeth. Ten days had passed since he had sent the missive by express; she should have been able to send him a few words in a week. To remain stoical and to be patiently waiting for Elizabeth to respond was insupportable. He was drifting in the wide sea of misery—rudderless in a tempest. To keep his promise and distance himself for three long months was not to be borne. How could he gather up the withered petals of her love and the ashes of her desire to wed him from a hundred and fifty miles away? It was in every way impossible!

He would afford her one more week to reply. If she did not respond, he would go to Longbourn and beg for her forbearance. Disheartened, he left for court—the last of his obligations to the Edensor estate. He chose to ride the seven miles instead of sitting idly in his carriage, and he rode hard to take his mind off Elizabeth.

His witness statement did not take long; the case was straightforward, and the jury was out for no more than fifteen minutes. The two thieves they had caught were brought before the judge and jury, looking rather nonchalant considering the seriousness of their crime.

"What is your verdict?" the judge asked the jury.

A Mr Burton stepped forwards. "Guilty, your honour."

"I sentence you both to death by hanging," the judge replied.

The thieves wrenched out of their guards' grip but were quickly caught and restrained. It was what they claimed that made Darcy flinch.

"It wasn't theft. Lady Baslow paid us to accost her as a lark. I swear, I'm innocent."

"That is a filthy lie," Captain John Baslow spat, while the judge called his court to order.

The thieves were led away, and the court room emptied. Darcy asked to speak to the condemned man who had made the claim against Lady Baslow, and he swore on everything that was holy that it was not a lie. The widow had promised no harm would befall them for their jest, and he had expected her to allow all of them to walk free by bribing the jury. Darcy was inclined to believe him; he offered a lot of details about her that convinced him. It was her motive that baffled him, until a dreadful thought settled in his mind. Had she done it to keep him from travelling to Hertfordshire? It was farfetched, but he could not think of any another plausible reason.

Darcy spoke to the judge about his suspicions, but the man

waved it off as a thief's desperate attempt to escape the noose.

Once home, he retreated to his study and glanced out of the window. A solitary figure was sitting on his garden bench. She dabbed her eyes and bowed her head. *The nerve of that woman! What is she doing here, in my garden?* He had to enquire. It would not do to let a lady cry alone, regardless of how much he despised her.

"Lady Baslow." He bowed formally and remained standing at a safe distance with his hands behind his back. Her cheeks were dry, and there was not a blotch on her countenance, which convinced him of her guile. "A pleasure to see you."

"Is it?"

He was surprised. If he was to be completely honest, it brought him no pleasure at all, but polite platitudes fell from his lips without thought. *'She is tolerable but not handsome enough to tempt me.'* As easily as untruthful insults it would seem. But he had learnt his lesson in that respect; Elizabeth had taught him what it truly meant to be a gentleman and the importance of respecting the feelings of others.

"Are you wool-gathering, Mr Darcy? You have the most peculiar expression on your countenance."

Darcy jolted back to the present and the unpalatable task of questioning Lady Baslow on a disagreeable subject.

"You look like a child deprived of its sweetmeats. What *is* occupying your thoughts?"

It was the best invitation to address the unpleasant topic he would receive, and he leapt into the fray.

"I must introduce a disagreeable subject, but it cannot be helped. I am at a loss, Lady Baslow, to how my betrothed came to believe that more than a comforting embrace happened between us during the thunderstorm. Not to forget the inexplicable actions of your servants and tenants. I suspect the two events are linked."

He closed his mouth and waited impatiently for a reply. Lady Baslow regarded him with no outward appearance of discomfort.

"It was unfortunate that both my maid and my butler happened upon us in that swift, unguarded moment. I am sorry to relate that their tongues ran away with them, and untruths have been added by the numerous mouths the story has since passed through. I have done my best to refute the outrageous claims but to no avail. I was appalled when I heard what had happened to you, and all the servants and tenants involved have been severely reprimanded. I beg your forgiveness for the part that I, unconsciously, played."

She looked contrite, yet she must be lying.

"Yet it was your tongue, not that of a servant nor a tenant, that related an exaggerated and plainly false account of events to Miss Elizabeth."

"I thought it was best that she hear the truth from me rather than the embellished version bandied about by servants. My maid admitted to me that she spoke to Miss Elizabeth whilst you were being so abominably abused. I feared that she might have exaggerated the event and thought it prudent to correct Miss Elizabeth's perception."

It was getting increasingly difficult to temper his replies, but not even pressing his lips together could prevent him from remarking upon the most glaring contradictions.

"What I fail to understand is where details of my body came into the conversation."

Lady Baslow chuckled, and all the contrition that had been displayed on her countenance disappeared.

"Oh, that was completely unrelated to the events of the storm. I thought she had the right to know those interesting facts your old friends were privy to. It was an innocent attempt to lighten the gloomy atmosphere that had descended upon us."

Despite Lady Baslow's calm appearance, Darcy was not fooled. He did not believe her, but he was appalled at how easily and convincingly she lied. She held herself under perfect regulation at all times.

"I am sorry I could not be of more assistance to you. We are old friends, and once we were much more."

It was the moment he had waited for eight years to discover. Wounds, long since buried, reappeared.

"That was eight years ago, and I dare say we have both matured since our youthful folly. But I would like to know why you chose to marry Sir Lawrence."

"I had to," she admitted before falling into a silence that stretched and grew like a wall between them.

"You must explain yourself fully, because my imagination is conjuring the most distressing circumstances."

"I loved you both, but I believed that I loved Sir Lawrence more. In retrospect, I own that I was mistaken."

Darcy's blood turned cold, and the last reminiscence of affection he held for the lady was encased in ice. Not for a second did he believe love had played any part in her choice.

"You were unattainable, ensconced at Cambridge. I had only Wickham to entertain me, and Sir Lawrence offered me respectability. I could not reject him," Lady Baslow continued when he said nothing to show he agreed with her sentiments.

"That was generous of him," he replied.

"Oh, he treated me with the usual resentment of a husband and killed the woman in my soul by his humbling attacks on my pride."

Darcy wondered what she meant, considering the circumstances, but said nothing. The description fitted poorly with the impression he had of the gentle baronet. Was she hinting at the lack of marital relations she had mentioned before? He imagined he would take umbrage should it turn out that Elizabeth had no interest in him once she had familiarised herself with the concept of giving and receiving love.

"But a woman needs a man, Fitzwilliam. I have written to Mr Wickham, or should I say Captain Wickham now. Did you know he is currently stationed with the regulars near Newcastle?"

His blood boiled at the mention of the reprobate's name, but he tempered his response. "Yes," he replied measuredly.

Was she aware of his involvement in finding Wickham an occupation and was trying to wheedle the story out of him, or was she trying to incite his jealousy? It might surprise Lady Baslow that what had appeared in his mind was not envy but disgust.

"I wrote him a letter, and the reply came this morning."

"Wickham is a married man now," he cautioned.

"Oh yes, I have heard about that patched up affair. Miss Catherine has a loose tongue… But with the execution of the will dragging out for what might be years, someone has to manage the Edensor estate in the interim. I have no such skills." She laughed coquettishly. "I have enquired whether he would be interested in being my advisor."

Darcy's pulse quickened—as it always did when the blasted steward's son was mentioned.

"Edensor has a steward, and an excellent one to boot," he reminded Lady Baslow.

"I have no concerns about the steward's capabilities. I simply require a man of business who has my interests at heart. Mr Morris is very loyal to the Baslows, and I am in need of personal assistance. Someone to go over the ledgers and make sure my steward, housekeeper, and butler do not cheat me. I also have investments that need managing and new ones to consider. I do not understand these things and require someone I trust to manage my affairs. Are you offering to stand in his stead?"

"No, I am not. There is no doubt in my mind that you wilfully deceived Miss Elizabeth into believing that we had a liaison on the night of the thunderstorm, and I shall never forgive you for causing my betrothed pain."

He waited a moment for Lady Baslow to refute his claim, but she said nothing, just regarded him steadily with her pale blue eyes. Not a shimmer of emotion was discernible on her countenance.

"By the bye, I am leaving for Hertfordshire in a week. After that, I shall be much occupied with my wedding—and my wife."

It was thrilling to voice it aloud—his wife. However, he had wrongs to correct. "I suggest you request that your father or your brother manage your business. Or...you could hire another criminal... The ones you employed to steal your necklace will hang tomorrow. How you can live with yourself, with two lives on your conscience, is beyond my comprehension. You did me a great service the day you married Sir Lawrence, and for that I shall always be grateful. But from this day, you are not welcome at Pemberley or Darcy House. I dare not imagine what atrocities would have befallen Elizabeth if you had succeeded in your scheme to include her in the funeral procession. But rest assured, I shall never allow you near her again. Your father and brother will be informed, directly, about everything you have done. What consequences your despicable actions will entail for you, I leave in their capable hands. If it were up to me, you would be chained and locked up in Bedlam."

Lady Baslow rose, inclined her head, and glided calmly away from him without another word.

How could he have defended the unfeeling creature, and to Elizabeth of all people? He who prided himself on the superiority of his mind had just proved that he was nothing but a fool.

#

Darcy managed to postpone his departure for five days, but his impatience to see Elizabeth burnt bright and steady in his chest.

Without the constant interruptions from Edensor, to set his affairs in order was easily done. He had heard nothing more from Lady Baslow, and neither did he expect to. He had made his sentiments abundantly clear, and the lady proved self-sufficient when required.

There was a knock on his door, and he called, "Enter."

"Mr Baslow to see you, sir."

He was surprised when it was Robert and his wife who entered.

"I have come to inform you that I shall no longer dispute the will. The Derbyshire climate does not agree with my wife, and she wants to travel south for the winter. I shall inform the House of Lords, once I reach London."

Darcy glanced at his pretty and much younger wife. She was fiddling with a diamond bracelet he recognised as Mr Conksbury's gift to his daughter on her seventeenth birthday. Was there no end to her deceit?

"How much did Lady Baslow pay you to contest the will?"

Mr Baslow puffed out his chest, but his posture sagged again at the hard look Darcy gave him.

"Nothing. She does not have any money. All her pin money is spent, and she has no access to her fortune. We had to settle for some pitiful jewellery. After all we have done for her..."

"I fail to comprehend Lady Baslow's motive for her deceit. What could have possessed her to do it?"

"You arrived at Pemberley with your young and pretty betrothed. She must have believed you could be worked upon, if given enough time..."

Darcy rid himself of his guests and soon embarked upon the two-and-a-half-day journey with a calmness he had not felt since his youth—more committed to his choice of bride than ever and determined to prove his affections. If he could just be afforded some time in Elizabeth's company, he would explain it all—how they both had been deceived. Preferably on solitary walks to Oakham Mount, where they could converse unrestrainedly and act in a manner that bespoke the nature of ardent lovers. He yearned to practise further the kiss he had bestowed. The brevity of that was not what he had in mind for their next moment of privacy...

The carriage rolled to a stop at Longbourn, and his stomach fluttered in anticipation. Mrs Hill greeted him at the door and whisked him away to Mr Bennet's study before he had a chance to see Miss Elizabeth.

"I appreciate your speedy response to my letter," Mr Bennet said the moment he set foot on the threshold.

"What letter? I have not heard a word from you or Miss Elizabeth since I left five weeks ago."

"Then your arrival must be due to divine intervention."

"Please explain." A vague and unknown sense of dread began to churn in his stomach.

"Elizabeth has vanished. She left more than a week ago."

Darcy fought for composure. If that was the case, why was Mr Bennet reading in his study?

"That is grave indeed! What has been done to find her?"

"She received an invitation from your aunt Lady Matlock to a musical soirée and was supposed to be residing at Matlock House. Sir William was going to St James's and offered to convey her to and fro. He watched her enter the house, but when he returned to retrieve her, Lady Matlock claimed that she had declined her invitation. Upon Sir William's return with the confounding news, I immediately set out for town to question your relations. Lady Matlock showed me Elizabeth's reply, and she had spoken the truth—Lizzy had declined the invitation, which means that she has deliberately deceived me. Further investigation revealed that the butler did admit a lady fitting

Elizabeth's description, but she claimed that she had come to the wrong house. He directed her to the neighbouring house of Lady Catherine de Bourgh, who I believe is another aunt of yours, with whom my daughter claims an acquaintance."

By Mr Bennet's raised eyebrow, Darcy surmised that he was less than impressed by his relation.

"Since the knocker was down, I went round the back, and a servant swore that none who fitted her description had been to the house. Your aunt had not been in residence for months, so she might have knocked on the door without anyone hearing her. I have searched for her all over London, but all trace of her vanishes at the steps of Matlock House. Her detached dullness made me suspect she had set out for Derbyshire, and I sent enquiries to every hostelry in the northern direction. I am certain she is not with family."

"Is there not a distant cousin or the like that she might have sought shelter with?"

"No, we have a small family, Mr Darcy. She is not at my brother Gardiner's in Gracechurch Street, neither has she sought shelter with my cousin in Hunsford. I have even written to my mother, as far-fetched as that is, but I have yet to receive a reply."

"Where does your mother live?" Darcy enquired as nonchalantly as he could muster. He had never heard it mentioned that Mr Bennet's mother was alive, and that in itself raised his suspicions.

"She lives…in the west."

"How far west?"

"Ireland. She and my wife do not see eye to eye, and she has an elderly brother there to tend."

Darcy wondered what constituted elderly in Mr Bennet's mind. His mother could not be so young herself. It occurred to him that the elder Mrs Bennet may be a Catholic, which would explain why they were reluctant to reveal her existence.

"Would she hide Miss Elizabeth from you?"

"Believe it or not, my mother is rather fond of me, her one and only child, despite our long separations. My father died when I was young, and for years it was only the two of us. She would not conceal Elizabeth from me. Besides, it is a long journey to Limerick. And may I remind you that Ireland is an island. I cannot imagine Elizabeth would manage to travel that far on her own."

"Dare I question whether you would conceal her whereabouts from me?"

"I have no reason to, Mr Darcy. I am not the one who dallied with an apparition before her eyes until she sought to escape you."

"Mr Bennet. I am not here to force Miss Elizabeth to marry me. Though I believe she would reconsider if she knew all the facts. Not all was as it appeared at Pemberley. I am a private man who does not often display my sentiments. I fear that Miss Elizabeth misconstrued the respect I feel for her and interpreted it as indifference. Which could not be further from the truth. My heart belongs to your daughter, and at the risk of appearing preposterously proud, it is my firm belief that her heart belongs to me."

"You should save your breath and tell Elizabeth—if you can find her."

Darcy could not fathom why Mr Bennet was mocking him. It served no purpose but to fuel his anger.

"I have added a clause to the marriage settlement relinquishing all rights to compensation due to breach of contract."

"If only you had done so five weeks ago, Mr Darcy, I would not be at a loss as to the whereabouts of my favourite daughter."

Darcy's ire rose, and he fought to keep it under regulation.

"Mr Bennet, I shall leave no stone unturned until I discover

Miss Elizabeth's whereabouts. But…if I should discover that you were, deliberately, hiding her from me—not even allowing me a conversation with her—hell hath no fury equal to mine." Then a thought so foul he barely managed to draw breath hit him full force. "Is there, perhaps, another gentleman who has caught her fancy?"

"No. There is no other man my Lizzy has ever taken an interest in."

"What about Wickham?"

"My favourite son by marriage? Wickham flattered her vanity with his compliments, but she never had any real interest in the man himself. No, the only gentleman I have ever worried would take her away from me was you, Mr Darcy. And you have succeeded. She has run from her home to escape your company."

Darcy could not believe him. It was a known deflection for a culprit to heave the blame onto anyone but themselves, and he had to know with certainty…

On his way out, he accepted Mrs Bennet's entreaty to take tea with the ladies, and he gladly suffered her vapid chatter whilst he studied her two remaining daughters. He supposed Miss Mary would be Elizabeth's choice for a confidante, and he approached her tentatively when Mrs Bennet left to hurry along the refreshments.

"I have a question to ask, and I want you to answer with complete honesty. I promise I shall not think less of you or your sister as long as you speak the truth."

Miss Mary sat up straighter and nodded. Her self-importance reminded him of his discussion with Elizabeth about vanity and pride at Netherfield. The memory made him smile—a gesture he quickly stifled before revealing his purpose. "There is no way to politely make this enquiry, so I shall simply ask you. Do you know whether Miss Elizabeth ever showed any interest in a gentleman besides me?"

Miss Mary hit her hands on the table and rose with fury written on her face.

"You must take me for a fool to ask such an utterly despicable question! Just because I do not prattle on like other females are prone to do does not mean that I am lost to the power of observation. I can assure you, Mr Darcy, that the three weeks I spent at Pemberley left me with no wish to return. To watch you parade your mistress—"

"Lady Baslow is not, and has never been, my mistress!" he interrupted her before her raised voice drew the notice of Mrs Bennet.

"Your knowledge of whom I am speaking of must confirm my claim. But it is not only that which has set me so firmly against you. I had to watch a most beloved sister, so very deeply in love, be constantly disappointed by your failure to please a woman worthy of being pleased. How could you watch her being ridiculed, even laughed at, by your friends and family?"

"Of what are you speaking?" he gritted through clenched teeth.

"You cannot claim to be ignorant of it!" Miss Mary exclaimed whilst narrowing her eyes. "You cannot have missed the barbs, the disdainful looks... Mrs Conksbury accused her of flitting all over the country to ensnare you. Heavens! Miss Bingley even forced Elizabeth to repeat your insult from the assembly, encouraged by the ever-present Lady Baslow. After Miss Bingley made some inaccurate suggestions of her own, my sister could not let it stand that you had ridiculed our mother's lack of understanding!"

"What did Miss Bingley accuse me of saying?" he asked, not bothering to hide his vexation.

"*She a beauty? I should as soon call her mother a wit.*" Miss Mary emulated Miss Bingley's grating voice.

His ire vanished instantly, whilst his breath was forced from his lungs.

"In front of everyone—the Baslows, the Conksburys, your relations... With the exception of young Mr Conksbury and Lady Matlock, they all laughed at her!"

Darcy rose and readied himself to defend his honour—he had not been present at that particular moment—but Miss Mary held up her hand.

"I do not want to hear it. There is nothing you can say that will redeem your actions. I suppose you have long wanted to absent yourself from my presence. Do not let me keep you from your *business*," Miss Mary spat with emphasis on the last word.

"Mary?" Mrs Bennet entered the room with her mouth agape.

"Thank you for your hospitality, Mrs Bennet. I wish you and your family health and happiness," he offered before striding out of the room.

Darcy left the Bennets and Hertfordshire, enraged by Miss Mary's revelations. He supposed he now, at least, had an explanation as to why the letters he had sent had gone unanswered. Elizabeth had not been there to receive them. With his glaring failures laid out before him, he questioned his purpose. How had his efforts to always behave impeccably rendered him the object of such wild accusations? Was there any truth to Miss Mary's claims? Had he, unconsciously, injured Elizabeth in his endeavour to contain the ardour burning so brightly within him and alienated her in the process? Yet Miss Mary was unaware of his more substantial mistakes. In addition to his inability to woo Elizabeth, he had failed to protect her. Only God's grace and her stubborn nature had saved her on the night of the funeral. She might have been beaten and captured, right under his nose, whilst he was occupied saving Lady Baslow's bloody diamonds...

From beneath his flame of anger, a calm and deep sorrow emerged. A mournfulness so profound he could not weep, but he clung to hope. Their brief period of happiness could not be the only one he would ever experience; nor could memories be his only comfort.

Persistence must be the remedy. He was certain that distance would do nothing to repair the damage he had caused. He had to act, and he needed time to prove his affections and constancy. He had to find Elizabeth and grovel at her feet. Whatever it took, he would do it in a trice. It was a relief to take action as opposed to remaining idle and waiting. But first he needed to address the slights he had been remiss in noticing. At ten the next morning, he knocked on the door of Hurst House and asked to speak to the master. He was led to a dining room, where the ladies and Mr Hurst were having breakfast.

"Mr Darcy!" Miss Bingley jumped to her feet and curtseyed low —no doubt to make sure he caught a glimpse of her bosom. Darcy fought the urge to shudder. "How good of you to come. Please join us. Robert! Fetch Mr Darcy a plate."

"That is not necessary. I have already breakfasted and came for the sole purpose of discussing an urgent matter with Mr Hurst. I shall wait for you in your study if you do not mind?"

"Of course not. Make yourself at home. I shall be with you in a moment."

"Thank you."

Darcy stalked out of the room and made himself comfortable in Hurst's sanctuary. A maid delivered a cup of tea, which he set aside while he gathered his thoughts. Perhaps it was not so bad that Bingley was unreachable on his bridal trip. Darcy had mentioned the actions of his sister multiple times, but the improvement in Miss Bingley's behaviour had been slight and short-lived. Mr Hurst had been born into the gentry and might be more amenable to his request. Darcy would be direct and leave the man in no doubt of his sentiments.

Mr Hurst entered a few minutes later. Despite the hour, he busied himself filling a glass of port and offered Darcy the same. He declined whilst listening for the footsteps he knew would be approaching. Miss Bingley was easy to predict, and her penchant for eavesdropping proved dependable.

"What brings you to my humble abode with a cloud hanging over your head?" Hurst enquired as he made himself comfortable.

"It has come to my attention that whilst I was occupied with Mr Conksbury in my study at Pemberley, Miss Bingley had the nerve to disparage and ridicule my betrothed. In front of my friends and relations."

"I believe I know what you are speaking about, but you must admit that she said nothing that was not true."

"To my eternal regret, that is correct. Yet that does not remove her culpability in repeating those words that would be best forgotten, and that it was done with malicious intent to belittle and hurt the person most dear to me. It shows an abominable degree of conceit and spite to believe that is acceptable under my roof. I have tolerated her atrocious behaviour for the sake of my friendship with you and her brother, but I am at the end of my forbearance. Her mean spirit and cruel remarks will no longer be tolerated in my house. It is unfathomable to me that she can think herself so high above an impeccably mannered gentleman's daughter that she will stoop to ridicule and derision. Her frequent references to fortune, or the lack of it, are positively vulgar and prove what a mercenary parvenu she is. She will not be included in any invitations from me, and she will not be granted admittance if she defies my wishes."

Mr Hurst held up his hands. "You will meet no opposition from me. I have spoken to Bingley, but he is how he is. Amiable to a fault and assiduously shuns conflict of any sort. If she married, she would be off his hands, but I do not know any gentlemen who would have her that are not deeply indebted or in their dotage. She is determined to marry up, but we both know that is unlikely to happen."

"No, she is going to remain a spinster, which makes it even

more urgent to curb her inflated opinion of herself. She is the most supercilious woman I have ever had the misfortune to meet. A true lady would not try to raise herself above others or boast about her accomplishments. She would be kind and compassionate, which are traits that Miss Bingley is utterly lacking."

"You are aware that she is eavesdropping on our conversation?" Hurst smirked.

Darcy allowed a slight smile to erupt. "Yes, or I would have used words to describe her that are unfit for a lady's ears. I have made my sentiments known and now have only the regrets of my own past behaviour to reflect upon. Good day, Hurst. I hope our conversation has been enlightening to Miss Bingley."

He opened the door and encountered a wide-eyed, open-mouthed Miss Bingley on the threshold. He looked her in the eyes and left without a goodbye.

Darcy went directly from Grosvenor Street to visit the Gardiners in the hope they might know where Elizabeth was hiding, but upon his arrival, both denied any knowledge of Elizabeth's whereabouts. To be certain they spoke the truth, he hired men to watch the house day and night. He dispatched a letter to Rosings' trusted steward. If she were hiding in the Hunsford parsonage, the steward would know and inform him. When both proved to be futile endeavours, he had to admit that Elizabeth was a resourceful young lady who might have sought employment, and he decided to follow that lead himself.

In the employment office, a tired clerk yawned over a ledger, but once he saw that a smartly dressed gentleman had arrived, his bearing straightened, and he hastened to serve him.

"I am looking for a young woman and wondered whether she is registered here."

"She might be. What are her specifics?"

*What an odd question*, Darcy thought, but he could describe her, he supposed.

"She has auburn hair, uncommonly beautiful green eyes, and is about average height."

"I beg your pardon, sir. I meant her occupation."

"Ah! She is a governess—" He could easily picture her doting upon a brood of children. But that entailed threats from the children's father he could not bear to contemplate. No, it was better she had found employment with a lovely old lady. "—or, perhaps, a companion," he mused.

"And her name, sir?"

"Miss Elizabeth Bennet."

The clerk searched his list repeatedly, but he had made no note of any girl with that name.

Darcy returned in despondency to his house. Amongst the stack of letters awaiting him, only a note held a slight interest. It was from Richard and might contain news about Elizabeth. He was soon disappointed because he did not even mention her. The colonel was in town and requested to see him as soon as possible.

Darcy sent a reply to Matlock House, and the colonel entered his study an hour later.

"Richard! Please sit down, and I shall pour you a glass of port. I suppose you do not mind, even though it is a bit early in the day." He glanced at the mantel clock that revealed it was already four in the afternoon, and he served the tawny beverage. "So, what was the urgency?" Darcy enquired, mostly out of politeness. The note had mentioned the viscount, and he could not imagine any news about Crawford could have the slightest interest to him.

"I wanted to bring you this news myself before you heard it from someone outside the family," Richard explained.

"Is the viscount in trouble?" Darcy worried he had gambled away a fortune.

"No, not per se, but that depends on you..."

"Me? Why do you suppose that I would cause Crawford any discomfort?"

"The Conksburys arrived in town yesterday. He wasted no time in offering for Lady Baslow, and she accepted him," his cousin related with a graveness belying the happy occasion.

"I wish him very happy," Darcy replied. He meant it, though he did not believe it. Regardless of his concerns about the lady's suitability, it was too late for Crawford to withdraw without creating a scandal. He only regretted inevitably being forced into the lady's company when she became family, which was a moot point because he had no intention of visiting Matlock with any frequency, and with this addition to the family—not at all. But he was disappointed with Mr Conksbury and Cornelius. They had been outraged when he had related Lady Baslow's treachery and had spoken about sending her to a distant relation. How that had turned into marrying her off into polite society was a conundrum he must contemplate later.

"Is that all you have to say?" Richard enquired sceptically.

"Do you want me to object?"

"No, but I did not expect you to be utterly indifferent."

Darcy sat back in his chair and pondered his cousin's words. If Richard, who knew him well and should know better, still believed he had an interest in Lady Baslow, it was not so strange that Elizabeth was convinced it was so. Where had he erred for his sentiments to be completely misunderstood, even by those closest to him?

"Do you want to retract your felicitations?" Richard enquired.

"Do not be absurd. I care not two figs whom either marry, as long as it is not me or Miss Elizabeth."

"Then what has you buried in brown study?"

"My failure to convince Miss Elizabeth, and even you, that I have no romantic interest in Lady Baslow."

"It was not so long ago that you were less certain..."

"I was confused for a very brief moment, but never did I waver in my feelings for Miss Elizabeth."

"How was I to know? You did not express it with words nor deeds."

"I prefer not to express my most private thoughts. But I do remember telling you specifically that Miss Elizabeth was whom I want to marry."

"Yes, immediately after you had lauded Lady Baslow's fine attributes. It was not clear to me whom you preferred. You were once very much in love with Celia."

Darcy scowled at his cousin. "So were you!"

"We all were, at one point," the colonel admitted with no sign of regret.

"Not Wickham," Darcy stubbornly objected.

"You are wrong on that account. Wickham was as smitten as the rest of us. He just acted with indifference because he knew he could never have her. Miss Conksbury's preferences for wealth and consequence were clear from an early age. It behoved him to pretend so as not to lose face."

As much as Darcy would have liked to object, he did not. Wickham had been cunning even as a child.

"You do not seem bothered by your brother's engagement. When did you lose interest in the beautiful Celia?"

"Long before your understanding was broken. As I came of age, I realised that she was not what I wanted in a wife. She is too cold and indifferent. I would like someone with more warmth."

"Like Miss Elizabeth?"

Richard smiled. "No, I would not like to be outwitted by my wife. My taste runs more towards the nature of Mrs Bingley.

Someone who would not mind being the wife of a second son. And she is very romantic, like her sister."

"Miss Elizabeth is a rational creature and not romantically bent."

"Of course she is. Why did you think she rejected your first offer?"

"Because she did not like me."

"No, because she did not love you. Many a lady has overcome a hearty dislike in return for connections and wealth. Miss Elizabeth is different. She is not practical in her affections."

"I wish she was."

"No, you do not. When is the wedding?"

"Tomorrow, if I can find her..."

"I assumed she would have been found by now."

"No, she is hiding from me, my friends, and my family because we treated her with indifference, disrespect, and ridicule."

"You are too hard on yourself. I would not call it ridicule. At least it was not intentional."

"I am not speaking of me but of Miss Bingley and Lady Baslow, who forced her to repeat my insult from the assembly as a piece of entertainment. My friends and family thought it a great lark and laughed at her."

"I did not know. I must not have been present."

"It was at the dinner at Pemberley when I was speaking to Mr Conksbury after the reading of the will."

"Ah, I stole away with Mr Bingley for a moment to look at one of his steeds."

"I am relieved. I could not believe it of you, to behave with such disrespect, and your mother I must also exclude. She did not participate in the mockery, but the earl and the viscount owe Miss Elizabeth an apology. If they ever disrespect her again, I shall have no choice but to sever the acquaintance."

"How are they to apologise when she has disappeared?"

"You are going to help me find her."

"Me?"

"Yes, you."

Darcy untied his cravat, overlooking his cousin's widening eyes. He was not about to undress but to pull out the locket he carried close to his heart. He had begged Georgiana to paint a miniature of Elizabeth's likeness that he kept on his person at all times. The removal of the locket left a cold spot on his skin. Though not as cold as the fear that had a firm grip on his heart. But he had to stay strong, find Elizabeth, and right his wrongs. For her to exist in the world thinking so ill of him was insupportable.

"Here, take her likeness and show it to all the soldiers under your command that can be trusted to act with discretion. I do not want her escape to become commonly known, mind you. I have her reputation to consider."

"You think that she is still in London?"

"I have found no evidence to contradict it. There have been no reports of her at any inn in any direction, and she is not registered in any books at the dock. She has not sought employment..."

The colonel nodded, took a large gulp of his port, and reverted into his thoughts. Darcy followed him, and they sat in comfortable silence, pondering the turn of events.

Weeks later, a dejected Darcy returned to his ancestral home and attended the wedding at Matlock. His aunt had pestered him to come, to prove he held no ill will towards the bride and groom. Rumours claimed that his long absence was on account of his cousin's engagement to his former intended. It could not be further from the truth, and Darcy decided to accept the invitation to put the gossip to rest.

His search for his true intended had come to a standstill; he had run out of paths to investigate. It was like the earth had swallowed her whole. However unlikely, his only hope was that she would reappear when the allotted three months had passed.

Darcy swirled the glass of brandy in his hand. He could not decide whether to swallow it in one large burning gulp or throw it into the fireplace. The explosion of flames would be fascinating to watch, despite the risk of rousing Lord Matlock's ire by wasting his best brandy—a lot more interesting than watching his gloating cousin and his odious bride. Why had he not noticed her excessive use of powder before? And her cheeks were most certainly painted with rouge—a most disgusting object to the eye. But even worse, Georgiana had asked whether he could purchase her a bottle of Pear's Liquid Bloom of Roses. As if she needed any unnatural enhancement to  sweeten her countenance! Preposterous!

The walls of Matlock's library closed in on him. From a distance, he heard the incessant humming of Viscount Crawford's wedding guests. Let them believe he was sulking over a lost love, because it was true. He had erred, failed, and lost. It was time to face the truth. She no longer loved him, if she ever had… She certainly had no wish to marry him—a fact abundantly proved by words and deeds. Deservedly so, when he had allowed himself to be worked upon. No, he alone must carry the blame. What miserable excuse for a husband he would make. Tending to the needs of everyone unconnected to himself but failing the two he held dear—Georgiana and Elizabeth. His failure in protecting Georgiana he had contemplated ad nauseam, but he had yet to examine his behaviour at Pemberley. How well he suited Elizabeth's description of inflated pride and repugnant conceit. Strutting like a peacock around Edensor House, trying to impress the woman he no longer held in affection and make her repine her rejection of him. He should have spent his time lavishing Elizabeth with flowers, escorting her to his favourite haunts, and showing her the squirrel living in the oak tree outside his study. Elizabeth would have loved to feed it a biscuit and would have admired him for his affection for the furry creature.

Mr Conksbury, wholly unconnected to him, had wanted to complain about his daughter's inheritance—a circumstance he had no hand in and could do nothing to rectify. How willingly he had taken the man to his study to discuss a hopeless matter, leaving Elizabeth to fend for herself amongst the vultures.

Had she been secure in his affection—assured of his loyalty—no stratagem could have turned her against him.

Elizabeth...

Darcy bowed his head in defeat, gripping his glass so tightly that it broke and cut into his hand. He looked at the blood dripping onto the carpet. He should probably do something about that, or Lady Matlock would have his hide when she discovered it. Not that he cared. He deserved reproach.

"Darcy! You are injured. Let me fetch a maid."

"No! Please, do not. I cannot abide the thought of being civil."

He turned slowly towards Mr Cornelius Conksbury, who was approaching with a handkerchief in his outstretched hand. He put what remained of the glass on the table, removed a shard embedded in his palm, and tied the cloth around his wound.

"Miss Elizabeth will return to you."

How could Cornelius immediately discern that it was Elizabeth and not Celia who had brought him low when Richard still believed he harboured feelings for the despicable bride?

"What made you draw the conclusion that I was thinking about Elizabeth and not your sister?"

"Mainly your incensed rage when you revealed her perfidious nature at Edensor. Disgust is still visible in your eyes every time you look at Celia, but I suppose your confession about your disastrous Hunsford proposal convinced me. When you returned, months later, betrothed to the aforementioned lady, I deduced you were in it very deep indeed."

He had no will left in him to reproach Cornelius for the nonexistent punishment the new viscountess had been dealt by her father and brother. He should not have left it to her family but seen to it himself. Another one of his many failures. Nothing untoward would have happened if he had not allowed it.

"She is gone. Elizabeth left Hertfordshire for London and evaporated on the steps of Matlock House. I have searched everywhere and found no trace of her in London or beyond. I might as well give up and return to Pemberley as the bachelor that I am. Perhaps, one day, I might stomach the thought of looking for someone else to wed."

Cornelius settled into the chair beside him and stared into the fire.

"I have a theory—that we experience three loves in our life. The first you experience when you are young. A kinship kind of love that leaves you with warm memories, but in retrospect, you do not regard it as a romantic love.

"The second love is when you fall deeply, but it is also the one that hurts you. You are left bruised and battered, but it teaches you valuable lessons, so you know what you want and what not to accept.

"The third love reaches much deeper into your soul and fortifies you. You and your lady become one—a stronger entity than anyone can accomplish in solitude. That is the one that lasts. You were intended for Anne until you grew old enough to realise that she did not suit. I hardly need mention your second and third."

Darcy had listened intently but failed to understand the purpose. "Why are you telling me this?"

"Because you cannot give up. It is not in your nature, and I am certain that you will regret leaving any stone unturned."

He was tired—utterly exhausted, which must account for him raising his voice. "I have turned over every bloody stone in London. It does not change the fact that she does not want to marry me. Hell and damnation, she even believes that I love Celia more than her!"

"But you do not," Cornelius replied with a calmness he found vexing.

"Certainly not! I am sorry for speaking so coarsely about your sister, but the truth is that I loathe her. What scant sentiments her rejection left were doused by her despicable actions and the lies she told to ingratiate herself with me. What I fail to see is the direction of this conversation."

"Miss Elizabeth is wrong in her assumptions. Until she knows the truth, there is still hope."

# Chapter 12 Wistfulness

Weeks passed before the sisters allowed Elizabeth upstairs to tend the sick. She was a gentleman's daughter and deemed of a too delicate constitution. That she was the niece of the Marquis of Limerick must also take some of the blame for Sister Honora's reluctance to employ her. But Elizabeth eventually managed to convince the nuns that she was indeed both hardy and healthy. A bout of the grippe had sent several children of working parents to their care, and Sister Honora, Sister Catherine, and Sister Erin could no longer cope. One of the children was an infant that had just been weaned. It was all too much for Elizabeth, who had discovered that she had led a protected, sheltered life, unaware of the true unfortunate souls who had so little. She needed just a few minutes to herself, but with every room filled to the brim, except for one room in the attic that Elizabeth believed was the nuns' private quarters, she hoped they would not object to her stealing a quick rest behind a closed door. She would not pry into their personal affairs.

The door was not locked. Elizabeth hurried inside, shut the door, and let herself fall against it with closed eyes. She breathed deeply through her nose. The little boy was so terribly ill, and she was not certain they would be able to save him. He was burning with fever.

The rustling of skirts put an end to her horrible thoughts. It was strange; she would have sworn Sister Honora, Sister Catherine, and Sister Erin were all downstairs.

Elizabeth opened her eyes and found two girls in the last stage

160

of pregnancy sitting by the window. Both were sewing tiny garments in preparation for the forthcoming event. She could not help the gasp that escaped and immediately covered her mouth with her hand.

"I am sorry our presence has shocked you," a pretty redhead drawled in disdain.

"Oh no. Please, I am not shocked, only surprised as I believed the room to be empty. I just need a respite. It was not my intention to intrude upon your privacy. I am so sorry. If I had known the room was already occupied, I would not have entered."

Elizabeth turned and clutched the handle but did not open the door.

"What I meant to say is that I am sorry for any inconvenience my intrusion may have caused. No judgment intended."

"Please stay," the redhead allowed. "I have so little society these days, a fresh face is welcome. I am Bridget, and this is Sophie. She was assaulted by her employer. Whilst I am entirely at fault for my predicament, Sophie is quite innocent. But I suppose you will not believe her either."

Elizabeth spun round to look at the girls.

"Why would I not believe you? I have no reason to gainsay you."

"The doctor said otherwise. Even though she had bruises enough to prove she was forced, the fact that she conceived belied that she was an unwilling participant."

"I had no idea that was the widely held opinion!" Elizabeth cried.

"That is because women in general know that is not true, but men..." Bridget spat out with vehemence.

"Yes, they are a loathsome lot, are they not? I find little to admire in the stronger sex," Elizabeth conceded.

"Who hurt you?"

Bridget's question threw Elizabeth off kilter. Compared with the women before her, she had not been injured; it was her trust that had been shattered.

"Oh, nothing as dire as you have suffered. I was once engaged to be married but was disappointed. I have no intention of repeating the experience."

"Are you to be a nun?" Sophie asked.

"I have no immediate plans. But if I can be of any assistance to either of you... I cannot but help thinking that if you took it to court, the judge could not overlook such a despicable action and would grant you compensation. Is there no hope from the law?"

"None whatsoever. I did go to the magistrate. It was he who ordered the doctor's examination and agreed with the conclusion," Sophie whispered. "But it is not true. I fought the ugly old beast, but he was too strong. The magistrate suggested that I should have closed my legs."

"The magistrate must have been a simpleton for not considering the difference in strength," Elizabeth replied in disbelief.

"Gentlemen always look after one another, and neither justice nor sense has any influence on the outcome. I have been working the streets long enough to be intimately familiar with their hypocrisies," Bridget said. "So, I am entirely at fault for my condition. It is the lot of the trade. One begets a child now and then."

Elizabeth did not believe her bravado to be entirely genuine but a defence against society's prejudices.

The conversation with Sophie and Bridget left Elizabeth with an indelible sorrow and a determination in her mind and her heart, lamenting the social, economic, and political oppression the maid struggled against. Turned down by a government institution with little sense of the urgency of her situation, yet she had been fortunate enough to find shelter with the sisters.

What would have happened if she had not?

Loud voices drifted up the stairs. Elizabeth hastened down to see what the trouble was about and found Sister Honora standing toe to toe with a priest.

"You are an upstart. A proper lady is unfit to work with the poor, and the unlearned sex should never meddle with the tasks of the clergy. I shall ensure that your work here is at an end. I suggest that you pack your trunk and move back to Dublin with immediate effect. I am certain your landlord can be worked upon and have you and the rest of the riffraff you host removed within a week."

"I have the support of the archbishop of Dublin," Sister Honora defended herself.

"He will retract his approval when I inform him how you are deflecting support from the work of established religious orders and are imitating them without abiding by their rules. Yet you demand to proceed. Your neighbours are complaining about beggars leaving notes on their doorstep, seeking blankets and clothing for the reprehensible women you shelter here."

"And where is your charity for those who have nothing?" Sister Honora protested.

The priest huffed and did not deign to answer her accusation.

"I shall carry my point. I shall brook no disappointment in this." The priest glared at Sister Honora before he turned on his heel and marched out of the house.

An eerie silence descended upon the stunned nuns. No one knew what to say.

"What am I to do? I cannot find a single soul willing to sell me a plot. We quite depend upon the Grange for our work," Sister Honora lamented. "And they are not afraid to say it to my face, that a school for the poor will ruin their fashionable neighbourhood."

"Have you enquired of Lord Dunraven whether he might have a suggestion? He has reroofed the Holy Trinity Abbey Church and added the north transept—he must be a man of God," Elizabeth suggested.

"God is the only man I confer with and the only one I ever listen to," Sister Honora replied.

"Yes, of course," Elizabeth allowed.

#

"You are pale, *Eilís*. You should stay at home and rest. I would appreciate some help planning our removal to town."

"Are we going to London?" Elizabeth enquired with dread in her voice.

"Of course. Henry must attend the Session. He is in the House of Lords and is the Clerk of the Crown!"

Why had she not thought about that?

"Am I expected to join you?"

"Certainly. You cannot stay here unattended, and I shall not leave Henry in the lurch. He needs me to keep house for him."

Elizabeth felt betrayed, though she knew the sentiment was not sound.

"I dare say she looks uncommonly pale," Uncle Henry agreed. "I say you need a day's rest, Elizabeth. Are you certain that you have not caught the grippe that is ravishing the town?"

She nodded her confirmation, but her verification was disregarded. Henry, the marquis, did not brook opposition. An odd feeling settled in her breast, and her mind niggled like she had forgotten something substantial.

"Pray, what day is it?" she enquired whilst bringing a morsel of bread and cheese to her mouth.

The marquis looked at the front of his paper.

"It is the eleventh of February, which leaves two months and a week until Easter Sunday. We shall travel to town in exactly two months."

Elizabeth swayed in her seat and heard her grandmother call out to her from across the breakfast table. She managed to regain her composure, but her heart continued to pound in her ears.

"That settles it. You almost fainted, dear. You are to have a day of bed rest, and I and Mrs Finnegan are going to take turns to sit with you."

"Should I summon the doctor, Maeve?" the marquis enquired of his sister.

"Yes, I think that would be best," Mrs Bennet agreed.

Steadied by her grandmother, Elizabeth returned to her room and was tucked beneath the covers.

"Do you want me to remain, *a leanbh*?" her grandmother offered.

"No, thank you. You are right. I am excessively fatigued and shall sleep until I am restored."

Thankfully, her grandmother acquiesced and left the room. Elizabeth curled up into a ball and willed her heart to calm, but it did not comply. It kept fluttering in her breast while she acknowledged that it was supposed to have been her wedding day. Mr Darcy would know that she had fled if he did not already. How would he respond? He appeared before her inner eye as clearly as ever. His regal bearing ascended the steps of Longbourn only to find...what?

Elizabeth suffered for her actions most acutely. She had no trouble imagining her mother taking to her bed with her concern. Jane would be summoned from Netherfield as the only one who could appease her mother's spasming nerves. Her father would lock himself in his study and ponder his mistakes. But he had once stated that he would not feel it as long as he deserved. Would he greet Mr Darcy with mockery and contempt?

*'I love you.'* How those words continued to haunt her in her dreams. Expressed with such fervency, she had almost believed him. There had been earnestness in his countenance, but she had been too furious to give his proclamation any consideration. Driven by jealousy and unmitigated anger, she had spurned any notion of affection. Was she ruled by her pride as Mr Darcy had once accused her of being?

She closed her eyes to rest in Morpheus's arms, but her dream was far from soothing. Mr Darcy's tormented eyes rested unfailingly upon her whilst she, quite against her will, kept insulting him in a base manner. It was a relief when her grandmother woke her up.

"*Eilís,* dear, the physician is here, and he would like to examine you. Is this an inopportune moment, or are you ready to receive him?"

Elizabeth rubbed the cobwebs of sleep from her eyes and sat up.

"I am quite well. You may send him in."

Mrs Bennet fetched the doctor who was waiting just outside the door. He asked questions and commented on her pale complexion.

"Have you experienced any great anxiety or an oppression of the precordium?"

"Not so much anxiety, but I sometimes feel a fluttering, like my heart is a butterfly."

"It might be palpitations. Are you coughing much?"

"No, not lately."

"Do you experience shortness of breath whilst exercising?"

"No, I do not think so, but it has been a while since I have taken a long stroll."

Elizabeth had been too busy at the Grange to keep up her daily walks.

After feeling her pulse, the doctor laid his ear against her chest for an inordinately long time.

"The good news is that Miss Bennet's ailment does not appear to be of an epidemic nature. It might be a peculiar disease of the heart. It is beating in an irregular rhythm, but the throbs are not strong. It is a simple case of too much blood. Miss Bennet needs to be bled," the physician informed her grandmother.

He pulled out his scalpel and a tray to collect her fluid. He cut her arm and let it bleed into the basin, then he dressed the wound and studied the blood.

"Let me confirm with my Pharmacopoeia Londinensis. It is the Royal College of Physicians' own publication and contains the latest in modern remedies," he boasted whilst leafing through a heavy tome. After finding what he was looking for, he said, "I shall leave this with you. You need to take two spoonsful in the morning and one in the evening. In combination with a week's rest, I believe you will soon recover."

Her grandmother left to escort the doctor out. The room spun, and she rested her eyes in the hope of a dreamless respite.

She slept for most of the day and the following week, then awoke one morning finally feeling well-rested and famished. Uncle Henry was the only person present in the breakfast room, and she greeted him cordially.

"Should you not be in bed?" he answered.

"I promise to rest, but the physician did not confine me to bed for more than a week, and it has been eight days."

"Very well."

Uncle Henry ducked behind his newspaper, allowing Elizabeth to fill her plate with victuals in a comfortable silence. She sat down, buttered her roll, and glanced out of the window. It was a frigid day, but the sun had risen above the treetops and was basking in the white snow. A barren horse chestnut tree caught her eye as a sheet of snow fell and tumbled down the trunk. It reminded her of the one her aunt loved, by the smithy in Lambton. From that thought, the route was short to picturing Mr Darcy. On one of her trips to Lambton, she had seen him standing under that very tree with his hands behind his back, listening to the blacksmith. She had stopped to admire him, and he must have sensed her eyes upon him. He had turned his head and smiled when he caught her ogling him. With a slight incline of his head, he had continued his conversation with the blacksmith, and Georgiana had called for her attention.

"Good morning. You look well. Has your fatigue improved?"

Her grandmother walked briskly up to her and studied her face.

"Yes, I am quite well. Thank you."

"You are still pale," she continued.

"It is February..." Elizabeth reminded her.

"True."

Mrs Bennet was not convinced, but she filled her plate and joined her brother and granddaughter at the table.

The marquis lowered his newspaper. "I noticed your longing look out of the window, Elizabeth, but you should not venture out of doors. At least not on foot."

"No, Uncle Henry, I promise that I shall not."

The spirit that had returned that morning shrunk before she had finished breakfast. She joined her grandmother in the east-facing parlour to take advantage of the morning sun and picked up the novel Evelina by Frances Burney. It was an epistolary novel about a modest, beautiful young woman of questionable parentage. Evelina had fallen in love with a lord who had sent her an insulting letter—a confirmation of Elizabeth's belief that no gentleman was truly honourable.

The butler entered with the morning post. Ironically, her father had told her mother and sisters that she was visiting her grandmother. It was considerate of him to take so much upon himself, but it had led to a conundrum for Elizabeth. She occasionally received a letter in her name, and notes from her mother and sisters were added to her grandmother's letters, but she could not reply, as that would confirm her whereabouts. Jane's letters had become more frequent after she had returned from her bridal trip and her visit to Mr Bingley's Yorkshire relations, and Elizabeth could tell she was becoming increasingly exasperated with the lack of reply.

Mr Bennet had clearly concocted the ruse to prevent her mother and sisters from worrying unduly while he was looking for her—a search he was conducting in his usual leisurely manner. According to his letters to his mother, the search was limited to the occasional missive to her uncle Gardiner in London and perusing the mysterious death articles in the newspaper. Today, there was only one letter, and Mrs Bennet sighed heavily after reading only a few lines.

"What news?" Elizabeth enquired, looking up from her book.

"Only the usual. It is from Lydia, and she is requesting more funds."

"Oh."

"Mr Wickham is a very unfortunate man. It appears like every friend, foe, and all his fellow soldiers are set upon depleting his pockets."

"Indeed."

"Yet I cannot help but feel sorry for the girl. She is foolish but so noticeably young. I shall send her a ten-pound note."

"I am certain she will be grateful. Does she have any news?"

"Not if you disregard the dreariness of Newcastle this time of year. The weather is inclement, and there are no parties to be had."

Elizabeth smiled and closed her book. Lydia was the same, married or not.

"I was thinking about returning to Sister Honora for a short while on the morrow. I want to see how baby Killian is faring."

"You may call upon them, but I shall not have you engaged in education or nursing just yet."

Elizabeth acquiesced and went to make the arrangements.

Unfortunately, when she arrived at the Grange the next day, the baby boy was not in his crib. The pang in her chest must have shown on her countenance because Sister Erin hastened to her side. Elizabeth steadied herself on the wall as a sudden spell of dizziness descended upon her.

"Baby Killian has fully recovered and returned home. His mother wanted to thank you in person, but since you were not here, she asked me to convey her regards."

"Thank you. I have been indisposed and have not had any opportunity to help you."

"You need not be concerned, Miss Bennet. Most of our patients have recovered, and no new ones have arrived. I dare say this bout of the grippe is over. But if you do not mind me saying so, you do not look well. I shall fetch you a chair."

"Oh no, there is no need. I have been on bedrest for a week, and my body appears to have forgotten how to stand upright. I am in need of exercise. Would you mind if I visit Bridget and Sophie?"

"Of course not. They will be happy to see you."

Elizabeth ascended the stairs and hoped she would soon be able to continue her daily walks because she was rather winded when she reached the top. For the benefit of the ladies, she composed herself before entering. She forced a smile and tried to hide her struggle for breath. They were not fooled.

"You look exceedingly pale," Sophie commented.

"I am not fully recovered from my fatigue," Elizabeth admitted.

"It is not unusual to be tired in my condition," Sophie whispered softly.

"There is no chance of that," Elizabeth stated firmly before she hastened to soften her statement. "Oh, I meant no offence. It is just that…"

"You know how it is done?" Bridget enquired.

Elizabeth's cheeks warmed, and her heart fluttered. It was not something a maiden should admit to knowing, but her mother's friends were loud and indiscreet.

"Yes. I am quite certain."

The image of Lady Baslow in Mr Darcy's arms flashed unbidden before her inner eye; the room spun before it went black.

Elizabeth revived and was embarrassed to find herself prostrate on the floor. Sister Honora had been called away from her duties and hovered above her. To her mortification, she insisted that Elizabeth should be carried to the carriage.

Her arrival caused an uproar at Áth Dara. Her grandmother and Mrs Finnegan fussed, and even Uncle Henry made an appearance, blustering about sending for doctors, the priest, and the apothecary.

"Please, there is no reason for concern. I was too impatient after my bout of fatigue and should not have ventured to the Grange so soon."

"Hush, *Eilís*. You should rest until the doctor arrives. It is not natural for a young and healthy lady to faint so readily. But do not concern yourself. I have an inkling as to what ails you. If I am right, you will be back to your usual constitution ere long."

"How long? I am not a patient soul," Elizabeth readily admitted.

"I know! In a few short months you should be fully recovered."

"Months!" Elizabeth cried and sat up too quickly. The giddiness returned with the addition of a ringing noise in her ears, and she dropped in an undignified fashion to the mattress.

Her grandmother patted her on her head like she was a child and pulled her brother out of the room.

Elizabeth must have fallen instantly asleep because they were back but a moment later with the doctor in tow.

"At least four months," her grandmother informed the doctor. What she was referring to, she did not say.

The doctor ushered everyone but Mrs Finnegan out of the room before he lifted the cover to press his fingers into her stomach. She groaned, but that did not deter him. He continued with an embarrassing examination before her grandmother and Uncle Henry were allowed back in.

"I can find no evidence of graviditatis. After four months, I would have been able to detect the expansion of the uterus. She is not with child."

"Of course not!" Elizabeth was furious; the noise in her ears increased, and her heart was palpitating when a fierce pain stabbed her chest. She gasped for breath and clutched the painful area.

The doctor removed her hands and put his ear to her thorax.

"My first assumption was correct. She has an ailment of the heart. The action of the heart is so strong that I can hear it distinctly, and the violent pulsation of the carotid arteries confirms it.

"I can feel no fluids in her abdomen, nor are her legs oedematous, but those are the serious signs to look for as the disease advances, in addition to rheumatic fevers. Mr David Dundas described nine cases in his account of peculiar diseases to the heart as recently as 1808. Though the earliest case described was in 1770. Seven died, and during the autopsy they found an enlarged heart and the left ventricle particularly affected, but not in thickness. This is usually seen after an episode of acute rheumatism, and I wondered whether Miss

Bennet had suffered an attack."

"I have never suffered from rheumatism in my life," Elizabeth protested.

"Well then, there is only one other affliction known to affect such a young person."

"And what exactly is that?" Lord Limerick enquired.

"Broken heart syndrome. Has the lady suffered a great disappointment of a romantic nature?"

The quiet in the room was exceedingly uncomfortable for Elizabeth.

"I see…" Lord Limerick mused. "Let us adjourn to my study and discuss her treatment over a tumbler of whiskey."

The guests in her chamber left Elizabeth to wallow in solitude with only her disturbing thoughts for company. Never had she imagined there could be something seriously wrong with her. To have a disease of the heart confirmed made the palpitations increase and caused her pulse to quicken.

Fear seized her, and she struggled for composure. To redirect her mind, she grabbed her book, but her attempt to distract herself failed miserably. Lord Orville had not written the letter Evelina had received. It was a forgery concocted by the troublesome Sir Clement Willoughby because he disapproved of the match.

What if Lady Baslow had staged the entire rendezvous, aided by a loyal servant? Elizabeth shuddered; it could not be—she was not that easily fooled.

She was fond of studying character, and other than her misjudgment of Mr Wickham, who was a practised liar, she was proud of her discernment. However, she had been utterly mistaken about Mr Darcy's character. Or had she? Charlotte sprung to mind. She had been more industrious than Elizabeth had believed her capable of when she had hoodwinked Mr

Collins into proposing.

Could she be wrong? Had she been fooled by a practised deceiver—again?

Her body flushed with heat. A sheet of paper fell out of the book. Mr Darcy's letter. Elizabeth ripped off the seal and perused the few sentences he had written, disappointed it was not a longer letter.

*Dearest Elizabeth,*

*It was never my intention to hurt you, though to my immense sorrow, I have.*

*I am counting the hours until we meet again.*

*My deepest wish is to be the recipient of your love and to love you in return.*

*Yours heartily and affectionately,*

*Fitzwilliam Darcy*

She dropped the book, which bounced off the bed and landed with a thud on the floor. Mrs Finnegan was at her side at once, offering her a sip of wine. She gulped down a few mouthfuls and lay back to close her eyes. The dam broke, and her sobs sang a threnody.

Her grandmother entered and spoke quietly with Mrs Finnegan. They mentioned the priest and the Anointing of the Sick. He was there the next day to confer the sacrament and lay his healing hands upon her.

#

The passing of the days became indistinct, but her mind was much occupied with reviewing past events. Repeatedly, all her interactions with Mr Darcy played in her mind, and one fact could not be denied—Mr Darcy was unfailingly honest, but she had sensed a penchant in him for the beautiful and impeccably bred Lady Baslow. Was it a small sort of inclination, exaggerated by her jealousy, or was duty binding him to his promise to her?

The hurt in his expression when she had told him she would not marry him haunted her. That and the dejected posture of his usually so erect body the last time she had watched him ride away from Longbourn. But she comforted herself that there had been little evidence of his deeper feelings when she visited Pemberley. He had made scant romantic overtures, he had not singled her out when they were in the company of others, and he had treated her without any symptom of peculiar regard. Mr Darcy had been pleasant but had not expressed any romantic sentiments. Exactly like her sister had acted towards Mr Bingley in Meryton. But Jane's feelings were so little expressed.

The hypocrisy of her thoughts was nonsensical. She searched her mind for something to contradict herself and was relieved when she remembered his marked attentions towards Lady Baslow. If she could find one occasion where *he* had instigated the intimacy, she would forget him entirely...

'*I am sorry to have occasioned pain to anyone,*' she had once stated in his presence. The first time she had injured him it had been unconsciously done. In her defence, his explanations had done nothing to conciliate her. Elizabeth could not claim such leniency at the last event. '*In vain I have struggled. It will not do. My feelings will not be repressed.*' Why had he fought against his inclinations? Because Lady Baslow had broken his heart... Perhaps she was not ill at all but suffered from a bad case of guilt-ridden conscience. She snickered at the ridiculous thought. Perhaps her ailment was of the mind, tilting her towards dark madness...

Two weeks later, Elizabeth was still abed. The fatigue had not relented, and her tongue was thick with thirst, but her bouts of pain and palpitations came less frequently.

Her grandmother was ever so diligent in her care and helped her to a glass of water while the linens were changed. *Móraí* gasped and exclaimed, "Oedema!" when Elizabeth's legs were exposed, which niggled at a memory in the far recesses of her mind. She could not recall what, but the priest returned the next day and offered her the viaticum—the body and blood of Christ.

"May the Lord Jesus Christ protect you and lead you to eternal life."

The priest further enquired whether she had any last confessions to make. Cold dread enclosed her heart, and the pain was unbearable.

"I might have been deceived and mistakenly judged a man harshly. I have brought distress upon my family, but my greatest sin is that I am exceedingly stupid," Elizabeth mumbled, her thoughts changing so rapidly and appearing incoherent. She had a vague feeling that the doctor had visited, mostly because of her oppressed and laboured breathing when the man had pressed his ear to her chest.

They spoke over her head like she was not in the room, but she revived when they mentioned Mr Darcy. Something about a hopeless endeavour and a journey pressed for time.

Elizabeth just wanted to sleep, but the pain rarely left her. Only laudanum gave her rest, but it made her dreams become obscure.

# Chapter 13 Love is an Arbitrary Monarch

The three-month mark of Darcy's exile from Elizabeth had come and gone, and so had their wedding day. He had undertaken a futile journey to Meryton and had returned to Pemberley without a bride. Even his servants had looked dejected when he had arrived unaccompanied by the revered Miss Elizabeth Bennet. She had won their trust and loyalty during the three short weeks she had visited, which he acknowledged was no small feat.

He had planned the spring planting in minute detail, and he would have liked to join his men searching for Elizabeth in London—not that he had any hope left he would find her, but he craved occupation—yet he could not do so with a house full of unwanted guests.

Well, not full exactly, but certainly unwanted. Could he throw out the viscount and his wife? Crawford had come for the sole purpose of gloating, though he had appeared contrite about his treatment of Elizabeth. Darcy contemplated whether he could order his footmen to bodily remove them and carry them out to their carriage. It was highly improper, scandalous even, and the earl would certainly take umbrage at the treatment of his heir, but his family were out of favour with him regardless.

Darcy rose from his desk and walked with determined steps towards the parlour where Viscount Crawford was having tea with his wife. They were chatting amicably when he charged through the door.

"This will not do. I demand that you leave Pemberley and do not return until you receive an invitation."

"I certainly will not!" The viscount leapt from his chair, approached him, and halted inches from his nose.

Darcy was not impressed by his display. He had half a head on his cousin and a healthier constitution. He was confident he would win any altercation, and the thought of hauling Crawford out into his carriage appealed more than it should.

"I could have you and your scheming, despicable wife carried off my land. I am even tempted to do it myself. Well, not the viscountess. She I would not touch with anything but a fire poker."

"Preposterous! I shall not stand for such disrespect. I have already sent for the earl, and he will know how to act."

A fervent knocking on the door broke through his anger-induced haze.

"Enter!" he barked.

Mrs Reynolds opened the door and stepped inside.

"The Marquis of Limerick and his sister have arrived. I took the liberty of admitting them, and they are waiting in the hall, sir."

"Thank you," a stunned Darcy replied. He was not expecting any guests, and he could not fathom why he had been blessed by a visit from the Irish aristocracy. The marquis was a revered peer who had forwarded the union between Ireland and Great Britain with success. His list of merits was long and included the honour of Clerk of the Crown, who administered the preparations of warrants required to pass under the royal sign-manual, fiats, and letters of patent. His close ties with the Prince of Wales made him one of the most influential people in the country.

His exalted guests turned out to be a petite, grey-haired lady —whose squared shoulders and steady gaze belied that her diminutive stature was a sign of weakness—and an older, formidable-looking peer. Darcy bowed deeply.

"You do not know me, Mr Darcy, but I know much about you. Ah, I can see that surprised you, but let me first introduce myself. I am Henry Conyngham, Marquis of Limerick, Earl of Glentworth, Viscount Foxford, and Baron Minister, and this is my sister, Mrs Maeve Bennet."

The lady stepped forwards.

"*Eilís* is dying of a broken heart. She fell suddenly and violently ill, and the physicians fear for her life. You must come with us directly. There is not an instant to lose," the lady implored. There was something strangely familiar about her eyes. They were the colour of emeralds, and it occurred to him that *Eilís* was the Irish equivalent of Elizabeth.

"Dear God! Do you know where to find Miss Elizabeth Bennet?"

Darcy used Elizabeth's full name to make certain there was no misunderstanding. A jumble of dread and joy surged through him; there was hope, but Elizabeth was seriously ill.

"I certainly do! I am her paternal grandmother!"

*This must be Mr Bennet's mother and the feeble old uncle he briefly mentioned.*

"I can see she has inherited your eyes, but she never mentioned..."

The lady interrupted him impatiently.

"Of course not. We are Catholics. Well, not publicly, of course, or we would have lost our land."

"Mr Bennet?" Darcy enquired incredulously.

"Yes, he is my son," the matron confirmed with exasperation. "Do keep up! You can imagine my reception when I moved to England and married my Mr Bennet. We were shunned for decades. That is why my son hates town and why I chose to return to my brother when the earldom was created. I saw no reason to stay when my husband was dead and my son had married.

"No estate should ever have two mistresses, Mr Darcy. Longbourn House is rather small, and it was not fair to my son to be always in the middle of two bickering females." The lady lifted one eyebrow and looked at him with the same sparkling eyes as Elizabeth.

"I do not understand... Why the secrecy?"

"There is no secrecy. I saw my granddaughters, occasionally, in London. Mrs Bennet was none the wiser, but then she is so easily duped. My son married an ignorant child, Mr Darcy. She was seventeen and as brazen as she was beautiful. Jane looks a lot like her, but in her youth, Francine was even more handsome. Unfortunately, her beauty is only displayed in her appearance. Once she was mistress of Longbourn, she forbade me from mentioning my Irish ancestry. Which is why I did not tell her when the barony nor the viscountcy were created in my brother's honour. When the earldom was resurrected from a century of extinction and Henry was appointed to the House of Lords, I moved back to Ireland to keep house for him. Although I seldom saw my granddaughters, the absence of Mrs Bennet from my life made the deprivation bearable. You should count yourself truly fortunate that there is such a great distance between Pemberley and Longbourn."

"I must inform Mr Bennet that she is found. He has been searching for her as long as I have."

"I told my son not to concern himself with Elizabeth's whereabouts. I dare say he is familiar enough with my quirks to know that I would not have done so had she not been with me. He is also quick-minded and would draw the conclusion that she journeyed alone with just cause. My omittance allowed him to claim ignorance when you visited him."

How unfortunate that Viscount Crawford and his wife were present and chose that very moment to clear their throats. He had to perform introductions when his mind yearned for more information about his beloved. When the reality of Mrs Bennet's words sunk in, Darcy had to steady himself on the pianoforte. Elizabeth had been found but was dreadfully ill. What if it was already too late?

The viscount offered the marquis his hand. "I have seen you in the House of Lords. From the gallery, of course. My father still holds our seat. He is the Earl of Matlock, and you are one of the original eight and twenty Irish Representative Peers."

"I am," the marquis replied with pride.

"How odd." Mrs Bennet addressed the viscountess. "I assume, from my granddaughter's description of your beauty, that you were Lady Baa-baa-baas-slow. Viscount Crawford, you have my sympathy. Though I suppose you must take some of the blame for your poor taste in women. Yet I cannot help but feel that you have been taken in, like your cousin."

The viscount cleared his throat, and the viscountess turned crimson.

"I was Lady Baslow, but I have recently married. Pray, who is your granddaughter?"

"My darling *Eilís*. She is an extraordinary young woman. So virtuous, compassionate, and kind. She is not like the guileful young ladies nowadays who think of nothing but themselves."

"I am certain I know no one by that name," the viscountess replied coldly.

"You may know her as Miss Elizabeth Bennet."

"How is she?" Darcy enquired impatiently, but what he really wanted to know was where.

"Why are you not packing?" the old lady admonished without replying to his question.

"You cannot leave your guests, Darcy. It is simply not done," Viscount Crawford whispered fervently in his ear.

"I certainly can. You came uninvited, after I specifically told you that you were not welcome."

"You are just jealous," Crawford snarled and stepped forwards.

Viscount Crawford's unsolicited visit, directly following their bridal trip, made their purpose clear. The former Lady Baslow had shown she would stoop to any underhanded method to remain in his company, and Crawford was renowned for his hauteur. Stealing Lady Baslow out of Darcy's grasp was his greatest triumph yet. The cousins were both of a competitive nature, and no victory tasted as good as their opponent's loss. But Crawford had been too engrossed in the contest to notice that he did not have a rival for his intended's attention. Darcy had avoided Lady Baslow completely since their last conversation, after he returned from court. The new Lady Crawford was not the young girl he had admired, and she probably never had been.

The viscount had misinterpreted his silence and shifting moods as a sign of defeat in vying for the former Lady Baslow's attention. He knew nothing about the painful turn his engagement to Elizabeth had taken. As far as the viscount was concerned, the marriage had been postponed because the groom had moved his affections elsewhere, not because the bride had changed her mind.

"When you and your wife have apologised for your appalling behaviour towards Miss Elizabeth, and on the condition that she is inclined to forgive you, I might receive you. Until then, you have your own estate, less than an hour's ride away. I expect you to repair to it before I leave mine. You came only to gloat, but your mission has failed. There is only one lady whom I hold in affection, and that is Miss Elizabeth Bennet. Until there is a Mrs Darcy to send an invitation, you may consider yourself banned from all my properties."

"I have already informed Father about your atrocious—"

"I care not," Darcy interrupted. "You may as well tell the earl he is banned too. Lady Matlock is welcome because she had the wherewithal not to laugh at Elizabeth when she was ridiculed by a tradesman's daughter who was conspiring with your abominable wife."

Crawford was regarding him in earnest. Darcy returned his gaze with a steady one of his own and saw the truth of the matter occur to his cousin. The viscount nodded and glanced at his wife.

"There are only a couple of hours left of daylight. Should you not wait and leave early on the morrow?" Crawford suggested. Despite the healthy rivalry between them, they were family.

"No. And neither will you."

Darcy rang the bell, and Mrs Reynolds entered shortly afterwards.

"Order my valet to pack for a long absence, and have one bag sufficient for a week's travel. Grey will come after me in the marquis's rented coach. Have my town coach[4] readied in half an hour, and Mrs Reynolds…"

"Yes, Mr Darcy?"

"Have the viscount and viscountess out of my house before nightfall by any means necessary."

The stunned housekeeper nodded briskly and left the room.

In the absence of Mrs Reynolds, a young footman in training was guarding the door and did not dare to stop the incensed Earl of Matlock from charging through the house. Darcy heard him stamping down the hall, giving his poor footman a reprimand.

"Let me through. Do you not know who I am?"

"Darcy!" he shouted, and the door hit the wall. "What is the meaning of this? I received a note that you are trying to evict the viscount from Pemberley, and I immediately set out to make my sentiments known. Outrageous! I will not stand for such—" The earl discovered the illustrious guests and stopped mid-sentence, staring at the marquis. "Limerick! What a pleasant surprise. You must excuse me. I was not aware that Darcy had company. What brings you to this area?"

"My sister's granddaughter, who has been residing in my house these many months, has fallen gravely ill. Mr Darcy might have the remedy to her ailment, and I have come to request his assistance."

"Do not let me keep you. Pray, shall I see you in the House of Lords for the Session?"

"Yes, after you have apologised for ridiculing Miss Elizabeth Bennet. She is the daughter of my heir, who will be appointed Earl of Glentworth at the opening of the Season. I know everything about her appalling treatment at the hands of your family. Your eldest son's wife in particular. It is my understanding that only the countess behaved with the dignity one would expect from nobility."

"You will have it immediately. I am sorry I did not make the connection. Bennet is a common name, and he did not mention anything to me about his future elevation of rank." The earl turned an accusing glare on his nephew. "And neither did you."

"I did not know," Darcy whispered, chagrined. Miss Elizabeth had mentioned she had something important to relate about her family, but he had been too busy to afford her the time to do so.

"It is not me to whom you owe an apology," the marquis thundered, "but a young girl betrothed to your nephew. In my family, we support each other and certainly do not ridicule—"

The marquis's rant was stopped by a dainty hand on his sleeve.

"May I remind you about the urgency of our mission and that the real culprit is the lady who barely warrants the title?"

The old lady might also have remembered her son's penchant for making sport of his wife and wanted to stop her brother from stating an untruth.

"Yes, you are correct, Maeve. Excuse me, Lord Matlock, for losing my temper, but Miss Elizabeth is particularly dear to me. She is the kind of young lady one cannot help but love and admire. I cannot slander any lady, but I implore you to guide the viscountess in the future. Your family's honour depends upon it."

"For what it is worth, I like Miss Elizabeth. She has a keen wit and a lively disposition. She is an asset to any family, and I shall be honoured to call her my niece."

"That remains to be seen," Mrs Bennet added wryly.

The earl had not noticed the sarcasm directed at Mr Darcy. "Yes, I shall keep your granddaughter in my prayers and hope she will soon be restored to health," the earl promised before turning to Darcy. "You have much to atone for."

"Yes. In my misguided sense of duty, I aided a baronet's widow, who staged her own fall from grace, and failed to give the attention to my bride that she deserved. The family's intervention did neither Miss Elizabeth nor me any service, but I shall not repeat my mistakes. And should I succeed in convincing her of my undivided affection, no one will ever come between us. She alone deserves my loyalty."

"How astute of you to notice, if somewhat belatedly," Mrs Bennet drawled. "Loyalty is an essential character trait if you are ever to wed a Conyngham. We marry but once. No one could ever replace my Mr Bennet, and death has not parted us, for we shall be together again in heaven. Is that not so, Henry?"

The marquis bowed his head. "From your mouth to God's ears. Me and my Sinéad were afforded two years of bliss before heaven claimed both her and my son. No other lady could ever compare..."

The earl nodded and ushered his relations out of the parlour. Darcy was ready in an hour, and the Irish peer and his sister joined him in his carriage. Their hired hack would follow with Darcy's valet once the horses were sufficiently rested. Mrs Bennet studied him from the opposite seat, and he fought not to squirm under her scrutiny.

"I am an old lady to whom it matters but little how I am perceived or whether I am palatable to people unconnected to me. So, I am frank enough to tell you that I do not care for your relations."

"Neither do I," he admitted, a bit more earnestly than he should.

"Except that sweet little sister of yours. I was watching you when you bid Miss Darcy farewell. You are a devoted brother, and that alone makes me believe there is hope for you yet..."

He surmised she was speaking about Elizabeth and their relationship.

"If there is a sliver of hope, I would be much obliged."

"Have you heard from *Eilís* since you parted in Hertfordshire?"

"No," he admitted dejectedly. "I have heard nothing of her whereabouts, what has occupied her time, or how she is faring. Please, relieve me of my misery and tell me what you know."

The corner of Mrs Bennet's mouth twitched—a habit she shared with her granddaughter when she was about to deliver a particularly witty retort.

"She joined a convent."

"She is a nun!" If he had to reveal their kiss to get her out of there, he was fully prepared to do so. Elizabeth did not belong in a convent, subjected to strict rules and regulations. It would mean a long and slow death of her spirit—the very essence he loved the most.

"No, not as a nun. She worked there to help with the sick and the education of girls."

"Worked?"

"Well, not as a paid occupation but for charity. It can be work if you are as compassionate and devoted as *Eilís*, and the need is great indeed. When she fell ill, I initially thought she had toiled too hard, but rest did not restore her—quite the contrary. Her health declined even more rapidly when left too much to her thoughts. Beaten by fatigue, she became confined to her bed, suffering from shortness of breath and palpitations of the heart. She deteriorated further, fainted, and suffered severe chest pains. I summoned the doctor, and he said her heart was beating in an unsteady rhythm. She is suffering from a broken heart[5], and it may very well kill her. I cannot let that happen, Mr Darcy, even though I despise you for hurting my granddaughter. If the remedy is you, I dare say you will rise in my esteem soon enough."

Darcy measured his words, wondering how open Elizabeth had been with her grandmother, but he would not leave her in doubt.

"I shall not disappoint you," he promised and turned his gaze to the passing scenery. If he had stared a moment longer into the reproachful emerald eyes of Elizabeth's grandmother, he might have lost his composure. And this was not the time to give in to weakness. He had a momentous task ahead of him, and he must not fail. If Elizabeth would give him a second chance, he would grab it with both hands because he loved her still—as ardently as ever.

It took three days just to get to the port of Holyhead, and one more for the ferry to take them to Dublin. The ride from Dublin to Áth Dara took another five. By the time they arrived, the argent moon rose in the shimmering sky as the mute arbitress of gloom. Darcy was overcome with foreboding about being too late. He looked and found no wreath above the door, nor were all the curtains closed. An oak loomed peacefully in the rosy hues of a setting sun.

"We shall make a swift call on Elizabeth before we refresh ourselves," Mrs Bennet informed him. "It is highly irregular to allow you entrance to her chamber, but she cannot leave her bed, and you are betrothed. You will, of course, be chaperoned at all times."

Darcy nodded, relieved that she was as eager as he to see how Elizabeth fared. They walked briskly in silence up a grand staircase and down a never-ending hall.

The old lady halted abruptly in front of an elaborately carved doorway with two doors that reminded him of the entrance to the cathedral of Notre-Dame in Paris. The matriarch breathed deeply before she turned the handle.

"How is she?" Mrs Bennet immediately enquired.

A woman rose from a chair in a darkened corner.

"Much the same, but at least she has not deteriorated further."

It was a relief to hear. He had worried they might be too late, and he knew Mrs Bennet shared his fear. He could hear the air rush out of her lungs and a muttered thanks to the above.

"You may rest, Mrs Finnegan. I intend to stay with her myself," Mrs Bennet offered once she had composed herself.

Mrs Finnegan closed the door behind her. The room was sparsely lit. A candle on a bedside table threw long shadows and illuminated the lithe frame of a reclining Elizabeth. She lay frail and lifeless, as though all her vivacity had drained from her body.

The god of love united all his lightning into one effective blaze Darcy was incapable of withstanding. Fervent passion coursed through him and robbed him of his breath, wit, and defence.

"Dear God, is this my doing? Name the penance, and I shall pay it."

"All she needs is love and constancy," the old lady admonished.

"I have loved her for eighteen months and never wavered," Darcy defended himself.

"Not even for a flighty moment in your thoughts?"

Darcy gave the matron a decided look.

"That may not be possible for anyone, but I have never regretted the offer of my hand, only grieved the days and nights we have spent apart."

"Let us not dwell on the past but think only of the present and, with luck, happier times to come."

Mrs Bennet inclined her head and retreated into the shadows, allowing him to direct his full attention to the girl who held his heart.

Elizabeth was sleeping, curled up on her side, blanketed by an abundance of luxurious auburn tresses. His heart quickened at the impropriety of seeing her thus—alone in her bed. He moved to her side and fiddled with a strand that hung across her face. She was pale but more beautiful than he had ever seen her. Lush lashes rested on her high cheekbones, her lips were slightly pursed, and her expression was one of youthful serenity. The carefully crafted speech he had prepared seemed conceited and inadequate with the reality of a dying Elizabeth in front of him. He whispered a desperate, "My love," too low for anyone to hear and sank to his knees. He folded his hands, bowed his head, and mumbled a fervent prayer for Elizabeth's recovery.

"She has never cut it." Mrs Bennet interrupted his reveries with a quiet whisper.

He did not immediately understand what she meant until he realised that he was still holding the lock of hair.

"She has been saving it until she marries. For the sake of her recovery, I hope there will soon be reason to cut it."

"Why?" he enquired with a feeling of distress but kept his voice low so as not to awaken the sleeping beauty.

"It is customary to cut a woman's hair to shoulder-length when she marries. It is easier to dress elaborately when it is shorter."

"I pray she will never do so."

"You do not want her to marry?"

"I do, with all my heart."

"Then we agree on something, Mr Darcy. The physician believes it is the only remedy for her failing heart. That only marriage to her true love will restore it to its rhythm. It is prone to afflict maidens who have lost their love. *Eilís* has been greatly reduced since she arrived on my doorstep four months ago with all the stubbornness and determination of a Conyngham. *Eilís* declared she was finished with love and set on finding another path in life. You young are so innocent of the facts of life. You cannot choose whom you love. It is chosen for you, or perhaps in spite of you. I know not, but I certainly had no desire to move to Hertfordshire when Mr Bennet entered my life. And the Lord knows I fought the inclination with all my might, but my efforts were in vain. The Lord works in mysterious ways and sorted it out for the best. I certainly have no regrets."

Darcy nodded in acknowledgement. If only Elizabeth shared her grandmother's philosophical approach...

"Please, Mr Darcy. I cannot bear to see her withering away," she whispered.

"You need not beg. I am devoted and decided. To me, there is not a woman alive in the world I would choose but her. Between us, we shall do everything in our power to ensure Miss Elizabeth's recovery."

In agreement, they left the sleeping Elizabeth to rest, and the matron escorted him to his chamber herself.

"I have appointed you the Nidaros chamber. I somehow thought the ornate gothic masterpiece would suit you."

"I observed that Miss Elizabeth's room was called Notre-Dame. Are all your rooms named for cathedrals?"

"Only the bed chambers, Mr Darcy. I wish you good evening

and hope we shall both awaken well rested on the morrow."

And with that, he entered a masculine chamber, exactly to his taste with a large, circular, rose-coloured window, but that was not what caught his attention. Over the fireplace hung a portrait of a young girl of perhaps fifteen summers. Her hair was down, and she was walking through a garden of blooming peonies. She was half turned away, letting her left hand graze the petals of a delicate pink flower, looking seductively over her shoulder at whoever held the paintbrush. Elizabeth...

He turned to the bedside table. On it stood a framed shade drawing of Elizabeth and a book of poetry by Thomas Moore. Darcy flipped it open, and a ribbon made it turn to a particular page. The marker had an inscription embroidered; *Eilís's favourite*. By the quality of the stitching and wear of the fabric, he surmised it had been done by the hand of a noticeably young Miss Elizabeth. The words on the page caught his attention, and he read the poem.

> *'Tis the last rose of summer*
>
> *Left blooming alone;*
>
> *All her lovely companions*
>
> *Are faded and gone*
>
> *No flower of her kindred*
>
> *No rosebud is nigh,*
>
> *To reflect back her blushes,*
>
> *To give sigh for sigh*

Darcy was trespassing on Elizabeth's innermost thoughts and could not help but think the poem reflected something of her essence. That she—who was one of the most vivacious of beings —in the deepest recesses of her soul was as lonely as he. An old soul with deep understanding but with no one to lean on. Who supported Elizabeth through hardship? Who lit her way like the moon's dusky beams brightened the raging sea it could not calm?

Mrs Bingley was a sweet and lovely lady but no match for her sister's wit. Her father came close but used his acumen to throw sarcastic remarks at his friends and laugh at his family. Mrs Bennet could not see past ribbons and lace, Miss Mary was too awed by Fordyce to think genuine thoughts, and Miss Catherine was simplicity in spirit. He had managed his affairs since he had left for Eton at the age of twelve. How old had Elizabeth been when she had discovered she was at the helm of her family? When her grandmother left...?

After a restless night and a light breakfast, he knocked on Elizabeth's door, hoping to find her awake and with a healthier pallor than the previous night. What would he not sacrifice for an earthly look or a sign of affection to quash the madness in his soul?

Mrs Finnegan bade him enter, and he crossed the threshold with hope that was immediately doused. Elizabeth looked even less hearty in the harsh morning light. Her pale cheeks and dull eyes were accompanied by sluggish movements. He tentatively approached her bed, ready to flee should she desire his absence. When she turned towards him and did not immediately tell him to leave, he knelt by the bed and gave a short prayer for that blessed mercy.

# Chapter 14 The Sweet Deluge of Love

In the silent room, the heavy creeping shadow took the form of a gentleman. Elizabeth turned her head towards its owner and discovered Mr Darcy hovering above her.

"Mr Darcy! Why are you here?"

"For love," he replied. "A love strong enough to brave your rejection, and the boldness to strive to charm you. I even anticipate being the object of your raillery, because without you in it, my life is but a dull, wide desert. Tell me. Is my suit in vain?"

A fleeting wish to tease him made her want to laugh, but she had not the strength to do so.

"Please, if you are to tell me an untruth, let it be anything but a proclamation of love."

"I come in earnest. For you, I would do anything you ask of me," he stated simply. "Upon my honour, I would..."

Elizabeth studied Mr Darcy, his expression torn by remorse, open and unguarded. Their eyes met, and she could not look away. The chair squeaked as he bent towards her, and she held her breath in anticipation.

"Elizabeth?" he whispered. His tormented countenance transformed into tender concern. "Please, do not speak. Rest until your health is recovered." He tucked a wayward strand of hair behind her ear, and she savoured the slight touch with a twinge of regret.

"I am dying."

"No!" he grumbled. "I shall not allow it. You cannot leave me, Elizabeth. I am desolate without you. You must fight. I have searched for you everywhere. I have raged against you for concealing your whereabouts and tortured myself for giving you even a moment of doubt of my constancy and my ardent affection. Fight to recover, Elizabeth. I cannot bear the world without you in it! If you would give me but a small part in your life, I shall be in your debt."

How she wanted to believe him! His speech, so passionately delivered, made it difficult to accuse him of perfidy, and she sunk back into the pillow, releasing a precious pearl to her cup of sorrows.

"Please, forgive me. I should not have upset you."

Mrs Finnegan poured a glass of water, but Elizabeth was not strong enough to sit up on her own. Mr Darcy must have seen Mrs Finnegan's struggle and decided to help. His arms reached under her haggard frame and supported her whilst she drank.

#

Elizabeth slept most of the time during Mr Darcy's first week in residence. The gentleman naturally assumed the task of lifting her when she took sustenance, but they were never alone to discuss the chasm that separated them.

It was a scene of melancholy that the elder Mrs Bennet observed as she watched Mr Darcy's tireless vigil over their beloved girl. The days of parched black despondency were fading away, and Elizabeth slowly began to improve. She no longer suffered as much pain, and the doctor reduced the amount of laudanum she was given. Her colour brightened, her eyes resumed a sliver of their vitality, and her spirit was gradually recovering. It was as if Mr Darcy's presence had breathed new life into her heart. Their fortunes seemed to have turned, and Mrs Bennet was loath to lose the progress made but recognised the tension between them—the unspoken words necessary to heal completely.

Mr Darcy had injured her dear girl, but she sensed in him a fierce determination to right the wrongs he had committed—of which some might be misunderstandings. His love was fierce; she could feel it rolling off him when he sat by *Eilís'* side.

They had experienced but the beginnings of love, a brush of Cupid's dart, before her dear *Eilís* had left in utter despair. But love in its infancy was jealous. Looming threateningly above the sequel to their love affair was the curse of Lady Baslow. Mr Darcy was not a charming gentleman but rather staid and taciturn. Yet he appeared unfailingly honourable, and she could not believe him to be perfidious. Had she erred in judging Mr Darcy without a trial in his defence?

Begrudgingly, Mrs Bennet had to admit that despite Mr Darcy's lack of charm, she had begun to like him.

She would have to conjure up a plausible reason to leave them alone for a few blessed moments. Elizabeth looked hearty today. Mrs Bennet had called for the doctor, who was pleased with the patient's progress and congratulated himself on his correct diagnosis. She had vehemently objected when he had first broached the ailment he suggested. The Conynghams were a sturdy lot and did not suffer broken hearts. But Mrs Bennet was not one to shirk admitting being in the wrong, and in this instance, she was more than happy to do so. The doctor was so pleased with her granddaughter's progress that he had allowed Elizabeth short spells out of bed. There was no better time for an honest discussion than the present, but she could think of no excuse.

"Mrs Finnegan, the young need privacy. Will you join me in my drawing room?"

The direct and honest approach was best. Mrs Finnegan smiled and nodded, and the ladies left the young lovers to themselves.

#

Darcy was bewildered at first but soon counted the liberty Mrs

Bennet had bestowed upon them as a blessing. Elizabeth was well enough to leave her bed for brief moments and sat in a chair by the window. She was wearing a lovely maroon-coloured dress that brought out the colour in her emerald-green eyes, and her gaze rested on a family of ducks paddling across the trickling brook next to the house.

"Your dress is very becoming. Is it new?"

She turned towards him with a secretive smile curling the corners of her mouth. "Yes, my grandmother has been spoiling me."

"Are you comfortable, or shall I fetch you a pillow?"

"I am quite well, Mr Darcy. I am enjoying the view, so please do not return me to my bed yet."

"Whatever you say. Your words are my command."

"If that is true, I would wish for candidness more than anything."

"I always speak in earnest. Disguise of every sort is my abhorrence."

"I remember you telling me so once before, and that is why I am counting on you to give me a full, unalloyed disclosure of your dealings with Lady Baslow."

She did not look at him but stared blindly at the white clouds drifting across the sky. He owed her an explanation and could only wish he had given it much sooner. He should have taken the time—that was the crux of the matter. He had put all his duties before his betrothed, thinking he would have free time to spend with her if he just finished what was currently occupying him. But his responsibilities never ended. They were a continuous succession of demands upon his time, and he had failed to give her precedence. He could only reap the consequences, speak the truth, and risk a lapse in Elizabeth's recovery.

"I acknowledge that for a brief moment, my sightless soul

strayed. I was confused by notions of imaginary bliss, assaulted by memories painted in a favourable light by the years that had passed. From my childhood to the cusp of adulthood, I entertained the possibility of offering for Lady Baslow. Our parents expected it even. Our families were close, and we spent much time in each other's company. When she chose to accept another man, the rejection caused substantial injury to my pride. To protect myself from further harm, I built a wall with bricks of shame and distrust. I am not proud to admit it, but parts of me wanted to show her what a man I had become and make her regret her choice. It affected my weak soul like a disease. But I swear to you, I am no longer infected. My feelings for Lady Baslow were immature, if they can even be called love. They were founded in the shallowness of beauty, wealth, and connections. Without substance, feelings wither and die. No. The blinds have been pulled from my eyes, and only regret for the pain I have caused you remains. My ardent love for you has strengthened. Even our long separation has only solidified my resolve.

"Ashamedly, I admit I found it difficult to believe your claims regarding Lady Baslow's rendition of the storm. I am no longer in doubt, and although the woman in question has not fully disclosed her perfidy, I no longer hold her in any affection. Well, perhaps a little for the girl she once was, but nothing for the woman she has become. Her deceit was disclosed in court when the thieves were found guilty. I discovered that they had been hired by Lady Baslow to prevent me from travelling to Hertfordshire. I suspect she even planned an assault on you, because she admitted to me that she had tried to persuade you to join her in the funeral procession. To my immense relief, you declined.

"Later, Mr Robert Baslow admitted that he was paid to contest the will. Another deception to keep me from you. Lady Baslow has since married my cousin, Viscount Crawford, and I can honestly wish them happy with not a sliver of envy in my heart. But I shall not receive them in my home because of their atrocious behaviour towards you."

Elizabeth hid her face in her hands—but not quickly enough to conceal the tears rolling down her cheeks; nor could they cover her ragged breathing.

"While I appreciate your honesty, Lady Baslow's marriage has no effect on me. It was not so much the attention you bestowed upon Lady Baslow but your complete lack of affection for me. The night of the storm proved that you were not so opposed to intimacy as I had come to believe. I was simply not the one who tempted you."

"Your beauty wants but wings for you to be a heavenly inhabitant. After Lady Baslow's betrayal, I did not believe Cupid's quiver contained an arrow strong enough to pierce my heart. But those little delicacies, those trembling, aching flutters of my heart every time I occasioned to see you, distinguished ardent love from its counterfeit. My youthful infatuation was not founded upon reality but an airy emotion based on imagination and fantasy. As I grew into my maturity, my preferences changed. You alone hold my heart, Elizabeth. And I am not too proud to beg your forgiveness until you relent for a moment of peace. And I swear to never leave you in doubt of my affection. I predict that you will sooner tire of my admiring overtures."

To emphasise his earnestness, he knelt beside her chair. It had the effect of drawing her beautiful eyes to look upon him.

"How am I supposed to believe that, when nothing in your demeanour ever speaks of ardent feelings?" Elizabeth challenged in a trembling voice.

"I..." Darcy sighed, at a loss for words. It had never been his intention to appear cold and aloof. He was not; he was simply too zealous in his effort to behave like a perfect gentleman and show his respect for the lady he loved.

"It hurt that you kept your distance from me whilst behaving perfectly at ease with Lady Baslow and even accepting Miss Bingley's cloying attentions at Netherfield. Both appeared permanently fixed to your arm whenever you were together."

"As a boy, I flinched whenever a lady grabbed my arm. My father disapproved, and I taught myself to control the habit and not to show any outward aversion. It does not mean that I commend the behaviour. I am highly uncomfortable with public displays of affection."

"You have not even held my hand since you arrived in Ireland."

"We are never alone, but I would very much like to hold your hand. I suppose I have concerns as to whether you would appreciate the gesture."

"Perhaps I have not managed to convey my sentiments clearly enough for them to be perceived by the opposite sex. But if it has to be voiced aloud, I shall risk it… I would. Very much so. I understand the need to contain ardent displays of affection in public, but there are other ways to distinguish a preference. Like seeking out their company, engaging in conversation, or offering your arm to them to the exclusion of—other ladies."

It occurred to Darcy just how much pain and heartache he had caused Elizabeth—at Pemberley in particular but also at his aunt's musical soirée at Matlock. By trying to please everyone, he had harmed the person who mattered the most. He clasped her hand and lay it in his left one while he used his right to trace the contours of her knuckles. It felt very intimate indeed…

His thoughts reverted to another lady who always held herself under good regulation. Lady Baslow was unfailingly calm and collected. No emotions ever crossed her face that she did not allow. An apt description of himself, to be sure, but what had he gained by it? To be the recipient of Elizabeth's unguarded affectionate displays would be a most cherished position. Yet he had offered nothing in return, and she had made the assumption that he did not care for her. No, that he cared more for Lady Baslow. How hare-brained was he to have enflamed her righteous indignation?

Perhaps Richard had been right. That by avoiding what he perceived as improprieties, he had failed to convince Elizabeth of his affections. Were those gestures he avoided so assiduously actually preparatives for love? He, who prided himself in being a rational man of sense and education, had erred. Love and reason were incompatible, and rules had exceptions.

Absentmindedly, he lifted her hand to his mouth and bestowed a lingering kiss. Disregarding her sharp intake of breath, he closed his eyes to savour the feel of her soft skin. He brushed their entwined fingers across his cheek and relished the sensation of the touch before he turned her hand to let his lips graze the inside of her wrist.

"Cease being so charming," Elizabeth rasped.

He lowered her hand and opened his eyes to stare into the emerald depths of Elizabeth's soul.

Although possible to feign, love could never be concealed. Elizabeth's glorious eyes were true and perfect agents of the kindled flames in her generous heart—despite her contradictory words that were trying to persuade him otherwise.

She loved him!

And her love was not only confined to her eyes. There was something in her air, a breeze in her expression, her manner of talking, a whisper in her voice, the tremble of her lips, and a thousand other nameless clues. Even her attempts to disguise her feelings made their ardency more apparent.

"You have destroyed my equilibrium and cast me into a stormy sea. I cannot swim—I cannot rescue myself," Elizabeth whispered.

Darcy tempered his rapture, and a sudden urge to envelop her in his arms and kiss those quivering lips nigh on overwhelmed him, but to trespass on the strictest rules of virtue would not win her respect. A different method—a measured demonstration of his feelings—would win her love and earn her trust.

Incapable of expressing himself in words, he stared into her eyes and prayed the love he had discovered in hers was discernible in his own.

"Oh, it is no use..."

Elizabeth grabbed his hand and tugged it to her heart.

"Love is not a flashy flamed infatuation that effortlessly fuels its bewitched victims. Oh no, it is a arbitrary monarch that I find myself incapable of resisting. My rational mind condemns my weakness, but my heart demands sovereignty. Love cannot be resisted, expelled, or even alleviated. Despite my vigorous attempts to conquer the affliction, it does not yield to reason. Love endures absence, survives disappointment and cold, wintry indifference. Love's fiery blasts cannot be extinguished by a deluge of loathing. There is no consolation to be had— no chance of recovery. In vain my pride opposed the thorns guarding love's soft delicacy. Intolerable torment is what love is. It raised me up to the highest heaven of bliss only to send me plunging into the lowest hell of misery."

"I have no wish to be parted from you," Darcy acknowledged.

"You have me at a disadvantage, Mr Darcy," Elizabeth admitted in a weary voice. Her declaration appeared to have sapped her of her last bit of strength, and she closed her eyes. "I have no choice in the matter."

They would not have parted if exhaustion had not interposed as a moderator, but Darcy had received the confession he most wanted to hear. He would be patient. He picked her up, placed her on the bed, and tucked the covers securely around her sleepy form. Her hand shot up, and for a brief moment, he thought she was going to slap him, but her fingers trailed across his cheek before falling listlessly to the mattress. He kissed her forehead before leaving his love to rest.

For days, Elizabeth slept more than she was awake, but in her waking hours, her strength was slowly returning.

#

Darcy was deep in thought, watching the gentle flowing of the river. He was leaning against an old oak with his light summer coat unbuttoned. It was the informality about him that caught Elizabeth's attention. She was sitting on a blanket with a glass of wine in her hand, listening to the trickling water and the cheerful chirping of a robin. He was becoming bold and hopped ever closer, his beady eyes on a piece of cheese.

It was her first sojourn out of doors since she became ill. Darcy had escorted her to their little picnic a few yards from the house. He had deposited her on the blanket, made sure she was comfortable, and retreated to support the old oak with his impressive, manly figure.

Elizabeth wanted him closer, but to study him had its own pleasures. He must have been aware of her scrutiny because he spoke.

"I have been remiss in telling you that I have changed our marriage settlement. I removed any claim to compensation upon a breach of contract. If you ever want to marry me, it must be your wish. You are well aware of my deficiencies, but my love for you is not one of them. My feelings and wishes are as constant and persistent as the dawn. If you cannot love me, I would even settle for loving you enough for both of us. But I cannot and I shall not force the issue. If my heart must break, dear love, let it be for your sake..."

His voice cracked, and he left the oak. Elizabeth thought that he would join her on the blanket, but he did not. He walked away from her down the riverbank until he disappeared round the bend.

Elizabeth felt abandoned despite the number of servants at her disposal, three of which were standing at an unobtrusive distance. But it was Darcy's company she wanted. Had she exhausted his patience? Was he tired of courting her good opinion?

Elizabeth waited for half an hour, and when he did not return, she retreated to her chamber to rest.

#

Mrs Bennet was waiting for him when he returned, with a scolding he richly deserved. His actions left much wanting. It was impossible to explain, yet he must.

"You have severely disappointed me, Mr Darcy. I had begun to think better of you, but your actions today have left me with doubts that you are the right man for my granddaughter. I am bewildered, which does not happen often. I have watched you sit, day and night, praying and weeping at *Eilís's* bedside. Yet I must enquire whether you are having second thoughts about marrying my Elizabeth."

"None at all," he assured her.

"Then why did you walk away from her? It makes me wonder whether you have the stamina for a lady like my *Eilís*. She is not your usual insipid ornament, but I thought you clever enough to appreciate the rewards."

"I am. A moment of weakness came over me with such force and haste that I needed to rein myself in." He spoke more candidly and more directly than was his wont. Happiness was in his grasp; he could feel it, and he would not let his reticence guide him. "The travails of the last year hit me forcefully. I have kept my composure out of fear. Now that Miss Elizabeth is on the mend, and my hopes and wishes may come true, I have lost my good regulation. I would not have her upset or forced by a duty-bound compassion to accept me. It would be a dismal way of securing her affection."

"Why? Because you cannot show her you are a human and not a cold, hard rock? Believe me, Mr Darcy, a woman does not expect, or even wish, a man to be impenetrable. Neither must you trust the sense of a woman in love. She will always question her observations and more often than not favour her doubts. Be explicit in your address, or better yet, show her with gestures of affection. Words are never truer than when followed by deeds."

"What of men? How is a man to know for certain he has captured a woman's affections?"

"A gentleman always set the standards to which a lady rises. She cannot display her affections without being judged a wanton by society. Therefore, you must be her guide in this."

Darcy walked straight to Elizabeth's chamber and knocked on the door. It was a weary voice that bade him enter. Elizabeth was resting on the bed and did not turn to look at him. He had fled to conceal his weakness and had ended up hurting her.

He knelt by her side and saw the residual tears glistening on her eyelashes. It made his heart clench and his voice raspy.

"Forgive me!"

"I worried that you were not coming back."

"Of course I was. Always!"

"Then why did you leave?"

"I was overcome by a moment of weakness."

"You regretted pursuing me?"

"No! Never! I wept for the pain I have caused you. Do not for a moment doubt that I feel it. I was not aware how appallingly you were treated at Pemberley. Your sister Miss Mary gave me a lecture I shall not soon forget. Never again shall I leave you alone with Miss Bingley. If not for her brother, she would not have been welcome in my house. I have spoken to Mr Hurst, and he assured me that you will be treated with every deference should you meet her again. If you wish it, I shall ban Miss Bingley, Lady Baslow, and all my relations from setting foot in either of my houses. Yet I am the one who must carry the blame. Lady Baslow could not have worked upon you if you had been secure in my regard. And for that, I shall never forgive myself. I do not deserve your love, but I ask it of you regardless. In my selfishness, I beg you to give me a chance to prove my affections and constancy, but I shall not force you. You have a choice, and I shall respect your decision. It was the thought of your rejection that filled me with dread. You are finally on the mend. I suppose the terror of your imminent death held my feelings in check. When the threat subsided, all my emotions assaulted me at once."

"You promised me you would be honest. That includes sharing your pain."

"Even when I am crying like a baby because you are well enough to reject me?"

"Everything that you are, for good and bad," Elizabeth replied in a drowsy voice.

Darcy looked at his intended; her eyes were closed. She must be exhausted. He kissed her forehead and wished her sweet dreams before he tiptoed out of the room.

# Chapter 15 The Shadows of Absence

The incessant shifting from hope to dread racked Elizabeth with intolerable agitation. Her impregnable heart had surrendered after a mere moment in the presence of the object it coveted. Calm and cold indifference was unattainable because desire filled her with fervour—but also an equal measure of shame.

Her principles had crumbled at the sight of this man who had destroyed her faith in love. What would those people who had witnessed his betrayal and condemned him for his actions think of her if she forgave Darcy? Word had certainly spread about her humiliation. She harboured no doubt that the sordid tale about Darcy's involuntary dip in the lake and its cause had been bandied about as far as London's drawing rooms. Would she be ridiculed as the silliest country bumpkin, too ignorant or mercenary to relinquish the position as mistress of Pemberley? Or worse, pitied as a victim of the altar, burnt by the nuptial torches of her father and adulterous groom?

But his address had altered—so modestly delivered and artfully expressed—and his wit had been so utterly delightful. If she had loved him before, she now adored him. Her affections dictated to her—ungovernable and demanding. Was it not a credit to herself to be sensible of his change? Was not concealing her sentiments a form of disguise? Absence had not banished the ardour from her heart; quite the contrary. Time and change of scenery could not have been more damaging to her health, and it was life-wasting anguish to suppress her heart's desire.

THE SHADOWS OF ABSENCE

The torture of sleepless nights and restless days had followed her to Ireland. She had failed miserably in erasing him from her mind. Her love for him was fierce and infinite—a love of souls, uncommon but refined and noble. Her heart was forever his.

Elizabeth studied the object of her affections. He was sitting by her bedside, reading Melodies, a book of songs, wherein Thomas Moore had written lyrics to ancient Irish music. It had become a habit that he read her to sleep every evening. Properly chaperoned, of course.

He was reading Believe Me If All Those Endearing Young Charms, with earnest feeling, making her believe he was adding his own sentiments to the song. But strain was evident on his countenance.

#

"You look tired, Mr Darcy."

He regarded Elizabeth, uncertain how honest his response should be.

"I am exhausted. The struggles of the last year and a half have been a torment, and I can bear it no longer."

"Will you not lie next to me? Rest your weary body and relieve my tired neck from gazing up at you. You are so abominably tall."

Darcy hesitated whilst Elizabeth shuffled to the opposite edge of the bed and turned on her side to give him room. His eyes flickered to the corner, and she immediately understood.

"Mrs Finnegan, please leave us."

The lady rose and left without a word.

"Jane and I used to lie like this and talk into the night. Please, I have no intention of ravishing you. I just want the intimacy of a clandestine conversation."

What choice had he but to obey? Yielding gradually to the soft and balmy influence of this woman. He was poised on the brink; her cheeks blushed rosy in the glow of the setting sun.

He capitulated and positioned his tall frame as close to the edge as possible. Had he resisted, his honour would have been uncommon, and applaudable, and stupid... Elizabeth smiled when he rested his head on the pillow, facing his beloved.

"There. Much better. You are not so imposing whilst lying down."

His thoughts ventured in exactly the opposite direction. He could be formidable indeed if he were inclined to follow his deepest yearnings, to pull her close and position her beneath him. He would not, of course. This was one of those moments where his good regulation proved invaluable.

"I disagree. I am holding on to the last thread of my restraint not to ravish you, as I have been for the last year and a half. If you had been privy to my reflections, you would not have invited me to join you, especially not in your bed." He heard air rush from her lungs and hastened to lighten the mood. "What would you like to discuss on this glorious spring evening?" he enquired whilst an undertow of desire pulled them closer.

"Our hopes and dreams," Elizabeth replied with a secret smile and inched closer still. Her trust was endearing, if not somewhat misplaced.

"What are your deepest wishes for your future?" she enquired in a husky voice.

He held her gaze, only a nose length away from his. "I wish for a future with you in it and, I hope, a brood of children to dote upon and a prosperous Pemberley to support us. In time, I hope that Georgiana and your remaining sisters will marry well."

It was a heady feeling to yet again be the recipient of Elizabeth's radiant smile. "I feel faint when you smile at me like that," he admitted.

"Shall I summon the doctor?"

Elizabeth's dazzling gaze and the teasing pleasure in her expression further enflamed him in the competition of who could radiate the fiercest rays of passion. Elizabeth was not unaffected; her blushing cheeks belied her indifference.

With a tumultuous eagerness, Darcy hoisted himself up onto his elbow and hovered above her with their lips aligned. It was agony not to act upon his inclination and capture that trembling lower lip between his own. He groaned when her hand stroked his ribs with only his flimsy shirt for protection.

"Unless you move away or tell me not to, my good regulation will soon be a memory of the past."

"I doubt a slip once in a while would turn you feral, Fitzwilliam Darcy."

His name rolled off her tongue like a purr. It was the first time she had used his Christian name, though he had given her the right months past. He brushed a kiss over her impertinent mouth. "I beg to differ." He kissed her again and lingered with the softest touch. "Your boldness is enticing, but you know not what beast you are unleashing." Darcy let his nose graze the column of her neck and inhaled her scent. "Years of pent-up desire." Elizabeth's hand touched his nape and tugged him downwards; their mouths joined in a rhapsodic dance.

"Oh, too lovely," she rasped between kisses. Their panting chests collided, and hands began exploring unknown territory. Whilst hope crowned, passion surged through trembling bodies. They took liberties that he coveted but her modesty could not allow, and he tried to extract himself.

Elizabeth would not allow it and jerked his shirt from his breeches. A flush of desire overcame his principles. Who could stop spring's rapid whirl of a river? Not he! He grabbed her shift and tugged in an effort to rip it apart, when a clearing throat jolted them out of their desire-induced haze.

Darcy stilled his hands and dropped his head to rest on her trembling, exposed shoulder. Elizabeth was quivering—he hoped not in fear or disgust at his inexcusable behaviour. She giggled, and he raised his head to gauge whether she was descending into hysteria or found mirth in their mortifying circumstance. The mind of a woman would always be a mystery to him, even if he could read her expression, because Elizabeth looked blissfully happy.

"A wedding would not go amiss," Mrs Bennet wryly remarked. "I suggest we do not delay having the banns read. Mr Darcy, I expect you to write to your vicar and request he read them in your parish."

Darcy extracted himself from Elizabeth's soft embrace and rose from the bed. It was fortunate that his rumpled shirt hid the evidence of his ardour. He chuckled like he was a fifteen-year-old boy and raised his head to meet the sparkling eyes of his beloved's grandmother. The corner of her mouth twitched, and her eyebrows rose quizzically.

"That will not be necessary. I have purchased a licence from the Church of Ireland. It was necessary because Limerick is not my home parish."

"How thoughtful of you to study our marriage laws and prepare in advance. What date suits you, Elizabeth?" Mrs Bennet enquired.

"We cannot marry!" Elizabeth cried.

Cold fear seized his heart. He had let his passion overrule his sense and had lost her trust by moving forwards too quickly.

"I dare say you have no choice at this point, *Eilís*," Mrs Bennet admonished in a stern voice.

"I meant not immediately. I have every intention of marrying Mr Darcy, but I have not regained sufficient strength. When my health is restored, we shall marry."

"You did not seem too indisposed a minute ago," Mrs Bennet quipped.

It was clear from whom Mr Bennet had inherited his dry wit.

"No, I am much improved, but I do not feel strong enough to brave being the centre of derision. It is my fate, and I only lack the courage to face people's talk and not care three straws about it."

"Dear girl, you have nothing to worry about. The marquis is offering his support, and I dare say few would risk his displeasure. Besides, you need not brave the vipers' nests in London immediately. You can marry here, at Áth Dara, and go on a bridal trip where you may tarry as long as you like. What cannot wait is the wedding. In this I shall remain firm. It might seem incredible to you, but I was young once and know exactly what I just prevented."

Elizabeth was afforded a week while they made arrangements for a vicar to officiate the service. A marriage by a Catholic priest would not be legal, and their children would be considered illegitimate by the Hardwicke act.

#

The Child of Prague statue had been placed under a nearby bush on the night before the wedding to ensure clement weather.

Elizabeth's new friends—The Sisters of Presentation, Bridget with her infant daughter, and Sophie with her infant son—were at the church. Bridget waited for Elizabeth on the church steps and handed her a horseshoe to carry down the aisle.

"For luck," she said aloud before she leant in and whispered in Elizabeth's ear, "Not that you need it. You have been very sly, Miss Elizabeth. You completely forgot to mention that your gentleman was not only as rich as Croesus but devilishly handsome as well."

"He is the best of men," Elizabeth replied with a smirk.

"I wish you very happy, Miss Elizabeth, with your dashing gentleman. And you must allow me to express my gratitude to the marquis for saving the Grange. Speaking for us against I am their new cook."

"Thank you, Bridget, I am relieved you are allowed to stay."

"It is time." Uncle Henry cleared his throat, and interrupted the ladies' praise of him, to escort Elizabeth up the aisle.

Once the Holy Communion was over, while the congregation sung Ave Maria, Elizabeth laid flowers before the statue of the Virgin Mary. She said a prayer and took one stem from the bouquet. She intended to press it and give it to her mama in gratitude for her motherhood that had led her to this day.

On her way out, Sophie tried to toss an old shoe over her. Elizabeth ducked and barely avoided being hit on the head.

"Oh, I am so sorry. I tossed the shoe for luck, not to injure you."

"No harm done," Elizabeth assured her.

Breakfast was served in the ballroom. Elizabeth regarded the guests, and although they were all pleasant, she missed her family. She would invite them all to a ball, eventually, after they arrived in London. With any luck, that would alleviate some of the slight.

Tradition demanded the bride and groom open the ball, but Elizabeth had to forgo the lively Irish dances. Her stamina had not fully recovered from her illness, and Fitzwilliam had chosen to teach her to waltz in its stead.

Her health was mostly restored, and she looked forward to seeing Jane in particular. She had long since written to her family to let them know where she was. Her grandmother had sent an express to Mr Bennet the moment she fell ill, to inform him of his daughter's whereabouts and her dire ailment. Mr Bennet, who had long since guessed the truth, had not been pleased, and Elizabeth knew she had much to atone for.

"Dearest, you look pensive. Has the toil of a wedding sapped you of your strength?" Fitzwilliam enquired and slowed down the pace of their waltz.

"No, I am well. I was thinking about my family and the amends I must make. I was contemplating the bond we have tied and the ones I have done much to sever."

"Our links of love, albeit undone for a while, are firmly chained to last. You will reconcile with your family. No one who knows you can help but love you."

"Thomas Moore?"

"Not quite."

"Can such a delicate phrase be Fitzwilliam Darcy?"

Her husband blushed becomingly.

"You have been holding back from me. Do tell. Shall I find a book of poetry written in your hand in a secret compartment in your armoire?"

"No, but I do flatter myself that I have some artistic talent, though I should warn you not to expect any true proficiency."

"And in what direction does your talent lie?"

"That, I might show you, one day in the distant future when I am out of favour with you and I need to bargain for a smile."

"Ah, so mysterious. You are aware that I shall be searching for it."

"Of that I have no doubt."

"I wonder whether you are hiding it in London or at Pemberley."

Elizabeth studied her husband to see whether either of the locations might spur a response, and she detected a darkening in his eyes when she mentioned London. She would have to be patient and wait. It was most convenient to travel to London first, and it had been decided that they would all go together. Uncle Henry was needed in town for the Season, and her grandmother was eager to join him.

#

**A week later.**

Elizabeth acknowledged that long journeys were much pleasanter in late spring than during the winter months as the carriage pulled off Meryton's main road and entered Longbourn's avenue. The house looked exactly the same as when she left. Yet everything had changed. It was no longer her home; she was a guest.

Her mother must have been standing guard at one of the windows because she came running out of the house before the carriages had drawn to a halt. Her remaining sisters and Mr Bingley followed, but the latter lagged behind with Jane. Elizabeth tried to determine whether her mother was cross or pleased. She could not say for certain, but she was coming straight at her.

"How was... Oh, Mr Darcy. How good of you to come."

Mrs Bennet curtseyed to the master of Pemberley before she gave her hand to Uncle Henry whilst flagrantly overlooking her mother-in-law. Elizabeth had hoped that the rivalry between the two ladies had abated with time and distance. She was obviously wrong.

"Do come in," the current mistress of Longbourn tittered and herded them all towards the entrance.

Jane and Mr Bingley stayed in the background, and Elizabeth felt all the misery of not having written to her most beloved sister. But she was whisked away by a determined husband before she could do more than look at Jane, and she tried to convey her wistful remorse through her eyes. Fitzwilliam steered her towards Mary and bowed deeply.

"Thank you, Miss Bennet, for your frankness in conveying my deficiencies. It was a valuable lesson that I was in dire need of. I can assure you that none shall ever be repeated, but if you detect any inadequacy in my behaviour towards your sister, I give you leave to correct me."

"Thank you, Mr Darcy. You can depend upon my honesty regarding that subject."

With another deep bow in acknowledgement, Fitzwilliam led Elizabeth into Longbourn's west-facing parlour.

Her father stood in the middle of the room with his arms crossed over his chest.

"Elizabeth! May I have a word?"

"Shall I accompany you?" her grandmother offered, but she was brusquely denied by a scowl from her son.

Elizabeth was on her own, or so she thought, until she heard her husband's footsteps following her down the hall.

Mr Bennet stood, deprived of his usual philosophical composure, and leant heavily upon the back of his chair, like he was bracing himself before receiving some dreadful news.

"I suppose you too are entitled to hear Lizzy's explanation, Mr Darcy. Not that I would dare deny you anything at this point."

Her father turned his narrowed gaze at her, but she was not cowed.

"Have you any excuse for the difficult position you put your family in? The time I offered you to adjust has long since passed, and Mr Darcy has every right to demand satisfaction."

"Mary knew where I was. I confided my plans to her to be sure that if Mr Darcy came to claim the twenty thousand pounds, she could reveal my whereabouts and I could save my family from destitution."

"Why Mary?"

The hurt in her father's eyes was unmistakable, but he could not have seriously expected her to confide in him after he had failed to support her.

"Father, I married him."

All colour drained from her father's face, and he slumped into his chair.

"By him, I sincerely hope you mean Mr Darcy."

"Certainly."

Fitzwilliam stepped forwards. "You have nothing to fear from me."

"I was certain that you had discovered Elizabeth's hiding place and had come to demand compensation."

"You did not receive my letter?" Fitzwilliam asked incredulously.

"I did, but I have yet to open it. I could not imagine it would contain anything I wanted to hear."

Her father had not changed; he still avoided any unpleasantness—a trait Jane had inherited, but she eschewed disagreeableness with a sweetness and charm her father lacked.

"My grandmother must have informed you about Mr Darcy's visit."

"Yes, she did. But that was weeks ago, and she never mentioned anything about a wedding. Only that you were ill and that Mr Darcy had the means to your recovery. I supposed he had brought a physician, but I knew that would not sway you. Your headstrong and unwavering stubbornness would not relent for any mercenary reasons. Mr Darcy loves you, Elizabeth. It is obvious to everyone but you."

"I know. I was mistaken. I have been wrong in so many things, and I have nothing to offer in my defence," she admitted.

"Surely it is I who am culpable for not making it clear that my affections were solely fixed on you." Fitzwilliam would not allow her to be burdened with the blame she so richly deserved.

"Because I did not allow you to explain yourself," Elizabeth countered.

"Your quarrel about who is the most to blame is interesting, but I fear that Mrs Bennet has just received some news that will soon interrupt you."

*True enough,* Elizabeth thought as she listened to her mother screeching for Mr Bennet as she thundered down the hall. She flung open the door and entered.

"We are saved!"

"Yes, my dear. Mr Darcy and our Lizzy have married."

"Oh, I did not mean that. Did you know that Henry is the Marquis of Limerick and the Earl of Glentworth, Viscount Foxford, Baron Minister, and Clerk of the Crown? He is offering you the Earldom of Glentworth and a seat in the House of Lords. The patent is passed by a special remainder, like Admiral Nelson's barony, and it includes Henry's sister! He is begging for your assistance and claims that your vote would be invaluable. We shall no longer need to trespass on Mr Bingley's charity when you die because there is property attached to the title. It is in the south of Ireland, but one cannot be demanding when one may be homeless. And it is ours to keep. The title is secured by heirs of the male body. The first son born to one of our daughters will be the next Earl of Glentworth. Oh, I do hope dear Lydia will soon have a son. She has been married the longest..."

Mr Bennet shuddered and opened his mouth to speak, but he was not quick enough, and his wife had not finished.

"I am going to faint! Lady Glentworth has such a nice ring to it... Lord Limerick has a house in town, on Portman Square, and he has invited us all to stay for the entire Season! I shall go distracted with all the packing needed, and my daughters must all have new dresses. You should order a new carriage too. Heaven forfend! I must inform Lady Lucas."

"Mrs Bennet!" Mr Bennet raised his voice in an attempt to curb his wife, which went unnoticed.

"Lady Lucas has only one unmarried daughter remaining at home and must have time to aid a countess. I shall go immediately. I have no time to spare."

Mrs Bennet flung herself around the still seated Mr Bennet's neck and kissed his cheek.

"I am ecstatic. I have not been so happy since the day of your proposal."

Mrs Bennet sailed out of the room, tittering about sleeve lengths and jewels but returned immediately to envelop her daughter in a fierce embrace.

"I am so distracted that I almost forgot to offer you my felicitations. You are not to be disheartened because your Mr Darcy has no title. He is so rich he is as good as a lord, and Pemberley is everything lovely. But I shall do my best to have the old Austen earldom resurrected. I am certain dear Lord Limerick will make himself useful. I wonder whether the Prince of Wales can break an entail…"

Mrs Bennet released Elizabeth and left in a flurry of skirts. Mr Bennet rose to his feet and stalked after his wife but then changed his mind. He turned to the parlour where his mother was informing the flummoxed Mary and Kitty about the change in their circumstances.

"You have been very sly by telling my wife about the earldom," Mr Bennet said accusingly to his mother. "I shall have no choice but to remove to town for the Session."

"Precisely. I learnt from the master who impressed upon his wife that she would starve in the hedgerows upon her husband's demise. You have had enough time to *adjust* to your new circumstances and should be ashamed of yourself for not relieving your family's concerns about the entail on Longbourn."

Her father bowed his head.

"How could you put your family in such a difficult position? Not to forget Lydia's patched up marriage. Had I known you would hide in your library with your nightcap and powdering gown, I would never have left Longbourn. How could you let Lydia marry that ne'er-do-well? Not a month goes by where he is not in some sort of financial pinch or at odds with his superiors. I should know because she writes to me frequently, begging for funds.

"But it is done, and I blame you more than I blame myself. A grown man of nine-and-forty cannot shirk his duties, and I shall not leave my granddaughters to suffer such a misfortune. We shall, all of us, adjourn to town, where I shall find your wife and remaining daughters a governess. Mrs Bennet should not be allowed into polished society until she has mastered proper comportment. I can see that I have embarrassed you. Good. You ought to feel it."

Mr Bennet nodded, properly chastised by his mother, and had nothing to say in his defence.

"On that note, I might as well inform you that your time to adjust to your new rank is at an end." The marquis had remained quiet during his sister's rant but had some news of his own to relate. "At my advanced age, there are no certainties, and you have a lot to learn about the House of Lords before I retire. Therefore, I have addressed the matter of your title. Your seat is waiting for you, and from the first day of Session, *you* are the Earl of Glentworth."

"Am I to have no say in this?" Mr Bennet blustered.

"No," the marquis immediately replied.

Mr Bennet nodded; he knew his uncle well enough to realise he was immovable.

During the heated debate, Fitzwilliam had sought Mr Bingley, and Elizabeth approached Jane. She owed her a sincere apology for leaving and another for not writing to her. In retrospect, her mad dash to Ireland appeared nonsensical.

Jane's smile was strained, and even Mr Bingley looked stern. Elizabeth grabbed her sister's hands and caught her eye.

"Mrs Bingley, I have been utterly selfish and infinitely stupid. Can you ever forgive me?"

"Of course."

Jane embraced her, and even Mr Bingley offered her his hand. Neither could bear any form of animosity for more than a few minutes.

"May I wish you joy?"

"You certainly may, and I intend to atone for the slight of marrying abroad by hosting a ball as soon as we have settled in London. Would you mind taking a stroll in the garden with me? I need to stretch my legs after being cooped up in the carriage for so long."

Jane understood the need for privacy and acquiesced. They walked arm in arm out of the door, with Mr Bingley and Fitzwilliam following a few steps behind.

"I have been informed that you became terribly ill."

"I did, but I have recovered completely."

Elizabeth told Jane the abridged version of everything that had transpired since she went on her deceptive visit to Matlock House. Jane was charmingly forgiving and impressed by her clever sister. Elizabeth could not bring herself to address her concerns about the rumours that must be circling the parlours in London. She would know soon enough how they would be received by the beau-monde.

Elizabeth glanced at her husband, who was conversing with Mr Bingley. He wore a content expression, and it occurred to her that he had missed his friend.

"I shall forgive you if you promise me that we shall never separate again and that you will come to me with your troubles, regardless of their nature. Mr Bingley has been fraught with worry for his friend, and I cannot bear to see him thus."

"I honestly did not think my disappearance would injure Mr

Darcy," Elizabeth defended herself.

"Then you truly are stupid."

"Jane!"

Jane smiled but did not retract her words.

#

Within a week, they had all moved to town. Elizabeth and her husband were afforded a month of seclusion, as was usual for a newly wedded couple, and spent most of it tucked away at an unknown destination in the south of England. Their first call upon their return was Matlock House. Fitzwilliam had explained plainly to his relations that it was necessary to apologise, and even the earl relented after grumbling his displeasure about humiliating himself by begging for forgiveness.

A united family apologised to the newly appointed Lady Elizabeth. Mr Bennet had accepted his fate as the new Earl of Glentworth and had taken his seat in the House of Lords with more pleasure than he had anticipated. He thrived having a valiant excuse to leave his tittering females for the garrulous gentlemen.

Elizabeth chose to forgive the Matlocks without delay because her dear Darcy had so few family members left. She would not deprive him of the ones he had. Secure in her husband's regard, she even included the former Lady Baslow. She could not trust the viscountess, but she had every faith in Fitzwilliam. No man went to such lengths and grovelled so incessantly for a woman he did not love with all his heart.

# Chapter 16 *The Savour of Remorse*

"I must look a fright!"

It was their first morning after their return to London, and they were languishing in the master's chamber long after breakfast had been served.

"When I have you thus, in my arms, naked and possessed, your love declared and proved, trembling, yielding, fervently impassioned, and panting for breath, it creates the most beautiful, beguiling, bewitching image. Not even in my wildest imagination could I have conjured such a delight. If I could have a miniature to carry in my breast pocket…"

"How scandalous, Mr Fitzwilliam Darcy!"

Her husband smiled, branded her with burning kisses down her neck, and left their bed completely naked to rifle through his armoire. From a hidden drawer, he pulled out a sketch book and a piece of charcoal.

"So…it is in London you have been hiding your secret."

"Enchantress of my soul and body, will you let your worshipper draw your exquisite lines?"

"You know how to draw? Then you must teach me."

Elizabeth turned on her side without a stitch of fabric covering her body. To lie exposed and be immortalised on paper elevated her to rakish delight.

"I might not draw all your rich excess of lovely charms, as some are subject to my solitary devotion. I am not prepared to share them, even with my charcoal. The glorious, shapely—"

Want blazed through her body and encouraged her to act brazenly. She let her fingers travel the curve of her hip and upwards. His sharp intake of breath emboldened her further, and she continued her exploration of herself. Her hand grazed her breast, and in the periphery of her vision, she saw that Fitzwilliam had frozen in place with his piece of charcoal hovering in mid-air. Her husband was unable to resist the bliss only his wife could provide and was at her side in a moment.

"This is what drew me—akin to the divine." Fitzwilliam kissed the peak of her breast. "To enshrine yourself in a form so fair may prove fatal to your devout husband's welfare."

Elizabeth laughed. "Your poetry needs more practice."

"Did you know"—he laid his hand upon her knee and pushed it aside—"that when you touched my knee at the hunting tower..."

"Yes..." Elizabeth gulped whilst he drew lazy circles on her knee.

"I had to move away because I was imagining your hand travelling upwards, and you would have been scandalised indeed, had I not," he explained whilst letting his hand travel upwards.

"Are you that easily aroused?" Elizabeth teased, but her smirk proved she was pleased.

"No. Only when touched by a certain siren..."

Her husband demonstrated how his mouth could be used for purposes other than eloquent speech, and their winged passion took flight.

#

Darcy was expelled from his own home, or at least that was what it felt like. He had perhaps been too attentive. Elizabeth's bout of illness had made him protective in a smothering, oppressive manner. His darling wife had laughed

223

at his foreboding, assured him she was quite well, completely recovered, and in need of female companionship. He had not left her side since their month of seclusion ended three weeks ago.

Loath as he was to leave his bride for even the briefest of moments, the incentives to make himself scarce outweighed the lure she had on him. Elizabeth had made new friends the moment she entered London society and had invited twenty young ladies to the house for a salon in the name of art. She had persuaded the renowned sculptor Catherine Andras, who was best known for her wax models, to speak. The artist's list of merits was impressive, as her works were displayed at the Royal Academy of Arts, and she had been appointed modeller of wax to Queen Charlotte, but that did not entice him to participate as the only gentleman in attendance. Elizabeth had saucily begged him to stay and laughed gaily when he rejected the notion most vehemently. He dared not even hide in his study lest one of the tittering females got lost and entered his sanctuary, or worse, forced him to join them. No, he had best haul himself off to the safest place he knew—White's. The gentlemen's club would be free of those creatures he found so difficult to interact with. Well, not Elizabeth; he had to exclude his wife from his censure of the female population, but to be outnumbered by twenty ladies was insupportable. Hence, he was nursing a tumbler of brandy in the company of several of his male acquaintances.

He did not respond to the gentle teasing his newly wedded state induced but listened to the chatter that surrounded him in silence. He was yearning to go home to a house empty of guests. Once, when his business had dragged out, he had found her waiting for him, reading on the window-seat wearing only her shift.

"So, she finally said yes."

He nodded absentmindedly to the rhetorical question.

"I heard you tied the knot at the Marquis of Limerick's estate. I sit rather close to him in the Lords and could not help but eavesdrop when the surprising news was mentioned. Is Mrs Darcy connected to his lordship?" enquired Lord Grenville.

"Yes, Lady Elizabeth is the daughter of his heir, the Earl of Glentworth. Her paternal grandmother is his lordship's sister. He leaves no offspring of his own."

"I know, though it is quite irregular, but the peerage was determined to elevate him to marquis. He was granted the marquisate by writ, expressly stating that his heir presumptive would inherit the title. I have never met the heir, but I have heard that he is an indolent sort with no taste for politics. It is a shame because the marquis has been instrumental in my quest towards Catholic emancipation. Not that we have met with success yet..."

"I am sorry to hear that."

"Have you ever considered a seat in the Commons, Mr Darcy?"

"No, I cannot say that I have."

"What a shame. I am convinced you would do well."

Darcy made no reply. It was not his wont to boast, and he was no more interested in politics than Mr Bennet had been.

"Did not your family have an earldom that became extinct?"

"Yes, but that was a few generations ago."

"The earldom of Austen, was it not?"

"Yes."

"Mr Darcy!"

The Earl of Buxton was approaching, and Darcy could not say he minded the interruption.

"Good evening, Lord Buxton."

"I wondered whether I could have a word in private?"

"Of course," Darcy replied in bewilderment. The earl had recently rented a house on Grosvenor Square, but he did not know the gentleman personally and wondered why he needed to speak to him privately. He had been an acquaintance of his father's, not his. But Elizabeth had made his daughter's acquaintance and had invited her to her salon. That must be his reason.

"I am glad I happened upon you, Mr Darcy, for reasons that will soon be revealed."

Lord Buxton led him to one of the private parlours, where he found a very drunk Viscount Crawford.

"I am at a loss as to what to do with him, but I am convinced that he had better return home, if he can be persuaded to do so..."

The viscount was not only deeply in his cups but uncommonly maudlin. He was spouting a lot of nonsense, so Darcy ordered his carriage and took him to Matlock House. With the aid of the butler and two footmen, he carried him to his chamber and ordered coffee just as Crawford became violently ill. The cleaning took a while, and Darcy quickly penned a letter to Elizabeth, explaining why he would not return for the night, and gave it to the butler when he returned with the coffee.

"Have a boy run to Darcy House with this. Immediately. And under no circumstances should we be disturbed unless I ring for you." He handed over the note, resolved to suffer a night of vigilance. What he had discerned from his cousin's hardly intelligible mutterings should not become publicly known. To be certain, he locked all the doors and prepared to argue, but Crawford had fallen asleep. Quite soundly judging by his loud snoring.

Darcy pulled off his boots with great difficulty, settled on the sofa by the fire, and waited for his cousin to awaken. A frank conversation was long due.

The door to the adjacent chamber rattled.

"Darcy?"

*How the hell does she know I am here?*

"Be quiet. Crawford is sleeping."

"I would like a word with you. In private."

"I cannot imagine that we have anything to discuss, and I am rather busy at the moment."

"Will you at least come to me before you leave?"

"I very much doubt it."

"I did not know you to be cruel, Mr Darcy."

"I think of it as a kindness, to protect your reputation, and mine. Good night, Lady Crawford."

To his relief, her light footsteps moved away from the door.

#

It was rather early to receive guests, so Elizabeth surmised the knock on the door must be her husband returning from Matlock House. She waited to hear his voice, but it was a lady who answered her butler.

She had missed Fitzwilliam dearly and could not be at peace until he returned. It had been her first night without him since they married, and a much longer time since he had not wished her good night in person.

Mr Murray entered with a calling card that made her heart flutter. She procrastinated for a few seconds before she asked him to send the guest in. Given a choice, she would have preferred to have Fitzwilliam present at all her encounters with the former Lady Baslow.

"Lady Crawford to see you, ma'am."

"Thank you, Mr Murray. We need a fresh pot of tea and some lemon tarts."

The butler bowed and left.

"Please, be seated," Elizabeth offered, and a wary looking Lady

Crawford did as requested. She had dark circles beneath her eyes that she had tried to cover, but it was to no avail in the harsh morning light.

"I just wanted to inform you that your husband spent the night at Matlock House."

"I already knew. Fitzwilliam sent me a letter to that effect last night."

What was her purpose? If she expected a willing ear for one of her fanciful stories, she would be sorely disappointed.

"Yes, he spent the night in our private quarter—"

"Let me, before you continue, disabuse you of any notion that I shall listen to or believe any sordid tale you fabricate about my husband. Not even if it is confirmed by your trusted lady's maid. Especially not then."

"I swear that I have never lied to you."

"You most definitely have, and this conversation is over."

Elizabeth rose to demonstrate her resolve. Mr Murray was there immediately, ready to escort the lady out of the door. Fitzwilliam must have left special instructions should Lady Crawford visit when he was not at home. His solicitous consideration warmed her heart and settled its pounding rhythm.

"No, please. Mr Darcy and my husband have sequestered themselves in Crawford's chamber and have not allowed anyone to enter since last night. My husband's mood has been dreadful lately, and I cannot help but worry that his intentions towards his cousin might be sinister."

Elizabeth scowled.

"What have you told him?"

"Nothing!"

"I do not believe you, but I shall accompany you to Matlock House."

Lady Crawford winced as she left the house. Her step faltered, but the Darcys' butler had followed his mistress and came to the lady's rescue.

"Are you well, Lady Crawford?"

"It is only a headache. I was blinded by the sun, that is all."

"I have willow bark and could make you a tisane if you like."

"No, thank you. I have found that willow bark only makes it worse."

The two ladies walked in silence up the steps of Matlock House, where they were met by several loud crashes and a blood-curdling howl. Elizabeth ran up the stairs, but a footman was there first. He had already tried the door and found it locked. The viscount shouted for him to leave, and for a brief moment, Elizabeth worried that Fitzwilliam was injured. It was a balm to her soul when he confirmed his cousin's order, and the few words she heard through the door convinced her that the servants, at least, should not be present. She shooed them all downstairs and was happy to find the countess in the hall.

"Lady Elizabeth, what a pleasure to see you so soon after your lovely salon. I have questions about the ball and one of a more private nature. Please join me in the parlour."

Elizabeth acquiesced, and Lady Crawford followed. She tugged off her gloves, and Elizabeth noticed brownish spots on her palms. That must be the reason she had not taken them off at Darcy House. She put on a pair of lighter ones for indoor use, and Elizabeth found other things to occupy her thoughts.

"What can you tell me about Lord Buxton's daughter, Lady Ada? I understand that this is their first year leasing a house on Grosvenor Square."

"It is, but why do you ask?"

"It occurred to me that she might suit Richard. I quite despair he will ever marry because he is so fastidious, and beauty is not enough to entice him. He tends to like quiet, intellectual women, and she is very handsome—"

"And old," Lady Crawford interjected.

Neither the countess nor Elizabeth paid her any mind and refrained from pointing out that she was about the same age as Lady Crawford herself.

"Pray, what is her fortune?" Lady Matlock enquired.

"It is fifty thousand pounds." Elizabeth smiled.

"That is a substantial sum," Lady Matlock mused.

"Yet it is the least of her virtues. I like her very much and would welcome her into the family, but I can only introduce them. It must be up to Colonel Fitzwilliam and Lady Ada whether they would suit."

"Of course. I was not suggesting we should sign a marriage contract, simply ensure that they meet," Lady Matlock assured her.

It was a scheme Elizabeth did not oppose.

#

Darcy must have dozed off, because the next time he blinked, the sun had risen. His cousin was sitting up in his bed, looking somewhat the worse for wear. Not only did he look ill from his night of revelry, but he was thinner than he had been the last time they met.

"She was not a virgin."

Viscount Crawford did not mince his words. Darcy understood whom he meant and what he was accusing him of.

"Do you want to know the most pathetic part?"

"I am not certain…"

"I paid my father's physician a thousand pounds to state she was untouched. My father demanded an examination to prove her claim before he would sanction the marriage. I paid the doctor to tell a lie should it prove to be false. Is that not rich? Despite her urine being clear as crystal[6], I had my suspicions, and it has been irrevocably confirmed."

Crawford launched out of his bed and took Darcy by surprise. His hands grabbed his neck before he had the wherewithal to defend himself. But Crawford did not regain his balance, and they tumbled to the floor, knocking over a table in their descent. Unfortunately, he landed on his back with his opponent on top. A vase smashed into hundreds of pieces, and the harsh sound made the viscount flinch. It was enough of a distraction for Darcy to gain the upper hand. He pushed his arms between his cousin's and grabbed his head, pressed his thumbs into his eye sockets, and butted his head into his face.

With a loud cry, Crawford let go of Darcy's neck to cradle his nose. Darcy pushed him off and jumped to his feet. They were both panting hard when someone banged on the door and rattled the handle.

"Leave us!" the viscount ordered.

"But sir—" a Matlock footman protested.

"Do as he says. You can clean in here later," Darcy added.

Crawford rose too, but his anger had abated, and he slumped into a chair. The footman walked away, leaving them eyeing each other warily.

"It was not my doing," Darcy claimed with conviction.

"Are you absolutely certain?"

"Quite."

"You admitted that you *embraced* her on the night of the thunderstorm. It happens that close intimacy evolves, and caution is forgotten in the heat of the moment."

"That was as far from *a heated moment* as you can possibly imagine. Lady Crawford was hysterical, screaming like an Irish banshee...I should probably not call her that."

"No, you should not."

"Elizabeth might take umbrage about me using a derogatory remark about the Irish. She is of Irish descent after all. What other things scream shrilly besides Mrs Bennet? Oh yes, a piglet."

"Are you calling my wife a piglet?" the viscount enquired incredulously.

"No, but she sounded much like one when she ran hysterically around her chamber. Perhaps a headless chicken is a more apt description... I contemplated slapping her, but I dared not hit a lady. I caught her wildly jerking arms in an embrace to restore her to her senses, and she calmed nicely as soon as her butler entered the room. I conveniently left her in his care and returned to my guest room. I am certain the maid that stoked my fire through the night can confirm it."

"Let me see your hands!"

"Why?" Darcy demanded to know, but Crawford grabbed his hands and turned them over to study the palms whilst mumbling to himself.

"And the soles of your feet."

"I demand to know why you are examining me!"

"Sit down and be quiet."

Darcy worried that his cousin had lost his mind completely and acquiesced in sheer bewilderment as Crawford pulled the stockings off his feet. After a quick look, he released them abruptly.

"I do not suppose you are willing to pull down your breeches and let me inspect your manhood for sores and the running of the rains?"

"Absolutely not!"

Darcy grabbed his stockings and crossed to the opposite side of the room, as far away from his deranged cousin as possible, to right his attire.

The viscount slumped in defeat and asked aloud to no one in particular, "If not you, who could it be?"

"Her husband seems to be the obvious choice," Darcy reminded the viscount.

"You would think so, but I have it on good authority that Sir Lawrence was uninterested in that sort of pursuit, with a female..."

"I am not surprised. I have had my suspicions."

"In danger of repeating myself, then who? A footman? A gardener? I cannot imagine she would stoop so low as to cuckold her husband with one of his servants, but she has led a sheltered life without much access to male company..."

A fanciful notion hit Darcy like a bolt of lightning from a cloudless sky. It was farfetched, and he had no evidence but for a correspondence that appeared suspicious. Why had she sought *his* aid in financial matters when no one was less fit for the endeavour?

"You have someone in mind. I can tell by your scowl," Crawford accused him.

"I do, but I have no proof, and it is highly unlikely."

"Who?"

"Wickham. She wrote to him after the funeral, requesting his help dealing with her financial matters."

The viscount chuckled mirthlessly.

"He is the last man I would ever ask for financial advice. But... is he not married and living up north?"

"He is married to Lady Elizabeth's youngest sister and is currently enlisted in the regulars in Newcastle. But this most likely happened years ago."

"I doubt I shall ever know."

"You could have an honest conversation with your wife—or

let the matter rest. Whilst we are speaking about wives, I shall return to my own, now that we have resolved our differences."

"She is barren."

"Elizabeth?"

"No, Celia."

"You have not been married long enough for such dismal thoughts. You should try to take your mind off your bleak conjectures and engage in something pleasant. Like a trip to the sea. I have heard that sea bathing is beneficial for your health."

"It is not that. I suppose you know about a lady's monthly indisposition?"

Darcy nodded; the conversation had taken a decidedly awkward turn.

"She has not had one since we married, yet she shows no sign of increasing. I browbeat that infernal maid of hers, and she admitted that Celia only has them once or twice a year. I have conferred with several doctors, and they all concluded she will not be able to conceive."

"I am sorry to hear that."

A long silence ensued, and Darcy was about to take his leave when his cousin spoke up again.

"That is not even the worst of it."

Darcy waited patiently for his cousin to continue.

"She has an advanced stage of the French disease, and it can no longer be concealed. She has demanded to attend your ball, even though I strongly advised her not to. The flesh around her nose has begun to decay, and only a bucket of Pear's powder can conceal it."

Darcy did not know what to say and dearly wished Elizabeth was there to comfort his cousin.

"Do you—"

"Yes. It has been months since I was first alarmed by the unexpected evil. A certain heat appeared in the part of my body sacred to Cupid. Very much like the distemper that Venus, when crossed, brings upon her votaries. I have had the rashes and sores, but they are gone for now. For how long, nobody knows, but probably much longer than Celia. It has gone to her head, and I suspect it already had last year when she made up that story about you seducing her. If I am to be honest, I could not believe it of you. It is not in your character.

"I only wish that I had seen the signs of her illness at that time and saved myself a lot of heartache. Can you believe that I was never clapped during my promiscuous years, frequenting every brothel and bagnio in London, but contracted the great pox from my wife?"

"I do not know what to say," Darcy remarked in earnestness.

"Of course, I used an English riding coat, you know, one of those preservative sheaths to protect myself whilst tumbling with the light-skirts. My health has always been of great consequence to me, but I had not imagined that I would need protection from my own wife...

"The sheath is an armour against satisfaction as well as disease. You have been much wiser. I should have paid more heed to *The Surgeons Assistant* by John Brown."

"That old rubbish is more than a hundred years old."

"It clearly states that you are more likely to be infected by a beautiful woman than an ugly one. Something about the level of heat and desire that makes you more receptive to the disease than a less passionate embrace. You should be safe, Darcy. Elizabeth will not inflame you as much."

"I resent the implication. Elizabeth is the most beautiful woman of my acquaintance."

"She is pretty, but her allure is not her countenance. It is her wit—and perhaps her figure, which *is* displayed to best advantage."

"I could demand satisfaction for such a speech," Darcy gritted through clenched teeth.

"I do not give a damn. In fact, I would prefer to die on the field of honour. You know the saying—'one night with Venus, a lifetime with Mercury'. The earldom will go to Richard either way."

Darcy's ire depleted when he could not gainsay his cousin. He could not promise that all would be well; and even should he outlive his wife, it would be dishonest and irresponsible of him to afflict the disease upon another lady to beget the sought-after heir.

"Are you receiving any treatment?"

"Yes. I have been covered in poultices with mercury, China-root, the root of soapwort, and burdock. I have also used the scrotum truss. It is working, so I am having the month of fumigation after the end of the Season. Celia will have the same."

"Does Lady Crawford know that she is ill?"

"Not that she has the French pox. She believes she has scurvy."

The viscount lay down on his bed and covered his eyes with his arm. Darcy took that as a sign that his cousin needed privacy, and he righted his apparel as best he could. As he turned the door handle, his cousin spoke up.

"For what it is worth, you got the better deal. Lady Elizabeth is lovely and vivacious. She will make you an excellent wife because she has substance, and she obviously adores you. Do not squander it, Darcy."

"I have no intention of doing so," he promised as he closed the door.

As he descended the stairs, the melodious voice of a woman tickled his ears, and his feet steered him towards the silvery notes. He entered the parlour and found his Elizabeth having tea with the countess and the viscountess. The latter he deliberately overlooked.

Elizabeth welcomed him with a smile, while her eyes roamed over his dishevelled appearance. Wrinkles of worry bloomed between her brows. After a distressing morning, he needed his wife's calming presence. Preferably in their private rooms.

"Shall we go home, dearest?"

"Yes." She rose with alacrity. "Lady Matlock and I have the details for our ball perfectly in order. Good day, Lady Matlock, Lady Crawford." She dipped into a perfect curtsey and hastened to take the arm he offered.

The light touch did much to relieve his grief, and he escorted his wife out of the room.

"How was your evening? Did the salon turn out well?"

"It was a remarkable success, and I made a new friend—Lady Ada Buxton. She is Scottish and the daughter of Lord Buxton. They have a town home here on Grosvenor Square, and I predict that Cousin Richard will like her very much because her fortune is fifty thousand pounds."

He dared not ask why but relished basking in the twinkling of her eyes.

"I see that you dare not ask, but I had an enlightening conversation with him whilst touring Rosings Park. Amongst other things, we established that the price for a second son of an earl is that exact amount. Now you and the viscount have married, the countess is as eager as ever to marry off her last son. Why, I know not, but what kind of relation would I be if I did not endeavour to aid her in any way I can?"

"I am inclined to endorse any venture that brings a sparkle to your eyes. If I must sacrifice a cousin, so be it."

"Excellent. I shall invite them both to dinner."

"Minx."

Later, after they separated to ready for the night, Elizabeth came to his chamber as agreed. Darcy was sitting in front of the fire, studying the palms of his hands. He hardly noticed her entrance until she leant over his shoulder and kissed his cheek.

"I want you to study the palms of my hands, Elizabeth."

"Why?" she asked in bewilderment.

"I want you to see for yourself that I have no rashes or brown spots."

"No, I can see that you do not." Elizabeth traced the lines in his hands. "But I noticed that Lady Crawford does."

"Do you know what it signifies?"

"No, I have to admit that I do not."

"She has the French disease."

"Syphilis?" Elizabeth whispered.

"I am afraid so, and it is far gone. There is no doubt that it has affected her brain, and I cannot believe that I missed the changes in her personality. My only excuse is that it came on so gradually that I failed to notice. I should not have questioned that you sent her from the house, nor should I have doubted your words when you told me about the accusations she made in the aftermath of the thunderstorm. For that I am heartily sorry, but I am relieved to vanquish the last of your doubts regarding my constancy. As you see, I have no rash. According to her lady's maid, Lady Crawford caught the disease eight years ago, about the time she married Sir Lawrence. If I had lain with her, I would have contracted the pox too. The viscount has…"

"I already knew you were speaking the truth. Have I not said so?"

"You have, but I was not certain whether you were mollifying me, sparing my feelings, and not being entirely truthful."

"I value honesty above all else and would not prevaricate, even to spare your feelings, and I hope you will offer me the same courtesy."

"I promise."

# Chapter 17 Nocturnal Observations

"I hope that a polished society ball will not prove too dull and vain for such a vivacious creature as you, Lady Elizabeth."

"Fear not, Mr Darcy. I am certain I shall discover enough folly and nonsense to keep me entertained."

Ballet dancers were illuminated by a dozen torches as they performed on the steps of Darcy House. Their guests were led through a rose arch to greet the family in the receiving line. The Matlocks, the Glentworths, and Lord Limerick had joined them to offer their support at Lady Elizabeth's first major event.

It was not the first time Elizabeth had encountered the former Lady Baslow since her return to London, but it was the first time in full lady's armour. She looked resplendent in her green ball gown, and her skin was flawless. There were no signs of the dark circles under her eyes; they were hidden under a thick layer of powder. But Elizabeth knew what was amiss and what had spurred Lady Matlock's sudden interest in the colonel's marital state.

The Bingleys had yet to arrive, but the musicians were tuning their instruments, and the newly wedded couple was opening the ball.

"You should join the line of dancers," Lady Matlock prompted.

"I was hoping to greet my sister before the dancing commenced," Elizabeth lamented.

"We both know that Lady Jane is unlikely to be blamed for their tardiness. I shall stay until they arrive and convey your regrets for not being able to greet your sister upon her arrival," Lady Matlock offered without blaming their delay on the most likely culprit—Miss Bingley. She had received an invitation for the sole purpose of sparing Lady Jane's feelings.

Elizabeth decided to accept her ladyship's offer and expressed her gratitude. She owed her much more for making her feel welcomed into the family and for introducing her to her ladyship's eclectic group of friends.

Elizabeth laced her arm with her husband's and entered the ballroom. She called the minuet played at the close of the first act of Mozart's Don Giovanni. The slow, etiquette-laden steps' basic floor pattern was the letter Z, and the dance was prefaced with stylish bows and curtsies to partners and spectators. It behoved her to remove the Darcy name from the Edensor scandal, and she had decorated Darcy House in the colour of innocence. All the tablecloths and flowers were white, and she had ordered a ball gown to match, with embroidered lilies.

The Darcys' status as a newly wedded couple took precedence over social position, and they formed the top of the line. All eyes settled upon them, and Elizabeth's cheeks bloomed under the scrutiny. No one had said anything untoward to her in the receiving line, but that could have been because the Earl of Matlock, the Earl of Glentworth, and the Marquis of Limerick had been surrounding her. In the middle of the ballroom, she was on display, and the interest she perceived was not all good.

"You are blushing, Elizabeth. I wonder whether your thoughts are similar to mine."

She thought not, judging by his slightly hooded eyes, but his expression made her smile. His unwavering attentiveness inclined her to agree to every favour he asked for.

"I was thinking it is time for me to draw your likeness."

It was Fitzwilliam's turn to redden, but he was so fortunate that it was only his ears that turned pink, and they were conveniently concealed under his thick mop of hair.

"Do you draw?" he asked nonchalantly.

"No, not at all, but lack of accomplishment has never deterred me from pursuing new pleasures."

"An admirable trait, I am sure. Which reminds me…I have yet to convince you to go riding with me."

Elizabeth was trapped, and she pursed her lips for the lack of a witty retort.

"Are you afraid of horses?"

"No."

"Have you been thrown and injured yourself?"

"No, I have not."

"That is good news."

"Why?"

"I remember you once said that you were not a horse woman, and after our docile ride to Edensor, I mistakenly believed that you were afraid, or had taken a bad fall. While those can be difficult to overcome, the want of experience can be easily remedied."

"Not on Rotten Row?" she enquired with concern.

"No, of course not. When we return to Derbyshire, we shall practise in the privacy of Pemberley's paths. Until you are proficient, we can always take the phaeton or stroll in the park if you are so inclined."

"Perhaps early in the morning, before the fashionable hour."

"I very much doubt that any of us will rise early on the morrow. In town, events like these usually continue well after dawn."

"Yes, and I have a likeness to take. I have not forgotten, you see. Although you tried so eloquently to distract me."

Fitzwilliam chuckled and drew the attention of everyone in the room. Miss Bingley's ostentatious and late entrance went completely unnoticed. Even her friends shunned her. After they discovered that *Mrs Darcy's* Irish relations included the Marquis of Limerick and that her father was the Earl of Glentworth, most thought it best to keep their distance from the supercilious and disparaging Miss Bingley. Mr Bingley's new wife, Lady Jane, was much more pleasant, and she was the daughter of an earl...

#

Lord Liverpool returned Elizabeth to Darcy after their set ended. They had not spoken to each other for more than an hour. Her previous partner had been Lord Cromford, and Darcy had used the opportunity after their set ended to introduce his wife to some of his friends.

"I heard you took a dip in your lake, Mr Darcy. Rather late, in November, to go swimming..." Lord Liverpool snickered.

"Have you not heard? Ice bathing is all the rage. It is supposed to be beneficial for your health!" Elizabeth exclaimed and pinched the inside of her husband's arm to remove the scowl suffusing his countenance. The surprise he then sported was not the look she had hoped for. She had noticed that his expression usually softened when he looked at her, but pinching was obviously not the best way to garner his attention.

Lord Liverpool regarded her with disbelief but did not protest and soon removed himself to greet an acquaintance. It was the first time anyone had mentioned the lake incident at Pemberley, and Elizabeth found that she had worried over nothing.

"I do not care much for the Season in London," Elizabeth admitted.

"Have you not made any new friends this evening, my love?"

"None worth keeping. It appears to me that most society ladies are always hunting for a husband, and when they do marry, they covet someone else's husband."

Darcy tried to hide his pleasure; it was a relief to him that Elizabeth was not exceedingly enchanted with the society he kept mostly for appearance. There were those among the guests he counted as friends, but there were several he barely tolerated. He was loath to participate in every event of the Season, flitting from house to house morning, noon, and night. He preferred to be fastidious about which events he attended.

"An astute and accurate description, I am sure," he belatedly replied.

Elizabeth raised an eyebrow and studied him with an amused expression.

"Those ladies that descended upon *you* rushed away like a gale had blown them from your company. What can you have told them to have been left so utterly in peace?"

"I have discovered the most effective method to relieve myself of simpering females. I talk solely about my wife, to the detriment of every other topic. Any subject can easily be guided in that direction, and no one is offended by a devoted husband. I cannot claim to mind that they all perceive me as rather dull."

Elizabeth laughed quietly and let her hand travel up and down his arm. She was definitely pleased by his admission but should be careful touching him, or they would be ascending the stairs to the master suite in a trice. She knew exactly what she was doing; a twitch at the corner of her mouth betrayed her.

"I should like to dance, husband."

Darcy made a show of looking around for a suitable partner.

"Which of these dull gentlemen would you like me to introduce you to before the next set commences, Lady Elizabeth?"

His eyes landed on a portly, elderly baronet.

"I should prefer to forgo any more introductions and dance with you, if you would ask me."

"It is not proper to dance with one's spouse more than once."

"Then let us create a scandal before Georgiana is out and we must adhere to the severest strictures."

Darcy bowed and offered her his hand, and she rewarded him with one of her brilliant smiles.

"Your wishes are my command, my lady."

Elizabeth giggled and took his hand.

"I know, but with great power comes great responsibility. I shall be careful not to abuse my authority."

Darcy was right. The last guests stayed until the morning dawned. The clock had chimed six strokes before he fell exhausted into his bed, and he never noticed when Elizabeth joined him.

#

Elizabeth found her husband sprawled out on the bed, naked and soundly asleep. It was too good an opportunity to miss, and she tiptoed to the armoire and opened the drawer as quietly as possible. Withdrawing the sketchbook and a pencil, she set to work. She accomplished her aim within minutes, then she lay down beside her husband and fell instantly asleep.

The sun was high in the sky before she was awakened by a feather tickling her nose.

"Sleeping beauty, the day arrived a few hours ago judging by the position of the sun."

Elizabeth stretched and yawned. It might be afternoon, but her body did not know the time.

"You could draw my likeness, and I can lie completely still until you have finished."

Fitzwilliam chuckled; he was not fooled. She had never asked him to draw her before and usually became rather shy when he suggested it.

"Splendid idea," he remarked and rose from the bed.

Elizabeth pretended to yawn and hid a smirk behind her hand. She hoped he would not be offended by her meagre attempt to draw his likeness.

Fitzwilliam opened the drawer and pulled out his sketchbook. Elizabeth held her breath as he opened the book and laughed outright. It was an unfamiliar sound. She had heard him chuckle but not deep throated laughter. She sauntered towards him and peered over the rim to properly judge her stick figure in bright daylight. Certain parts were exaggerated, but it was Fitzwilliam how she perceived him.

"A true likeness if I ever saw one." Fitzwilliam smirked and straightened his posture.

"Yes, I am rather pleased with it myself. We should frame it." She grinned back at him.

"There are several framers in London," he quipped and walked away. "Which do you prefer?"

Fitzwilliam positioned the sheet of paper above the mantelpiece and stepped back to admire it.

"Perfect!" he exclaimed.

"You would not dare…"

"Would you rather hang it in the yellow parlour, or perhaps the blue at Pemberley?"

Elizabeth began to worry he was in earnest and chewed on her lower lip.

"Truly, I adore it. But it is best we keep it private, under lock and key with my drawings of you."

Elizabeth exhaled and hastened to fetch the drawing from the mantelpiece.

"Wait," Fitzwilliam urged. "I would like to draw you with the picture, just like that. Looking saucily at me over your shoulder, reaching for my likeness."

"I am rather hungry," Elizabeth complained.

"Just a few minutes so that I can outline it. I shall finish it later."

#

In the lingering rosy afterglow of the sun, the lovers reclined on the balcony. Swallows twittered in the eaves. Elizabeth rested in the crook of her husband's arm, enveloped in his warmth.

"I have received a reply to my letter from Wickham."

"What did he have to say? Did he confess?"

"Yes. He saw no reason to prevaricate since so much time has passed, and with the lady safely married. By his boasting, he thought it revenge on me too."

"You cannot leave it at that."

"No, I suppose not. Although I would rather not divulge the depravity of their actions, I know enough about your curious nature to know that you would not be content with anything but the full truth."

"You need no longer protect my maidenly sensibilities. I am a married woman now."

"Yes, I know," he replied huskily and let a hand travel down her thigh.

Elizabeth swatted his hand away and buried herself deeper into his embrace.

"Oh no! You are not changing the subject before you have told me everything."

Fitzwilliam sighed and kissed the top of her head.

"Wickham had a brief affair with the viscountess before she married Sir Lawrence. She worried that she had become with child and asked Wickham what the signs were. He explained that her courses would stop, which they had. Wickham proposed but was refused, and a month later she married Sir

Lawrence."

Elizabeth was afraid to ask but did so regardless. "What became of the child?"

"There never was a child. The viscountess suffers from a rare condition and has her courses but rarely. Only once or twice a year, and I know this because Crawford told me. He had her examined by several physicians, and they all came to the same conclusion. She is barren."

"How sad..."

"Yes, but that is not all. Wickham was the one who gave her the French pox."

Elizabeth let the repercussions sink in before she gasped. "Lydia!"

"I am very sorry to relate that she is infected too."

Elizabeth remembered all the sorrow, humiliation, and vexation she had endured since she set foot at Pemberley. Yet it was nothing to what poor Lydia had gone through. And now she was infected with a horrible disease that could be fatal. She had an indifferent ne'er-do-well for a husband and no Pemberley to support her. Elizabeth made a mental note to send her sister some money on the morrow, because at present, she was particularly comfortable and not inclined to leave her husband's embrace.

"Has it been worth all the pain, dear husband?"

"Yes, for the happiness we have obtained. Though I would be loath to relive it."

"We have trodden a thorny, winding path to happiness, worthy of a romantic novel, but I believe we have redeemed ourselves. The story about our love would be a literary work of art. I imagine two young lovers resting in a field of blooming apple trees, reading The Shadows of Absence."

"Is that the title?"

"Yes, it is fitting. Do you not agree?"

"Lady Mary had better not be penning that. I have noticed the pen and notebook she takes with her wherever she goes."

"I know not what she is writing, but she is very observant."

"Some events are best forgotten. Let time cover our mistakes and remember only the pleasures. Like the lock of your lush hair tickling my cheek now."

"What about when time has devoured all my beauty and your lust has turned to dust. In the silent-footed years, will you mock the old and grey?"

"I shall love you more when your hair grows argent lily. Nothing ages so advantageously as love..."

# *Epilogue*

Two hundred years later, a random but inquisitive American visitor at Pemberley found herself forgotten by the guided tour group. She had gone to the loo after high tea, and when she returned, her group had moved on.

Wendy walked up a flight of stairs and down several hallways whilst she listened for the voices of her party. Instead, she found a particularly ornate door that looked much older than the rest. It was locked, but she always carried a butterfly-knife, since she had learnt to use it during her karate lessons. She jiggled the knife in the lock, and it gave in. The door shrieked from disuse, and the bedchamber behind it was covered in decades of dust. The bed curtains had turned grey; only in the creases could the original forest green colour be discerned.

Wendy ventured farther inside and studied the paintings on the walls. Every single one depicted the same couple—a tall, dark, and handsome gentleman, greying over the years, and a vivacious brunette, looking adoringly into each other's eyes. Feeling drawn to the couple, she eyed the armoire hiding under a dust cover. She was fairly certain she knew who they were, but the thrill of finding a written testimony proved too strong, and she removed the cover to search the drawers.

There were several watercolours tucked deep into the bottom drawer, depicting the life of a loving family. Children of all ages and both genders were lovingly painted doing a variety of activities. Some were playing outside or had curled up in their mother's lap whilst she read to them. One was of a toddler crying in front of her mother with her hands folded as though in prayer. In the clouds was painted a horse. Wendy chuckled; it looked like a joint effort between father and daughter, to convince Her Grace that the child needed a pony. How adorable!

Tied with faded ribbons in two neat bundles, letters of love and devotion revealed their names as Elizabeth and Fitzwilliam Darcy. The one with the pink ribbon contained his letters to her, and the one with a blue ribbon contained his from her. Their correspondence spanned over five decades. The first one, dated April 1812, was not exactly a love letter, but the subsequent ones, until the last from 1862, revealed a deep and abiding love. She had to read them all, and a life of many blessings, eight bundles of joy, and a few sorrows, was related through the eyes of the lovers. Particularly heart-wrenching was the death of the duchess's youngest sister. At only sixteen, Lady Lydia's romantic elopement had ended in tragedy. Her husband had infected her with the French pox before he died in the Napoleonic War— not as a war hero but hanged for attempted desertion. One Miss Bingley had nursed her through her illness and subsequent death. The nurse had been ostracised from polite society for reasons the letters did not reveal.

She returned the letters to their rightful place, but her ring caught on a tiny button that turned out to be a latch to a hidden compartment. It was empty. The top drawer proved the most enticing. A collection of scandalous drawings lay haphazardly in a pile, like they had been thrown into it in a rush. Some were rough and unfinished, others were completed. Most were of the woman in the paintings, draped enticingly on the bed, a sofa, or a chair. Three of the drawings depicted both of them in burlesque positions. Wendy imagined he had used the large mirror standing in the corner to capture them in such explicit poses.

The bottom one was not of a lady but was a very amateurish attempt to draw the male form with an exceptionally large—

The door burst open, and Wendy almost suffered a heart attack.

"What have you done?"

"Nothing!" Wendy tried to slide the sketch back into the top drawer, but the guard pulled her away. There was nothing to do but to slide it into her tote bag and hope she would not get caught.

"A door is locked for a reason. A hundred and fifty years ago, the first duke of Austen"—the security guard gestured towards the paintings on the walls—"died in his wife's embrace on that bed. Both passed on the same night, after a love story so riveting that hundreds of books have been written about them." The guard pointed, as he did not believe her capable of discovering the obvious. "Their children decided to close the room for all eternity, in honour of their mother and father's memory, and you have just trespassed on this sacred part of Pemberley. Have you no shame?"

"Not overly much, no. But are you absolutely certain that the heir didn't close the room after finding these burlesque paintings of his mother?"

Wendy pulled out a half-finished charcoal drawing of a naked reclining lady, running her fingers over the swell of her hip.

"Get out!"

"There's no need to shout. My hearing is excellent."

Wendy put the drawing back into the drawer and closed it with a sigh. She strolled leisurely out of the room and turned in the direction she had come.

"Not so fast!"

The guard slammed the door shut and set out after her. He grabbed her arm, hauled her down the hallway and down a flight of stairs. He knocked on a door, and a deep voice bade them enter. A mature man in jeans and a button-down shirt sat behind a large oak desk. By his clothes, Wendy surmised he was the head of security. He had been present at the high tea and had sat quietly listening to her conversation with Melissa. Later, he had jokingly advised an inquisitive elderly Canadian couple to ask the Americans about Regency customs because they had a greater knowledge than he.

"Your Grace."

Or maybe not... Wendy studied the man who was obviously the current Duke of Austen. The smiley wrinkles around his eyes were deeper than the furrows between his brows. This mess she was in would sort itself out, she thought, and she curtseyed reverently.

"I found this woman—"

"Wendy," she interrupted.

"Wendy." The guard sighed. "Trespassing in the first Duke of Austen's bedchamber. She must have picked the lock..."

"Oh yes. With my butterfly-knife. It's very handy."

The duke studied her and sent the guard on his way.

"So, how much did you learn about my mythical ancestors?"

"Firstly, I must say that I don't think the children decided to bar the chamber because of their love story but rather the burlesque drawings of their mother and father. The pictures were thrown haphazardly into the drawer, as though in haste or disgust. The other drawings I found were neatly put away, and the letters were nicely tied in ribbons."

"Letters, you say. Were there many?"

"Not too many. It appears that they spent little time apart, but I would say there are twenty odd letters spanning from 1812 through 1862."

"Did you read them?"

"Of course!"

"All of them?"

"Yes," Wendy admitted. "Did you know that Her Grace aided the Duchess of Kent and Strathearn when she arrived in Dover in April of 1819. She was heavily pregnant with Queen Victoria and had become violently ill on the sea voyage. It was because of her that the dukedom was created in 1820. Though I don't think the duke was overly pleased. By their letters I assume he preferred to stay at Pemberley with their children over social events in town. What struck me was the deep and abiding love that shone through their words of affection. But their life was not all smooth sailing. The duke had a lost love that drove them apart, and Her Grace almost died of a broken heart." Wendy sighed at the romantic image it painted in her mind. "Their children are long gone, and their shame shouldn't prevent you from exhibiting the letters and the more modest of the drawings and paintings."

"You think it would be of public interest?"

"I do! I didn't know there was a connection between the Austen dukedom and the Marquis of Limerick. Her Grace's father was the second Marquis of Limerick. Her eldest sister's son Charles was the third. The Darcys' heir, named for his father, became the next duke. Their second son, Emerson, became prime minister, and Llewellyn, their third, was minister of foreign affairs. Their second child Vivienne married a Danish prince and—"

"All this is known."

"Without it, Pemberley's just another great house with beautiful grounds. A love story so profound and long-lasting could make Pemberley the most romantic venue in all of England, if not the world. Show your visitors that not all Regency marriages were arranged for connections or money. Display their letters and drawings. Make it Pemberley's main feature, and hordes of romance-lovers will take a pilgrimage to your estate."

"I'll think about it," the duke promised.

Wendy rifled through her tote bag and pulled out the stick-figure drawing.

"Look. It was not my intention to take it, but your guard scared the shit out of me, and I didn't know what to do with it. Here —" She showed him the drawing. "The stick-figure is rather well endowed. I wonder whether it's a true likeness or a joke, but it gets interesting on the back."

She turned it over, and the backside of a naked Duchess of Austen held the image over the mantelpiece whilst she looked saucily over her shoulder.

"Liam!" the duke called out to the security guard who, by the swiftness of his entrance, must have been waiting just outside the door.

"Take this lady," the duke gestured towards Wendy.

Her heart dropped into her stomach. She was most definitely in trouble.

"Show her to our private quarters and find Elizabeth." The duke turned to Wendy. "Elizabeth is my eldest daughter and handles all the events at Pemberley. Show her the drawing and tell her what you told me. I'll leave the decision of how to proceed up to her."

"Thank you so much!" Wendy exclaimed and smirked at the shocked security guard who was leading her to Pemberley's private wing…

# The End

---

[1] Charivari, skimmington, and stang riding were names for a custom you could be subjected to if you had done something that was regarded as shameful in villages and small towns. The villagers would approach banging pots and pans, pelt him or her, and occasionally throw you into a pond. (Sex

and sexuality in Georgian Britain by Mike Rendell.)

[2] In the Georgian Era, an adulterous man was called a gallant.

[3] From The Dictionary of The Vulgar Tongue 1811, meaning old man.

[4] The town coach was a four wheeled, hardtop, expensive carriage pulled by four horses.

[5] Broken heart syndrome, or Takotsubo Cardiomyopathy, causes the left ventricle to change shape and grow larger. The condition is caused by extreme emotional or physical stress and usually corrects itself after a few weeks. Source British Heart Foundation: https://www.bhf.org.uk/informationsupport/conditions/cardiomyopathy/takotsubo-cardiomyopathy#:~:text=Takotsubo%20cardiomyopathy%2C%20also%20known%20as,severe%20emotional%20or%20physical%20stress.

[6] In the Georgian Era, they believed that urine that was clear as crystal was a sign of virginity.

# Acknowledgements

I owe a big thank you to my bright and clever beta readers, Barry Richman, Wendy Luther, Sam, Rachel Collins and Kelly Miller.

Thank you, Marie, for your excellent proofreading.

A heartfelt thank you to my invaluable editor, Jo Abbott.

To all my friends and readers on Goodreads, Fanfiction.net and Archives Of Our Own whose reviews have given me courage to write and criticism to help me improve.

To the JAFF community that welcomed a Norwegian amongst their midst with open arms and shared generously of their vast knowledge.

Thank you!

# About The Author

## Elin Eriksen

Elin Eriksen is a Norwegian author of Austenesque dramas, a proud mother of four children, a grandmother and happily married to her own Mr Darcy.

She has exchanged chemical analysis of explosives and pharmaceuticals to stay at home with her children and write chaste and steamy, dramatic stories from the Regency era, Viking era and modern era, taking great liberties with the characters and the plot of Pride and Prejudice.

# Books By This Author

## Still Waters

It is not a storm that drives a grown man from reason, but still waters...

In the dark hours of the night, Elizabeth's most beloved sister succumbs to her illness. The aid of a solicitous gentleman is appreciated until her distraught mother misconstrues the circumstances and creates a situation more intolerable than she could ever have imagined.

Elizabeth is grateful when her betrothed leaves the area to let her grieve the loss of her sister in peace but the gentleman who returns for their wedding is not the same gentleman who left her behind.

She had not expected her life would be easy, moving halfway across the country, married to a man who found her only tolerable, yet Elizabeth is not made for misery. The decision to make the best of what life has given her was easy to make but the follow through breaks her heart as she must fight for her position and accept betrayal too despicable to contemplate.

Warning: Infidelity, betrayal and descriptive sexual encounters that are appropriate for a mature audience only.

## Silence Implies Consent

A heart is such a fragile thing, breaking too easily—impossible to mend once broken...

In this sequel to Pride and Prejudice, Mr Fitzwilliam Darcy

and Miss Elizabeth Bennet have exchanged their marriage vows and enjoyed their honeymoon alone at Pemberley. A few weeks of wedded bliss were bestowed upon them before their marriage broke apart in a short but dramatic confrontation—betrayed by someone dear.

Elizabeth turns to her father but there is little he can do to aid her, he has his other daughters to consider. Elizabeth must rely on her stubbornness and resilience until a reconciliation with the husband who showed her no mercy proves unavoidable. While her love never wavered, her trust has been shattered. Mr Darcy must prove himself while they fight the power that wants to rob him of more than just his inheritance.

A dramatic and chaste novel of approximately 49 000 words, which ends in a happily ever after for our dear couple.
Due to the theme, a mature audience is advised.

## The Beastly Mr Darcy

What if Mr Darcy was no longer a handsome man? Could a man with a disfigured face and body relinquish his inherent pride and find love where he does not expect it? And could even a love match overcome the prejudice of a superstitious society?

A disfigured and embittered Mr Darcy does not welcome redemption with equanimity. He perceives Mr Bingley's disruption of his solitude with vexation—until a certain pair of vibrant green eyes catches his attention. But rumours are running rampant in the town about the secluded master of Pemberley, and when unfortunate occurrences involve Miss Elizabeth Bennet in the sordid tale that his life has become, Mr Darcy is forced to act...

The Beastly Mr Darcy is a novel of approximately 49000 words, inspired by Pride and Prejudice with a tiny wink to Beauty and the Beast.

Certain things catch your eye, but pursue only those which catch the heart. (Ancient Indian Proverb)

Warning:
This is an angst-filled tale with a dark ambience and a dramatic backstory including off-the-page violent assault involving adults and children. Appropriate for an adult audience due to its description of violence and explicit sexual content.

## Lord Harpenden's Daughter

Thou, to whose eyes I bend...

Rumours about the imminent arrival of the beautiful daughters of the reclusive Earl of Harpenden had reached the superior society of London. It was the talk of the town; not even Mr Darcy could avoid hearing about it, with his best friend's loquacious sister in tow.

The sisters, dressed in their mourning garb, do not quite meet the expectations of the fastidious Mr Darcy, who soon finds himself in the unenviable position of trying to rectify a poor first impression. But then a dramatic event forces them to unite against a common enemy—a master of deception—to save their sisters.

A chaste Pride and Prejudice variation of approximately 63 000 words, appropriate for adults due to graphic descriptions of nonsexual violence. A forced marriage scenario with no compromise.

## Baby Blue Eyes

What would make Mr Darcy, a man who abhors disguise, resort to deceit and fraud to achieve his goal? Baby blue eyes...

The guilt of a certain regrettable event at the Netherfield

Ball has put Mr Darcy in an unusually low mood, even more so than Mr Bingley, who cannot seem to evict the fair Jane from his mind. When word reaches them that Miss Bennet has fled Longbourn for the wilds of Yorkshire, a very grumpy Mr Darcy follows Bingley on his search, only to have his heart captured by a pair of beautiful blue eyes. He cannot turn away, even if he had wanted to, but the road to a happily ever after is fraught with difficulties from the law and interfering relations—hardships that are easier to endure with your love by your side.

Be aware, dear reader, that our beloved couple's passion, although not graphically described, runs white hot and they do anticipate their wedding vows.

This variation of Pride and Prejudice of approximately 74 000 words is set in the Regency era. It is a low angst read with an early understanding between our dear couple. Appropriate for a mature audience due to the theme.

## Veni Vidi Vicious

Never a whit should one blame another for the folly which many befalls; the might of love makes sons of men into fools who once were wise...          ( Hávamál in the Poetic Edda.)

A unique story in the Austenesque catalogue—a Viking era variation of Pride and Prejudice. Set in the late 800s when King Alfred the Great ruled in Wessex and Harold Fairhair united tribal Norway into one kingdom.

Elizabeth's courage had risen when faced with the fierce Viking, but what will she do when she finds herself as a stowaway on a Viking ship, heading for a major sea battle?
Fitzwilliam has been taught since infancy that men do not love, but can he withstand the temptation of giving his heart to the one woman whose eyes he cannot resist?

The Bennets have travelled to London to trade and visit their relations when Elizabeth's brother, John, enters the house, battered and bruised, announcing they are expecting guests the next morning.

Elizabeth has no choice; she is forced to wed the savage Viking, Fitzwilliam Darcyson, to save her brother, to sail across the North Sea to a foreign country with pagan customs. Fortunately, her most beloved sister will travel with her as Jane has wed the amiable chieftain of Netherfield, in a double wedding with Elizabeth and the Jarl of Nidaros.

A ruthless time in history is brought to life through Elizabeth Bennet and Fitzwilliam Darcyson's eyes as they get to know one another and adjust to each other's customs through battles, hardships and bliss. Be warned, this is not for the faint of heart. This is an uncensored, unglorified medieval tale with all the gory details. Approximately 148 000 words.

Trigger warnings:
Violence, death, a few steamy interludes and the repercussions/ punishment of rape. Suitable for a mature audience only.

## Where Love Resides

An interruption at the church disrupts the reading of our dear couples' banns. A ghost from the past throws their engagement period into turmoil and threatens Miss Bennet and Mr Bingley's happiness. Elizabeth Bennet is not one to sit idly by, and she engages herself completely in restoring her dear Jane's felicity. Mr Darcy is no less eager to help his friend, as they unravel the mysterious allegations of the colonel.

Where Love Resides enters canon by the time of the second proposal. It is a chaste novella of approximately 26,000 words, a mash-up between Pride and Prejudice and Sense and Sensibility set in the Regency era.

## Convenience Of That Kind

A random suggestion from Miss Elizabeth Bennet had settled in Mr Darcy's mind. The convenience of a particular kind would alleviate some significant challenges in his life. If you had warned him his feelings would become engaged, he would have baulked, but we all know how the most carefully laid plans can go awry...

Convenience of That Kind is a novella-length farce with a platonic marriage-to-love plot of approximately 30 000 words.

Warning:
Before you read, beware that this author has often been accused of having an exceedingly dry and bawdy sense of humour...

## Master Of Puppets

What if Elizabeth stumbled upon a mystery? A secret of murder and betrayal, ripping a family asunder. Who is friend? Who is foe? And who is the Highlander hiding in Pemberley's hunting tower?

Seven gentlemen and twelve ladies were rumoured to be accompanying Mr Bingley to Netherfield. Mrs Bennet was relieved when the number of females proved to be grossly exaggerated, and for the most part—married.

Mr Darcy was Mr Bingley's particular guest and had brought with him his senior married sister, her husband, and a younger sister. Not to forget his mother, a straightforward speaking lady with an uncanny ability to understand human nature.

Mr Darcy was pleasant to look upon and an accomplished dancer, but neither he nor his mother perceived Elizabeth Bennet as any threat to his marital status. Elizabeth suspected that his affections might be engaged elsewhere when she accepted an invitation to Pemberley as Miss Georgiana Darcy's particular friend.

"My courage rises at every attempt to intimidate me," Elizabeth Bennet proudly proclaimed. The stubbornness that could never bear to be frightened by the will of others was about to be tested by the last man in the world she could ever be prevailed upon to marry.

Master of Puppets is an angst-filled mystery romance variation of Pride and Prejudice of approximately 94,000 words that spans several years.

PS: I solemnly swear that no matter what happens in this novel, it ends with a HEA for Elizabeth Bennet and Fitzwilliam Darcy. Best regards, Elin.

## Wistfully Beautiful

Mr Darcy had not envisaged that as a wealthy, educated gentleman he was considered an underdog.

Darcy had promised to teach his friend estate management, but Bingley's ideas changed so rapidly... He contemplated rescinding his offer when the estate turned out to be a hunting lodge, not even situated on the British Isles. Despite his concerns about the endeavour, Darcy could never have predicted the particular peril he would encounter across the sea, nor such a strong desire to prove his mettle.

Miss Elizabeth was clever, witty, and headstrong. But she was blind to the core timber of Mr Darcy, and she had little faith in the revered gentleman. Mr Darcy, who blew into her life—dismissed everything she held dear—rescued her—and left with her heart.

Wistfully Beautiful is a low to medium angst, Darcy rescues Elizabeth, Regency era Pride and Prejudice variation of approximately 58,000 words. It is appropriate for an adult audience only due to a steamy wedding night and graphic descriptions of the death of animals.

## Unforgivable

Forgiveness saves the expense of anger, the cost of hatred, and the waste of spirit, but there is something to be said for having a scapegoat...

What if Elizabeth fell in love with Mr Darcy first? After she had committed an offence he could never forgive. Would Mr Darcy still fall in love with her bewitching eyes?
Elizabeth loathed the mere sight of Mr Darcy after his slight at Admiral Livingstone's dinner party. He did not know she existed until they reunited under dire circumstances at Gretna Green. Even a shy and timid young girl can possess a core of strength in matters of the heart. We are all fools in love...

Unforgivable is an off-canon, chaste variation of Pride & Prejudice of approximately 72 000 words.

## Oblivion

His sister's troubles drive Fitzwilliam Darcy to drink a little more than he should before Mr Lucas's barbecue and when he stumbles into the night, a petite brunette comes to his rescue. His thank yous are swallowed by the consequences, to which he reacts with little grace.

In this modern reimagining of Pride and Prejudice, Darcy does not insult Elizabeth upon their first encounter. Instead, they have a cosy interlude under a starlit sky. He does, however, destroy his favourable first impression during their subsequent meetings, earning him a taste of Elizabeth Bennet's fury, and quite deservedly so.

A modern variation of Pride and Prejudice of close to 50 000 words. Appropriate for a mature audience due to a couple of steamy scenes.

## Two Components

What could make Darcy and Elizabeth venture into a marriage of convenience? A missing sister and stolen explosives…

The CEO, Mrs de Bourgh, is retiring from Lebon Explosives. Her nephew, the wealthy bachelor Fitzwilliam Darcy, arrives to find her replacement, but the theft of a secret military explosive and a certain green-eyed chemist disrupt his plans. Instead, he sets out on a wild chase into foreign and dangerous territory, with the chemist in tow.

Two Components is a contemporary, steamy, action-adventure Pride and Prejudice variation of approximately 59,000 words. The content is appropriate for adults only due to steamy scenes and violent altercations.

28939452R00154